Sense of Home

THE LAND OF THE GREAT LAKES

N.Z. KAMINSKY

D1521971

To Dean and Leia
Life is about moments.

Listen: there's a hell of a good universe next door; let's go.
– E. E. Cummings

Prologue

THE SHADOW AND I

Tyra was lying in bed, overwhelmed by chaotic images, hidden messages striving to break through immense pain. The pain penetrated her entire being—every part of her body. Her head and neck screamed in agony, and her bones pleaded for mercy. Tyra's mind wandered, trapped in a kaleidoscope of intrusive thoughts. She cringed, shivered, and twisted. Emotions burst and overflowed. Frustration. Anger. Sadness. Guilt. All at once.

Tyra craved answers. She couldn't endure this never-ending pain anymore. She needed it to stop, even for a while. Tyra wished she could take her body off like clothing and hang it in a closet until it got better. She tried to shake the pain—shift it off as if it were a grim cloak. But resentment brought even more pain. Disconnected, split, and isolated, she begged for help. But from whom?

Her head reeled as long-forgotten memories popped out, reemerging from the hidden dungeon of her psyche.

In a glimpse, the scenery changed and her surroundings transformed. Tyra looked around. Everything was different. The room, the bed, and even her aching body were all gone. But not the pain. The pain overshadowed her with the expression of a guilty, wounded puppy, waiting for help.

They existed as two independent entities, but they were bound, inseparable at their core. A hazy, bluish, amorphous cloud of shadow was clinging to her.

The shadow wasn't frightening, but it was hurting, and it was lonely. Tyra and her pain looked around. Nothing unusual, just an empty space.

In that void, images from the past started waltzing around. Dizzy and free.

CHAPTER 1

The Escape

> *"No man is an island,*
> *Entire of itself;*
> *Every man is a piece of the continent,*
> *A part of the main."*
> – John Donne

The barn they moved into from a beautiful city with a nice apartment, good people, and a decent life was a dark, gloomy place.

It was converted into a tiny house in a rush.

Grey and musty, peeling walls had abandoned hope ages ago. The wood was soft, almost spongy. The windows were hazy, flimsy, and covered with mud.

When Tyra's mom found a job at a local grocery store, they offered her this crumbling shack where cows and chickens had lived only a month before. There was no hot water and no bathroom. Nettle bushes surrounded a timeworn outhouse, squeezed in behind the barn. Every trip to the toilet was painful, especially at night.

Why hadn't her parents removed the bushes? Probably for the same reason everything else happened; they were grieving.

They were grieving for their lost life in their homeland, familiar and warm, the city of Moss, surrounded by green mountains, untamed forest, and an opal river. They missed their family and friends and their cozy neighbourhood with artistic houses and eclectic, vibrant balconies. They missed the colourful, cheerful markets with delicious goods of all kinds, the kind where they got to meet people and connect.

Moss was a place filled with joy, divine food, and, above all, the aroma and colour of life itself.

Tyra recalled the smell of juicy tomatoes from a local farmer's market. Whenever she held the tomatoes in her hands, she would close her eyes and smile. She would inhale deeply, slowly. The fresh, earthy scent revived memories of pure happiness. Everything else lost its importance at such moments, taking away the weight of day-to-day struggles for a moment.

Life is all about such moments.

The city of Moss was the only happy place in the cheerless parallel world of Azure. Those who strived for a better life in the realm of isolation had created an oasis of hope a long time ago. They shared mutual values of freedom, community, and collective responsibility. Integrity. Dignity. Such fine places create a sense of belonging, safety and warmth.

The people of Moss were cordial and joyful, as all carefree beings are. It wasn't uncommon to greet someone multiple times a day with a broad smile, reflecting normally sunny weather and the human need for connection. Nor was it unusual to hear the doorbell ring when they shared a nice Saturday evening as a family in their cozy living room in front of the TV. The doorbell usually indicated the arrival of a neighbour with a fresh homemade dish or cookies, smelling delicious, still warm and steaming. Such moments were precious, filled with life and kinship, the safety of childhood, and simple joys.

The realm of Azure was similar to yours, Terra, a non-magical world on planet Earth with rapidly evolving technology, a social media madhouse, and countless social issues.

The people of Azure were rational beings. They never believed in magic, but they knew a lot about darkness. Pandemics, wars between different continents based on religious prejudices or controversial, outdated, and irrelevant historical facts. Fluctuations in the real estate market, inflation, terrorism, corruption. Such a mad world.

The realm of Azure was far less polluted than Terra, and for a simple reason: they didn't produce much. They traded their rich natural resources of precious stones with Terra's massive production in every possible area. Even their books and art were mainly borrowed. And they spoke only one language—English. Centuries ago, multiple ethnic groups had merged into one colourful, mixed culture, except for faith. Faith came in various forms and provoked chaos across the realm.

The village of Marigold was beautiful. Nestled in the middle of a massive greenbelt, it was characterized by well-groomed streets and bleak, identical cottages. But the villagers were wicked, and Tyra's new home was inanimate.

Her parents, disconnected from their home, coped in different ways. Her mother, Scarlett, fell into depression. Logan, Tyra's father, started drinking.

Did they long to turn the wheel of time and return to things as they were, far away from that wild place, so cold and indifferent in its cruelty? Were they lost?

No doubt. But the wicked village in the middle of nowhere was their only escape from war. It was called "a special operation" that had emerged due to a conflict of interest between the citizens of Moss and their neighbours across the river. But it felt like war in terms of its destruction and terror.

Not all the people on either side were vile. They didn't all get lost in chaotic disruption. Many remained kind, good people who were enduring a bad time. Both sides were simply human. Some were evil, some were kind, and some were neither.

The aggressors invaded and claimed Moss as their ancient heritage. They refused to coexist in harmony or share the land. They attempted to enforce their religious values and murdered those who opposed them. Their primary goal was to destroy the roots of those who rebelled against them. The most terrifying part of this lunacy was that their leaders were still human, or at least they looked like humans.

However, in their familiar physical form, they hid the real insanity—lack of empathy.

The leaders enlisted monstrous creatures, the beasts, who inhabited the dense woods across the city. They were tall, skinny, bald, humanoid figures with slick grey skin. Their round eyes were empty, their lips narrow and tight. They had reptilian ears and wore filthy silver cloaks.

The beasts lived in isolated clans across the realm. It was unknown how and when they entered Azure or where they came from. But their ruthlessness was unquestionable.

In Tyra's nightmares, their bodies looked like rotten, smearing masses. They had no hearts, not anymore. Amorphous, legless creatures, shapeless beasts walking inches above the ground's surface. Their brains looked inflamed, fogged by a thick black cloud and bathed in the sickest idea—the idea of one belief, one philosophical and political structure for all.

Many people speculated about how to kill the beasts, but some knew it was crucial to aim for the source. Scientists searched for answers for ages, trying to invent different types of weapons. If only they knew that the darkness itself could not be destroyed. That or another sort of pure evilness would always be seeking a way to get into people's heads to make them cooperate *if* people let it.

The beasts and the villagers of Marigold were plagued by different types of cruelty on the scale of madness. The first kind was the ultimate fall into complete darkness with no escape because they became the darkness itself. The type where evil was hiding and waiting for an opportunity to strike.

The people of Moss knew the beasts existed among them and the beasts now lived outside their society, banished into the woods a long time ago. They lived in poverty and hardship, in the most difficult circumstances, even for the obscure creatures they were, neither human nor animal. Excluded, they became even more bitter across the centuries. They watched their more fortunate neighbours from the highest trees with rage and hunger. As they watched them thrive, the beasts were filled with rivalry and jealousy. Seeing the outer world constantly changing, ever flourishing, they craved a change in their ever-still, ever-gloomy kingdom without a king.

The people of Moss knew these creatures existed, but they tried to silence their fears with blissful festivals and delicious gifts from neighbour to neighbour. They tried to hide this undeniable fact with the sound of kids' laughter, the aroma of baked goods, and merry holidays. They became busier and busier in an almost ecstatic attempt to hush the distant whisper of truth. The truth that could barely reach their conscious minds anymore.

When the leaders enlisted the beasts, chaos arose. Suppressed forces went wild. Those were challenging times, filled with terror and death. Violence spread through the once-peaceful streets, sneaking into people's homes and hearts.

The safe, friendly bubble full of joyful people and peaceful lives, nice neighbours and good intentions, collapsed as if it had never existed, leaving no room for "happily ever after." Brotherhood. Union of all species. Friendliness. Home. Welcoming. Warmth and openness. Prosperity. Harmony. All such things were gone, smashed by the beasts who attacked unexpectedly, or so people believed.

Perhaps it was easier to dismiss the early signs of catastrophic events.

Tyra's last memories before the escape remained forgotten for a long time. Once they resurfaced, she couldn't push them back into the shadows.

Tyra was ten years old when the beasts struck. Her parents and her maternal aunt, Olivia, gathered at Tyra's grandparents' cottage. Tyra was sitting on the floor, gripping her head with her little hands. She pushed her head down as if it would protect her from harm. Her face was frozen in tension, petrified. Panicking adults surrounded her, muttering non-stop. Tyra felt an urge to go to the bathroom. Guns were shooting outside. Chaos was everywhere. Somebody said she had to crawl. Otherwise, she might die. So, Tyra crawled. Her heart echoed in her ears as if it were trying to escape the madness. Primeval fear took over as the sound of gunshots spun in her head, but she couldn't scream. Silence was crucial. Silence was hope. *Is there even hope?* Tyra wondered.

The adults babbled in hushed, anxious whispers about one of the savage gangs, known for its heartless cruelty, that was approaching their building. Normally, they would enter each home, bringing raw horror and traumatic death to destroy human nature at its core, to crush beating hearts with their unimaginable malice.

The adults lost it. They failed to cope, broken. They forgot about Tyra, shaking in the dark corner, so lonely and scared. As they chatted in muted whispers, they weren't individuals anymore but only a mass, a crowd, scared to their bones.

By that point, Tyra was well informed about the horrors that awaited once those creatures entered the building. She knew in detail how each of them would die, step by step. First, the beasts would burst in with loud, bestial excitement. Their wild, empty, deep-seated, shadowed eyes would glow red with an evil smirk. They would kill each adult with inconceivable atrocity in front of their children. Or they would torture them all with the most demonic actions first and then murder them. The bullets would whizz; dust and paint flakes would rain down. Walls and toys would turn red.

That was what had happened in other communities that dared to protest.

Kids screamed and begged for death. "End it now! Kill me, kill me, kill me!" But their voices were lost in their attackers' diabolical laughter.

The beasts danced and shouted, celebrated and rejoiced. They moved proudly through endless bodies. Infants, kids, and their caregivers—all massacred with such incomprehensible malevolence that their minds exploded, and their souls evaporated. Nothing was left, only burnt and mangled bodies, hugging each other—broken, piece by piece, spirits of once happy-living beings.

In those walls, nothing remained except silent emptiness and bloody madness—until *she* came in. Death entered with grace and kindness. She gathered those wounded fragments of human souls, healed them, and made them whole again. No pain or sadness, only relief.

The monsters aimed to destroy the essence of humanity by disintegrating every soul, crushing it with unthinkable cruelty. But they couldn't destroy something they didn't have. Not entirely, and not for eternity.

Death never came for the bodies. She brought a gift of love and compassion. She brought comfort and alleviation when there was no more life left. She restored, integrated, and returned them to nature for another circle of life.

When Tyra returned from this endless journey to the bathroom, she heard a burst of relief and exaltation.

"You won't find any rebels here," a neighbour yelled out the window. "Move along. We've already accepted your terms as a community." She had put her own life and the lives of her children at risk to save others.

The beasts moved along, and Tyra couldn't help but wonder, where?

It hurt. Fear and guilt. A wily combination.

Two silent killers. Soul eaters.

That period was about pure survival. Adults took turns sneaking out for groceries while others waited in terror for them to return home, safe and sound. The streets were dangerous, the markets even more so. Online services had been cancelled, but the need to eat remained.

Their good, cordial neighbours had split. Some stuck to their values, others to their fears. It was painful and sad. The cracks in the once-unified communities were unbearable. Their little paradise had been destroyed, and there was no way back, only out. So, they moved far away to a different kind of darkness, rotting from the inside.

"In each of us, there is another whom we do not know."
– Carl Jung

CHAPTER 2
The Wicked Village

"Thinking is difficult, that's why people judge."
– Carl Jung

If Moss was a happy oasis in the realm of madness, Marigold was a part of Azure's gloomy, shadowy side. Sullen and untouched by time, picturesque landscapes towered above it, casting a smirking shadow.

The barn was unsuitable for humans, lifeless and disengaged.

Tyra's tiny bedroom hosted a twin bed beside a cracked window and a bare, lonely wall. Weary dark-green curtains stirred, unpleasant to touch. The opposite wall was lined with furniture —a scuffed but functional desk, a few rusty bookshelves, and a red wooden closet with a broken mirror. Hastily applied floral wallpaper looked like an outsider in the otherwise grim but well-matched room.

The living room was dim and shabby. It looked sad with a previously green, old-fashioned sofa in the middle. Up front was a tired, outdated TV and a bleak, rustic coffee table. On the right wall, an antique cupboard with half-broken country dishes stood behind closed doors. The walls had been painted with basic white primer, covered in streaky brushwork. The only attractive feature was a large window with a spacious sill, softened by a cushion, which overlooked a neat street lined with grey brick cottages and age-worn trees. The tiny kitchen was dark and dispirited. Only a decaying square window peered into a yearning, uncared-for garden. And there was no hope left to make things better. Tyra and her parents were drowning, each of them lonely and lost.

Tyra's consolation was Moose, a shaggy, mid-size sheepadoodle with a mostly white coat. His nose, ears, and tail were coal black, and his paws looked like black-and-white slippers. When they'd adopted him, Moose made their lives happier, and now they were more bearable.

The villagers hated outsiders of all kinds, especially from the city of Moss, whose constant presence reminded them about a life they could never have.

Scarlett's free spirit and unusual appearance had provoked turmoil in their boring lives. She was young and beautiful. She had messy raven hair and wore eccentric clothes she designed herself. Scarlett carried herself with a fierce and unapologetic demeanour. She resembled Lilith, the goddess of night. In her previous life, she had worked as an accomplished graphic designer. Now she tried to adjust to customer service.

Logan Blair was a different kind: physically strong, closed off, and detached. His tousled red hair seemed to have a rhythm all its own, and his tall figure exuded a latent tension, like a storm waiting to break. Overall, he was a good fellow with simple endeavors and a difficult childhood, who couldn't quite understand how he ended up marrying such an interesting but uneasy woman.

Logan was obsessed with her. She didn't love him; she despised him. He knew it. Their marriage was his mother-in-law's arrangement. For an obscure reason, Alma thought it was a good match.

Logan had been raised by his kind-hearted uncle and aunt, who didn't have children of their own and who loved him with all their hearts. His mother didn't like or want him. She had him when she was young. When her husband died from an alcohol overdose soon after Logan was born, she remarried, had another boy, and mostly disappeared from Logan's life.

Logan had worked his whole life as a truck driver. He enjoyed traveling in his gigantic truck across the realm and spending time with his daughter.

As Scarlett often noted, they remained together only because they loved their one and only daughter dearly—once cheerful, always respectful.

Tyra was sensitive and a thinker, which wasn't an easy combination. By age eleven, she already looked like a petite, pretty woman. Her braided caramel hair was soft to the touch and a bit naughty. Her teal eyes already knew sadness.

She was the centrepiece of her parents' lives, but after the escape they crashed. And the long, cold winter only added another reason to sink.

Tyra was on her own. Sometimes she had to cook herself dinner, sticky and disgusting pasta. It looked miserable, mushy and gooey, in a rustic pan. Ketchup, a brilliant invention for all times, was the saviour. The miraculous red substance made everything taste edible.

The Blair family learned to wash themselves in a bucket, saving hot water for luxurious bath-time moments. The barn was cold, and they had to kindle an ancient stove with actual wood, always a struggle for city people. It seemed they were incapable of living a normal country life. How funny it would sound to Tyra when she grew older. The struggle wasn't a struggle anymore but an eager anticipation for a crispy sound of dancing fire, coziness, and warmth.

Such a perfect ambiance for reading a book.

Reading was Tyra's ultimate escape from the troubles of daily life—her saviour, her compass, her comfort. Even before she could read the words, she observed illustrations with absolute concentration. Pictures transformed into words, actions, and then adventures. Tyra would travel the world, meet thousands of characters, and participate in myriad scenes as if she were an authentic part of them all. She would laugh and cry. She would feel, learn, and grow wise. Books were Tyra's best friend, sometimes her only friends. They were her guides and the guardians of her sanity.

Tyra's favourite places in the village were the library and the forest. She avoided other places at all costs since local kids made her life even more miserable.

Hatred spreads like wildfire. It consumes people. Hatred feeds on jealousy and fear. Tyra and her parents were different, which was sufficient to evoke hostility in narrow-minded folks. Their lonesome family tried, if not to fit in, then to get along. It was futile. When there's no room for openness in beating hearts, there's no room for genuine kindness.

The entire village rose against the miserable trio and Moose, with few exceptions.

Every day looked pretty much the same for the entire school year.

Tyra would come home hurt after being bullied by the entire school, including the staff. Each time she found her mum lying on a weary sofa in a fetal position as tears dripped from her fireless eyes. Logan would probably be out drinking. Moose would be thrilled, over the moon to see her again. They played, ran, and snuggled. Tyra would take a book and cuddle on a worn-out sofa with a bowl of fresh garden carrots and Moose, curled up by her side.

Once a month, Tyra received letters from her aunt. Olivia valued old-fashioned correspondence. She liked the personal touch, saying it took an effort to frame one's thoughts, express one's feelings with thoughtful consideration, and deliver opinions with greater accuracy. Tyra adored this peculiar way of communication. It felt more intimate than a screen meetup. It felt like bonding.

Tyra took solace in Olivia's letters. Like a solitary lighthouse, they helped her navigate from afar through dark waters and obscure horizons. Tyra cherished them as a guide to help her survive on her own in the psychological desert of her new, unsettled life.

~

Over time, Scarlett and Logan moved past depression, or so it seemed. Sometimes they would even talk and smile. Tyra liked listening to them talk. She craved their company. But she had Moose, and it was almost enough.

Often, Tyra had dreams mixed with memories about a long line of people fleeing the city with their pets. Thousands of them were carrying their precious friends inside their jackets, tucked in with love and caution, huddled on their shoulders, or shivering inside carriers or even grocery carts. And some were plodding beside them. Cats, dogs, parrots. All shocked, scared, and disoriented.

The people of Moss treated their pets as beloved family members. It had been reported that the aggressors exploited this bond as a means of psychological warfare, damaging animal shelters. They aimed to shatter the integrity of their animal-loving victims, to scratch and ruin their spirits. They wanted to generate moral degradation.

Instead, the remaining pets had brought unprecedented comfort to their families, at times providing their only sense of purpose, meaning, and hope. Often, the pets and kids were the only things that kept the adults' sanity intact.

Moose was Tyra's safe place, her oasis of light and joy. He spent his mornings outside, running around and chasing offended chipmunks.

Scarlett and Logan were still too drained to take him for a walk.

On a hushed afternoon, when spring was attempting to arrive and bring revival, Logan was making tiramisu pancakes in the hissing kitchen. Moose bustled around, jumping in exaltation, licking his face in sweet anticipation of leftovers.

Logan squeezed out a smile. "No way, you goofy fellow. It'll make your skin itchy. Here, have your sweet-potato treats."

Moose turned his face away with a snort of contempt.

Scarlett stared at the murky window. Moose's enthusiasm reminded her of her own sense of joy and drive. "Logan, could you make one for Moose?"

"No," he grumbled.

Scarlett was too blue to get agitated. As weird as it sounds, her depression stage was Tyra's favourite. Scarlett was quiet and harmless, even timid. Tyra liked it. It was safe.

Tyra turned to Moose. "Oy, Dad's in a brave mood today. And *she's* a delight now that she's had her coffee." Tyra took a plate with piping-hot pancakes to the living room, followed by her devoted companion, who was never ready to give up on hope. Tyra blew on the pancakes to cool them, and then fed them to Moose as she gazed around with caution. "Itchy, not itchy. The soul also requires nourishment." She giggled as she cooled another pancake, the biggest and fluffiest of all.

As happy as could be, Moose wiggled his tail and then ran outside to chase the squirrels and chipmunks in the forest.

"Mum, it's dangerous for Moose to be all alone in the woods," Tyra said. "Besides, he chases cars like a crazy monkey. I'm scared something bad will happen to him."

"Tyra, you're a big girl, and you can certainly take care of him."

Logan didn't answer; he only sighed.

Tyra tried hard. She tried, and she failed. When Moose died, Tyra blamed herself. She had let him down, and she hated it. The day he died was one of the hardest days of her life. Grief mixed with guilt can be excruciating in its complexity and desolation.

Tyra was at school when they notified her. Her teacher approached her desk, looking upset. A wave of sympathy wrinkled her normally tight, restrained cheekbones. She touched Tyra's shoulder and leaned over her with peculiar softness. "I'm so sorry, Tyra. It's your dog. He's dead. It's unfair."

A drunk truck driver had run over him. Just like that. Snap, and he was gone. Nothing could be done. In such moments, a time loop was created, a loop in which all precious days and nights spent with loved ones were trapped forever.

Moose had adored chasing trucks, barking like a lunatic. It was his joy, his entertainment. Tyra's parents had feared it was coming. People across the village were annoyed. Bad people. Rumors claimed the driver had run him down in a fit of anger fuelled by hatred toward their family.

For the first time in many moons, Tyra sobbed like a wounded animal. She didn't care if the others watched her, giggling. Tyra felt free of their judgment, their looks, and their conspiracies, their vicious plans to smash her later, to punish her for her vulnerability. She felt free from all the consequences of her breakdown. She felt free from their malicious plans, ignited by mindless rage.

"How dare she be so free and careless in front of us?" they said. "She's a weak freak. We must eliminate her. She's a threat to our existence."

Tyra wept, releasing all of her defenses, all the pain they had caused her—the bruises and the humiliation they inflicted upon her. All of it was gone, drowned in sorrow. Tyra felt their wily gazes, their insidious intentions, but she couldn't have cared less. She felt liberated. It was a complete and total catharsis.

When Tyra came home, for the first time in her life, she found her dad sobbing like a child. Logan was sitting on a wobbly wooden stool behind the glass door in the tiny storage room. His elbows rested on his knees as he bent his head down, covering his face with trembling hands. Pain, depression, and anger were forced out by an enormous sense of guilt. His grief for the lost life had grown and expanded.

Scarlett also felt guilty. She loved that dog. But guilt found it hard to penetrate her guard. Somehow, she put it aside and concentrated on the disgust that Logan's meltdown had caused her. She couldn't tolerate weakness in men, let alone crying.

For a moment, Tyra felt immense empathy for her father. Then her mother's reaction confused her, and she abandoned him too. Guilt arose again and disoriented her even more. It paused, hopeless of gaining her attention, then crawled into the depths of her mind. There, it slinked to the bottom of her shadow, where all uncomfortable and controversial emotions hide when cast out.

It was draining and sad. All the freedom Tyra had felt a minute earlier, and all emotional outbursts evaporated, vanishing in a way that was wrong and unnatural. Only grief and guilt remained, ruining her piece by piece.

"Mama is a difficult woman, but she loves us in her own twisted way," Tyra said in front of Moose's grave in their small, untended garden.

> "Do not stand at my grave and weep
> I'm not there. I do not sleep.
> I'm a thousand winds that blow.
> I'm the diamond glints on snow . . .
> Do not stand at my grave and cry.
> I'm not there. I did not die."
> – Clare Harner

CHAPTER 3
Mother Wound

"If you can keep your head when all about you
Are losing theirs and blaming it on you,
If you can trust yourself when all men doubt you,
But make allowance for their doubting too . . ."
– Rudyard Kipling

When the school year was over, Tyra felt exhilarated. Happiness touched her soul again, and her starved heart felt almost full. She even forgot to be afraid that those moments would pass away sooner rather than later, leaving another hole in her chest. But this time, Tyra didn't care. She needed to feel good, to feel free.

Scarlett was resting on a comfy pinkish armchair in her mother's cozy countryside living room, a picture of a white owl with smiling eyes above her head. Her porcelain coffee mug spread a strong caramel aroma throughout the house. As Scarlett watched her daughter play, tears dripped from her tired cheeks.

Her gaze was full of love, compassion, and a forgotten taste of normality. The feeling of peace in a mother's heart when her child is safe and sound.

"Mama," she said to Tyra's grandmother, Alma. "Look at

20

Tyra. I haven't seen her like this for an entire year. I was afraid I would never see her smile or hear her laughter again."

Alma, a stunning, elegant woman with a slender figure and shoulder-length strawberry-blonde hair, stared at her yellow cup of double espresso, lost in thought. She was resting on a plush linen couch after a busy day in the kitchen, her legs nestled on a pile of colourful cushions. "Poor child. She's only twelve—well, almost, but she's already been through so much pain. Such a good girl. She didn't deserve it. I know she's resilient. Stronger than most of us." Alma frowned. "But she's just a child. What would you say about letting her stay with us for the next school year? We're in a safe place now. It isn't that bad. I'm glad we moved here. I told you, Scarlett, you should consider it too. It's heart wrenching to think about our girl returning to this horrible place and these people. You can try to find another job and get yourself together. I know it hasn't been easy for you, dear. You gotta get out of that wicked place." Alma sipped coffee and took a bite from an apple strudel sprinkled with brown sugar as she scrutinized her granddaughter with anxious eyes.

"Mama, how could I? I can't let my daughter live far away from us. *I can't* be far away from her." Scarlett stared at Tyra, who was swinging and dancing around the room with chiffon scarves, happy and carefree.

Tyra's hearing and observation were excellent. Always alert, she ran over to her mother, gliding in the air as if she were skating. "Mama, Mama!" she cried, flipping her hair, which was tied back in a boho up-do braid. "Please let me stay! I'll be safe here with Granny and Grandad. You know that. I'll be fine. Don't worry. I don't wanna go back there. Please, please, please."

Scarlett hesitated, pondering. She felt another wave of compassion, which caused her to forget about logic, logistics, and everything else. "All right. I want you to be happy." Then a thought arose and flew away. "I probably should've consulted Logan first."

Tyra spent almost a year with her grandparents.

When she was little, her grandparents' cottage had been her safe place, her anchor. Alma and Ethan Bach and their younger daughter, Olivia, lived in a beautiful suburban community, Willow. It was a part of the vast, dazzling city of Moss. Willow was quiet and full of greenery. The roofs of the red brick cottages with large mosaic windows were covered with moss. The front yards were elegant, well-tended, and flourishing. A tree-lined alley with colourful benches led to the lazy Main Street. It featured boutique shops, a tavern, a coffee house, and a bakery. A mellow emerald hill, an aquamarine brook, and a birch grove were all within walking distance.

Tyra spent most of her weekends and holidays in Willow. Sometimes it felt like she was living for those moments alone. Her real life was there, with a sense of stability and happiness. Luke, her best friend, lived next door. Alma was warm and caring. Her kitchen was the center of bonding and laughter. Alma's cooking was divine. She expressed her affection through crunchy pastries and country dishes. Each dish contained love, nourishment, and comfort. On holiday mornings, Tyra would sneak out to the clean, cozy kitchen, looking for delectable leftovers. Alma's kitchen smelled like fresh milk and homemade bread.

The hardest moments of Tyra's early life were when she had to leave for another long week. Her own house never felt like home. But in her dream house, she was a guest—a welcomed, loved, and cherished guest. Tyra wanted to belong to that place so much that each time, she would leave a little piece of herself to keep the ties intact. She longed for an unbreakable connection.

Each time they returned home, it was the same. Tyra would sit on her bed and cry. Her crying would get quieter and subtler, her face gloomier.

"Tyra, why are you crying?" Scarlett would ask repeatedly like a broken record. "For God's sake, this is your home! Your family is here."

"I wanna go back! I need to get back to Granny. I can't stay here until Saturday. It's too long." Tyra's anger would be replaced by sadness.

"Do you want me to sit with you until you fall asleep? I'll bring my crochet."

Scarlett wasn't a hugger. She craved hugs but had never learned how to give one, and Tyra had never received one. It felt like Scarlett's mum and Tyra's grandmother were different people. Alma didn't know how to hug her daughters, nor was she hugged when she was little. It had been passed from generation to generation for who knows how long until Tyra was born. As a baby, Tyra failed to connect with her mother but found warmth and love in her grandma's arms, melting Alma's guarded heart. It was a powerful bond that worked with tender care to heal them both.

Rare moments of coziness with her mother were dear to Tyra. She would watch the crochet hooks in her mother's hands, moving effortlessly, making a quirky sound, and calming her down, click by click. But little Tyra feared the moment Scarlett would get up and leave the room. She wanted the moment to last forever. Her mother's closeness and the safety of her silence could soothe Tyra's heartache and loneliness for a while.

But the most precious moments spent with her mother were their walks to school early in the morning when dawn, dressed up in a unique combination of colours, was still preparing to arrive and bring softness, calmness, and new endeavors.

At such moments, when nature was still slow and lazy, Tyra's mum was quiet and sleepy. It felt safe, almost like bonding.

Tyra chatted, commenting on every detail around them. Crispy snow beneath her new red boots, the smell of early spring, or a bird tweeting.

She tried not to crash the magic or annoy her mother. She treasured those mornings, but soon Scarlett would get irritated by Tyra's energetic spirit anyway.

"Tyra! Stop leaping, jumping, and running about! Stop it at once! You're giving me a headache. Behave yourself! You're a young lady, after all. Tyra! Look at your feet, or you'll get hurt. Why are you staring at your feet? It'll ruin your posture! Goodness, why aren't you like the rest of the girls? Sit quietly! Don't twitch! Chew carefully! Don't climb! Do your best not to hurt yourself! Don't make me worry! Stop laughing so wildly. It will eventually bring tears."

All at once, everywhere, in every interaction, non-stop.

Little by little, Tyra learned how to attune to other people's needs and recognize them way before she could get hurt, although she would get hurt anyway. She felt as if nothing she did would ever be enough or just right. From a young age, she suspected something was very wrong with her.

The year Tyra spent with her grandparents was a pleasant break from her regular life, a long holiday. She felt safe, but all the magic was gone. The new city was dull and downhearted. Tyra missed her mother dearly, which surprised her. Once, she even caught herself watching birds through her classroom window during a boring geography lesson, feeling melancholy. She sensed a salty liquid coming down her cheeks and touched it with curiosity and wonder. Only then did she realize how much she missed her mother, but the reason was a mystery.

When the school year ended, Tyra returned to her parents. She expected to face nagging disapproval from her mother, but the minute they met at the train station, Logan and Scarlett ran to greet her and hug her. Scarlett's pure and sincere happiness confused Tyra, but deep down, she knew it wouldn't last long. Still, she decided to enjoy the moment, to savour it and put it inside her memory compartments. The ones that kept her grandma's coffee on Sunday mornings when Alma was sitting in a white puffy armchair beside Tyra's bed. The memory of warmth, love, and safety. The smell of freshly made coffee with a pinch of coriander and a quilted blanket. Or a memory of a daisy field where Tyra used to play with her dad when she was little. When yellow dust circled, tickled, and marked their noses. Fluffy yellow noses are the funniest and the happiest ones.

When they entered the barn, Tyra and her dad were still happy.

"Tyra, watch where you're going!" Scarlett snapped. "Put your shoes where they belong, and don't make a mess."

Here we go, Tyra thought. It was fast. Too fast, too soon, too short.

Scarlett's mood change was always rapid and unpredictable. Tyra cringed. This time it was even more painful.

Logan sighed. "Don't mind her, Tyra. You know how she gets. This is the way she is. You know, I quit drinking even though I missed you terribly. I'm glad you're home, kiddo."

"I missed you too, Dad. This is great news!" Tyra paused to think, twirling her boxer braids. "I've just pictured my favourite moment with her. When we walked in a golden forest in autumn, picking withered leaves. Remember how we always made peculiar bouquets? They lasted the whole winter." Now it sounded ridiculous. When things went sideways, Tyra focused on the bright side. At times it would come out of nowhere. But even if it was forced, it was her way of coping. No one had ever taught her how to sit with her uncomfortable emotions, and as a child, she found optimism was a way to deal with sadness, frustration, and anger.

Logan nodded. "What's your favourite memory of me?"

"Oh, I have a few." Tyra chuckled. "We used to hang out a lot, right? Mum preferred to be left alone, cooking. I wish she'd let me into the kitchen sometimes. We could have baked and cooked together. Anyway, I really enjoyed our ice cream outings on the way to the farmer's market. Remember the tiny ice cream truck with the most delicious ice cream in Azure? You would ask what kind of ice cream I had in mind. I would say, 'I don't know; it's hard to decide. I'll have your favourite, chocolate.' And I *loved* our funny dancing routine. Before Mum would get back home and close the curtain, we'd have quite a party, wouldn't we?"

"Oh, yeah. They were the best! We certainly specialized in fooling around in these days."

"Yeah, and the one on my birthday. I was feeling sick, and you brought me to work. I felt so proud. I thought, 'Wow, my dad drives this enormous truck!'"

Logan moved with unease. His wife would never consider that an advantage. "I remember feeling anxious about spending my wage without consulting your mother, but I wanted you to have something special. Something *I* bought for you."

"Yes. Mama buys all the presents. I know that, even for your birthday. She might ask if you'd like a new kitchen device she's dying for since you never need anything." Tyra chuckled. "So, we visited this large kids' store that felt like heaven, with all the toys a kid could dream of. You said I could choose *anything* I liked, and you wouldn't make any unsolicited suggestions like Mum does. I was super excited and couldn't believe my luck, but I feared Mum finding out. Anyway, I put that thought away and got lost in decision-making. It was hard." She giggled. "We bought Jena, my favourite squishy doll with a happy face, a collection of clothes and a quilt blanket for her. It was fantastic! Then we stopped by a pastry shop and had multiple mini cakes *instead of lunch*." Tyra snorted. She nurtured such moments. "Later, Mama crocheted a suitcase for Jena's accessories. It was sweet."

"Right, your mum was okay with our little adventure. I guess we got lucky."

They both laughed.

"Let's make something to eat, shall we?" Logan suggested.

"Yes! Let's make our home-smell-like butternut cookies again!"

Their last summer together was almost a happy one.

"Men talk of heaven,—there is no heaven but here. Men talk of hell,—there is no hell but here."
– Omar Khayyam

CHAPTER 4
Unexpected Friendship

"Clouds gathered in the sky.
Drops of water began to fall.
My shadow settled within me,
I continued my way alone."
– Yehuda Poliker
"The Shadow and I"

In early August, Logan started drinking again. He lost one job after another, cheated on his wife, and then cheated again.

Tyra heard rumours about his affairs but denied them.

One day on her way home from the library, holding a pile of new treasures, she saw him on a dark, grim street. He was drunk and dancing with another woman. Logan struggled to remain stable, stumbling with every step.

"He looks like a different person—easygoing, dumb, and even more lost," Tyra whispered. Her half-halo moon-braided hair tickled, hiding her eyes and cheeks, but her hands were full, and she needed to remain unnoticed. She leaned back and tried to scratch her face with her books. She murmured as she watched her father giggling and flirting.

How quickly one can lose a human form and a sense of morality. Integrity. Dignity.

For a bottle of unfulfilled dreams.

Tyra clutched her books, then walked backward into the shadow. She remained invisible with no effort. At first, she felt like crying, but nausea overcame the sadness. Disgusting. Obnoxious. It was all she could think of. Absolutely revolting. *Who is this man?*

Tyra felt a rattling weakness inside her belly. Her shallow breathing caused an aching sensation in her chest, and she cowered as if a heavy truck had landed on her shoulders.

She knew the scene she had witnessed couldn't be reversed. Disappointment washed over her, hitting her harder than ever. At that moment, Tyra lost all respect for her father. She never told her mother about what she had seen because she had an unspoken obligation to protect her mother and shield her feelings.

Now she loathed her father. Hated him.

But Scarlett always used to say, "Hatred is a dangerous emotion. It will destroy you. If you let it in, it will eat you up."

Tyra wasn't allowed to have such potent feelings, no matter what. No anger, let alone rage. And surely, not hatred. Even the expression "I hate these beans!" was forbidden in their house. Tyra felt there was something wrong with her for daring to feel such things.

I must bury these emotions and lock them away, she told herself.

The moment she thought that, the shadow *moved.* Tyra didn't notice, but she felt an odd sensation throughout her body as if she had transformed into a cotton cloud, feeble and dim. Feeling better, she headed home.

Tyra was lonelier than ever. She dreamed about having a friend, someone her age to talk to and spend time with. That was all she wanted. Problems at home became too noticeable. Her parents struggled to cover things up. She never heard them yelling or arguing, but the air was dense and foul. The entire atmosphere at home was tense, filled with silence and secrets. Tyra knew her parents were fighting, and she knew why. Hanging out in that dilapidated barn was unbearable.

Tyra spent most of her days outside—reading, walking, dreaming, and imagining that one day she would meet a friend, and it would shatter her loneliness.

When the new neighbours moved in beside their barn, Tyra's life became somewhat less miserable. They had older kids who were nice to Tyra, but the age gap was too big. They built their lovely house in the heart of a flourishing, fertile garden. In a verdant pine tree in the garden, a mother magpie had built her nest and become Tyra's new companion, reminding her of Zoe, a gifted, extraordinary magpie who could speak like a highly intelligent parrot. The magpie and her offspring rekindled nostalgic memories of Tyra's happy life in Moss.

The new neighbours were good people and shared their bountiful harvest with the Blair family with sincere generosity. Carrots, cabbage, squash of all kinds, zucchini, cauliflower, divine fresh potatoes, aromatic tomatoes, crunchy cucumbers, lettuce, sweet-scented herbs, fruits, and berries. It was a natural paradise.

Scarlett often used to say, "One or two warm hearts can save a family from hunger."

Once a week, the neighbours would drive them to the public bathroom, where there were hot tubs and saunas. They collected books, and Tyra read them. They baked and cooked, chatting with Tyra, who was a frequent guest in their kitchen. And they all gathered from time to time to share dinner, stories, and laughter. Tyra felt grateful, but there was no one her age who didn't want to cause her harm.

"Why don't you befriend the new kids?" Scarlett asked her daughter as they folded laundry in their barren, sombre living room.

"What kids? Oh, the milk lady's grandkids?"

"Yes. They seem nice. But you're a loner. I get it."

"I'm not a loner. I like solitude, but I also appreciate company. Anyway, there's no point. They're here only for the summer. They'll leave eventually, and I'll be left alone. Again." Tyra rubbed the amethyst drop-pendant Alma had given her the day before they left Moss.

"You miss Luke?"

Tyra nodded.

"Well, you don't need friends. You have us. Besides, there's no such thing as genuine friendship. You can only rely on your family. Friends tend to disappoint or betray or simply become estranged."

Tyra fidgeted, tugging her braids. "But Luke and I . . ."

"Yes, you were kindred spirits, two peas in a pod. But such a bond is rare, and you two were still too young. It would've faded away anyway. It's good that you're self-sufficient. It'll keep you safe. Besides, you've always been our little white crow."

"Did you just call me an outsider?"

"Of course not, I mean, you're different. Nothing wrong with that. But I wonder how such a bookish child, whose head is always in the clouds, could be born into our family. Most people have simpler expectations from life than you do. And it's easier this way. Your grandad always worries about you. He says that life won't be easy for you if you don't find your ground."

Tyra crossed her arms and stared at a neat pile of crisply folded clothes. "And my ground is in our family only? Family is more than blood. Often, it has nothing to do with blood. But I love my family. You know that. In fact, I fear I'm too attached to it."

"Nonsense. Family is everything. As you already know, the outer world isn't a safe place."

Logan overheard the conversation from the midst of the sizzling, bubbling kitchen. "Right. Our world is a dangerous, grim place," he said. "You better stick with your family, kiddo."

Tyra shook her head in disbelief, then adjusted the braids and went out.

She entered the library and met another newcomer who had moved to Marigold the previous month. At first, the young librarian, in her early thirties, attempted to join the rest of the village in hating the Blair family, but then she surrendered and opened her heart toward Tyra, who would always walk in with wide-open teal eyes and a soft smile, eager to find interesting stories on the dusty bookshelves. Sofia would always hunt for and retrieve the best books for her little visitor, the books she remembered and loved. She liked watching Tyra leaving with an enormous pile of flavescent, rustling books.

Sofia had become a brief but important part of Tyra's unfolding life.

Tyra loved her walks to the library, travelling back and forth through the charming rural area surrounded by berry bushes, blossoming flowers, and fruit trees. The smell was celestial. She would stop and sniff, stop and sniff.

On a hot summer day, she dashed into the library and noticed a new painting in the sitting area.

"Do you like it?" Sofia asked. "I found it in an online store. It reminds me of my childhood. My dad and I used to fly a kite in a dandelion field near our house."

Tyra stared at the lush yellow dandelion field. Who knew a simple canvas could awaken such vivid, almost tangible memories? Images, scents, sounds, tastes, and textures came to life. Tyra could feel the gentle wind on her cheeks, a tingling sensation in her nose, and a faint memory of happiness. On a cool summer evening, Tyra was ten again, a few months before her life would change and crumble.

~

"Luke, wait! Wait for me!" Tyra shouted as she tried to catch up with a boy who was racing down a dandelion field. His wavy light-brown hair swayed in the wind with childish recklessness. He wore denim shorts and a soft brown T-shirt with a beaver emblem on it. Zoe, a black-and-white magpie, hovered above him, screaming in a squeaky voice. "Come back, child, come back!"

With a mischievous smirk, Luke raced even faster. Moose swept beside him. The kids ran barefoot on the juicy, plush grass. The field was moist, smooth, and tender. Tyra fell on the ground and rolled down the hill until she reached Luke. She grabbed his foot and pulled as hard as she could. He tumbled onto the lush grass, grabbed her, and they rolled over and over, laughing. The kids landed on a damp yellow surface and sprawled out as if they were floating. Weightless, carefree, and happy.

"Don't like it, me, me, me," the magpie muttered.

"Relax, Zoe," Luke said. "Have some fun for once."

"Fun? What fun? Dark soon, soon dark," Zoe squawked as she fluttered around.

Luke groaned. "Help us make a bonfire. Or fetch some mushrooms and berries, will you? Please? I brought some potatoes and corn. We'll eat and go home; I promise. I have a flashlight, so no worries. Besides, you'll give us a heads-up beforehand, right? I guess we have more than an hour." Luke chuckled, then began making fire from a pile of leaves and branches.

"Fine, and then *home*," Zoe cawed. She grabbed a small basket from Luke's backpack and flew away. In a while, Zoe returned with the basket full of elderberries, huckleberries, and savoury blue-oyster mushrooms. The kids made a dinner of roasted corn and potatoes in silver foil, pan-fried mushrooms, and fresh berries for dessert.

In twilight, they sat in silence, watching the flames dance and crackle as an owl hooted and grasshoppers chirped. Moose lay on the ground in pure chillness. His legs sprawled out, his shoulders relaxed, and his torso slack. His soft sapphire eyes wandered, surrendering to dreamy slumber.

Tyra broke the silence. "Luke, we should listen to Zoe. It's getting dark. Olivia and your parents will be worried sick." She squeezed Moose in a heartfelt hug. Tyra looked younger than she was, wearing two double-bun braids and an emerald dress.

"I got it, child. We have time."

"Child? You're only one year older than me! Besides, I'm a girl."

"What's that supposed to mean?"

"Girls grow up faster. It's a fact." She giggled.

Luke snorted.

Zoe shook her head, whistling. "Listen, yes, listen to our girl, boy."

Luke gave her a look, rolled his eyes, and stoked the fire. "Let's sit here for a little while longer. It's nice."

"It is. I wonder if we'll be different when we get older," Tyra mused.

"I hope not."

"I wish I could picture us as young adults, rolling down the dandelion hill." She chuckled. "But I bet you'll be a boring, restrained man by then."

"Me? No way! Never!"

"I won't be coming to your wedding, just so you know. I won't like her, your bride. Period."

"Why?"

"I don't know. It's weird."

"Why? Are you going to marry me, then?"

"Ew! You're my best friend. My bestie!"

Luke tapped her shoulder and smiled. "And you're mine. Let's go then. Zoe's freaking out." He put on his scuffed-up, ginger hiking boots and got up.

Zoe let out a sigh of relief and flew forward. Moose raced her.

In a while, Zoe entered a beautiful garden full of roses, orange trees, and passion flowers, landing on a tree stump with sweet violet flowers on top of it and fairy lights all around. Moose ran toward her, yelped with glee, and almost bit her as if she were another puppy.

Zoe flew inside the house. "Shameless! Shameless!"

When the kids entered the garden, Olivia, Tyra's aunt, met them with a well-prepared lecture. She was eighteen but positioned herself as an old lady in a quest to protect the two naughty children she had been assigned to babysit. Olivia was short, plump, and pretty in her striped linen dress. Her cropped, curly, sunburnt hair looked furious. She spread her legs, her hand on her hips. "Where have you been? This is unacceptable! Outrageous! You leave your phones here and disappear until sunset for the entire day? Thank God your grandparents are still at work, Tyra; otherwise, they'd be having a heart attack right now. And your parents asked me to keep an eye on you. Let them have their long-anticipated vacation instead of searching for you in the woods. And you, young man, you're certainly overstepping any boundaries!"

Tyra was nervous and guilty. Luke pretended to be.

"Okay, come inside. I lit the fireplace and made cherry hand pies. I gather you've already eaten?"

"Sure, but one last minute." Luke dashed to the well, scooped water into a blue bucket, and splashed it all over his friends. Moose ran around, absorbed in absolute happiness. Soaking wet and quivering, the girls roared. Then they rushed to the water hose, switched it on, and drenched Luke in perfect cooperation.

His face dripping wet, Luke almost choked with laughter. "Now we can go!" he declared as he wrung out his dripping T-shirt.

The girls snorted and ran to the cottage.

"Where's Zoe?" Luke asked as he followed his friends.

When the kids and the puppy had settled beside the fire to warm up, they heard a rattling noise from the kitchen. They got up to check it out. Luke lifted the blue-and-white linen tablecloth and peeked under the table. "Zoe? What did you do? It's not a nesting time, you fashionista. Besides, your nest is already packed. Show me what you've got."

"I did not, I did not steal," Zoe tweeted. "Not enough, packed."

The girls bent down to see what Zoe had snatched this time. The queen of nesting was sitting on a pile of pearl buttons, scattered fragments of silky fabric, silver threads, and a stick of maroon lipstick.

Luke's eyes narrowed. "Is there anything else?"

"Nope," Zoe replied too quickly and turned away.

"Zoe, you can't have the compass, girl," Olivia said as she spotted a glow under the pile. "The rest, I think Mama won't mind sharing."

"All right," Zoe said, nudging a golden compass with her tiny leg toward Olivia.

Olivia smiled as she took it. "Okay, girl, let's pack up your treasures."

"Wait, I sense there's more," Luke said.

Zoe made a sound resembling a chuckle.

While the kids searched for a secret stolen piece, Zoe, amused by all the commotion, shuffled and stretched her neck in different directions. Her eyes glowed as if she were smiling, her entire figure gleaming with joy.

"Got it!" Luke said as he retrieved a tiny alpaca figure from a wicker basket in the hallway.

"Zoe, I thought you liked me!" Tyra cried.

Her grandmother, Alma, had given it to her on the solstice holiday last winter.

"I do. I do like you, child. Can't help it. Take it, take it," Zoe said.

Olivia examined her mini cherry hand pies. "Let's have some pie. I overdid myself; I can tell."

Tyra sighed. "I wish I could move here for good."

The cozy four-season cottage her grandparents had bought when she was born was Tyra's favourite place.

"Tyra, you spend all your weekends and holidays here. Your parents miss you," Olivia said. "You know that?"

"Not enough."

Olivia checked her phone. "Luke, your parents texted me. They want you to come home."

He nodded.

"Do they still dream about the Land of the Great Lakes?" Olivia asked.

"Oh, yeah," Luke said. "Mum believes in all that magical stuff. She's been waiting for the invitation her whole life, you know? They both dedicated their lives to becoming 'worthy' of that ethereal realm. It's ridiculous. The realm's a myth. And my parents are the best humans. But common sense, yeah?" He rolled his eyes.

"Amy and Adam are great parents. You're so lucky to be their kid," Tyra murmured.

"I know. I just think it's absurd to believe in such nonsense at their age. And being too good isn't good if it makes sense. It doesn't feel right."

"Or realistic." Olivia nodded, and then chose another pie, nicely browned and toasty. "I don't think there's a marvelous place that can make you happy. I don't believe such a realm even exists. But if it does, it's probably just a regular place, only with magic. People are people."

To avoid disappointment, Tyra never allowed herself to have such bold dreams, but her heart pulsated with a disagreeable rhythm.

That summer was the last time Luke and Tyra spent time together kayaking, picnicking, building a hut from pine branches, and having breakfast in the oak tree. Happy and carefree. When chaos arose in their land, Luke, his parents, and Zoe left the city without notice and disappeared. There was no connection for a while, so the kids lost track of each other. Some said Adam had found an illegal job in the land of Terra, and they'd moved there for good.

Tyra missed Luke terribly. She shook away the memory, then grasped a pile of fairy tales, thanked Sofia, and headed home.

Tyra liked to act out her favourite scenes from her best-loved books. Once, she was Ronia, the robber's daughter. Then she was Gerda from *The Snow Queen,* Pippi Longstocking, Jo from *Little Women,* and Athos from *The Three Musketeers.* After the incident with her father, Tyra dove into her bookish world. When Logan wasn't around, she spent time in the kitchen with her mum, cooking and baking. Finally, they were having real fun. They laughed and talked like sisters. It felt so good.

Meanwhile, Logan tried to find another job, with no luck. He grew gloomier and gloomier and even more closed in. His gaze drifted, and his body looked tight and stiff, even more than usual. It seemed as if something dark was bottled up inside him, trying to escape. Tyra did her best to avoid him. She spent most of her time in nature, walking in the forest. She called it the enchanted forest. It was dense, chilly, and shadowy, but it was also vibrant and full of wonder.

One day while feeding chipmunks and squirrels, Tyra said, "I wish I could have a friend, a best friend, like Anne of Green Gables or—"

Before she could finish, she heard a squeaky voice behind her. "It's very nice of you to come here, always full-handed."

Tyra turned around and saw a large squirrel, about the size of a toddler, wearing a red scarf, funny glasses, and a green ragbag with straps that crossed its shoulders. The squirrel stared at Tyra with a mixture of curiosity and mischief.

Tyra shook her head and wondered if the heat was getting to her. She had spent too much time that day under the sun while gardening.

"Happy to meet you, Tyra!" the squirrel exclaimed.

Tyra heard a rustling sound above her head and turned around. On top of the highest tree sat a giant Maine coon cat, the size of overgrown lynx. It stared at Tyra and then sprang down and vanished into thin air. Weird.

Tyra closed her eyes and shook her head again. "I feel dizzy, to be honest," she said, trying to regain her senses. She fiddled with one of her dragonfly earrings, its blue and purple crystals twinkling.

"You needed a friend?" the squirrel asked as if it were a casual thing to meet a talking squirrel in a forest, offering friendship. "I'm Koda. It means 'a friend' in the Sioux language."

What's the Sioux language? Tyra wondered, but that was the least of her problems, so she let it go. "Am I dreaming? Perhaps I fell asleep, and my body's lying under a pine tree," she muttered with a fair amount of hope as she tugged her hair, which was trapped in a bubble ponytail.

"Daytime and dreams sometimes overlap," Koda said, crunching a nut. "Let me take you to my place. It's cute and cozy. You'll see."

Tyra frowned. "How can I possibly fit into your tiny home? Besides, I haven't been climbing trees lately. I used to. Actually, I was an excellent tree climber. My friend Luke and I used to build our tree fort with blankets and cushions. Grandma didn't mind. But . . . I really need to understand what's happening right now."

"Don't. You'll miss the whole point. Sometimes it's better to follow the natural rhythm of life," Koda said theatrically. "It's going to be a truly good thing for you—and for me. I could use some company. It's been pretty boring here lately." Koda rolled his eyes at the offended chipmunks.

Tyra felt puzzled, but she was a child, and what kind of child would turn down an invitation to visit a squirrel's cozy home? So, off they went, leaving the disappointed chipmunks to themselves.

"How am I supposed to get in there?" Tyra grumbled a few minutes later as she stared at a petite, colourful door above her head.

"Just hop up."

"Okay, it's just a dream, a weird lucid dream. Gosh, I feel like Alice right now." Tyra chuckled and hopped up, as Koda suggested. The door seemed to adjust to her height, and against all odds, she was able to enter and stand comfortably inside.

Tyra found herself in a bright, spacious room. *Cozy indeed.* She looked around. Tiny lanterns with a golden glow hung on the walls, filling Koda's neat, snug home with their soft light. Crafty shelves overflowed with a respectful collection of greenish acorns, mysterious seeds, edible flowers, and nuts, nuts, and more nuts, among other delicate treasures from the forest. The floor was carpeted with a thick layer of plush moss. Tyra dipped her toes into the soft, warm surface. She wiggled, curled, and nestled her feet there for a blissful moment. In one corner, she saw a bed of woven twigs and soft leaves piled with quaint feathers and miniature blankets made of spider silk and flower petals. The faint scent of fresh pine, lavender, and roses infused the room, making her dizzy. On top of a round cedar table rested a bowl of forest fruits, chestnuts, mushrooms, berries, and mini pies.

Tyra gasped. "This is above and beyond."

Koda pointed at the table. "Please, help yourself."

Tyra fetched some berries and treated herself to a chubby apple pie.

"So, Tyra, you like reading and acting the stories out, eh? Me too. But I have a different approach . . . more interactive. Would you like to try it?"

Tyra got up with a hint of caution and grabbed another pie. "Sure. Why not? Please show me."

Koda pointed to the oval window and snickered. In an instant, the window transformed into a rippling mirror, whispering in a foreign language as it projected a mischievous glint.

Tyra shivered. "Creepy."

Koda chuckled, looking pleased.

Then Tyra screamed. "What the nut?" She looked at her fluorescent hands in shock. Her body shimmered, and her hair glittered.

Koda set his glasses on the bed. "It's safe, no worries. Come, and I'll show you *my* favourite scenes." He winked with a hint of a grin, then entered the mirror.

Tyra hesitated.

Koda turned around. His bottom was inside the mirror, and his head was stretched out. He gestured to the pantry. "Grab some snacks, will you? There's a green bag on your left, on the coffee table. Oh, and put this brownish cap on. It'll make you invisible."

"Well, see, I probably should get going. My mom will be worried sick."

"Time's irrelevant here, sugar. No sweat. You'll be right on time for dinner."

Tyra tilted her head, bit her lip, and narrowed her eyes. Then she sighed, grabbed some snacks, and put on the invisibility cap. It was coffee-milk brown with a white anchor in the middle. Tyra peeked at the mirror and spotted Ronia and Birk jumping back and forth above the chasm.

"It can't be. No way! No, no, no!" she whispered.

"We must be quiet. Shh!" Koda waved, inviting her to take a step.

Tyra stared at her disappearing body, struggling to adjust. "What about you?"

Koda shrugged. "I'm just a squirrel with a red scarf. No biggie."

Tyra and Koda immersed themselves in their favourite scene, in which Ronia and Birk, the robbers' kids from two fighting clans, were making a bridge of friendship and kindness.

"It was . . . wow! Fantastic!" Tyra admitted a while later when they returned to reality in Koda's home.

Koda smiled with pleasure. Then Tyra heard a subtle, hushed whisper coming from the mirror: "There's nothing better than a friend, unless it's a friend with chocolate. Linda Grayson."

CHAPTER 5
Two Tales

"The wind moved about,
The fear seeped and dripped
My shadow in me made me shake."
– Yehuda Poliker

Tyra spent most of her daytime hours with Koda. In his domain, each day felt like a long weekend. Every morning, they raced to a cool, refreshing river and swam for hours. They built tiny homes for bustling, humming chipmunks, climbed sprawling trees to examine peculiar nests, and ate berries straight from the bushes. They visited books and stories through the oval transforming window-mirror and had picnics. They read aloud and chatted during long, sweltering midday hours under a gigantic mushroom where they created their mini book club of two.

"So, tell me, sugar, what story would you like to visit the most, but you've never dared? Wait, and most importantly, what story would you never visit?" Koda asked Tyra one afternoon when they sprawled under their mushroom, munching on red apples.

Tyra shifted from side to side on a pile of green leaves with a hint of yellowish dots, a bit restless. "Mmm . . . let's first visit the one I'd like to visit. The *Tale of the Wonderful Doctor*. Do you know that one? I heard it multiple times when I was little. It's a dark story, but for some reason, I was hypnotized by it."

Koda nodded and began to tell the story in a spooky manner. "A long, long time ago, a good boy and his widowed mother lived in poverty. One day the young boy woke up at dawn and went to the forest to gather firewood. Nearby was a large swamp; it was rumoured that the swamp was cursed. Suddenly, the boy heard a hoarse female voice, asking for help. It was an old woman with a black scarf who was stuck in the swamp. After the lad helped her get out, the old lady offered him a five-year apprenticeship as a reward for his open heart. The boy consulted with his mother, and she was glad her son would become a learned man, but she was sad to be left alone. If she fell ill, no one would be able to get her water. But her maternal instincts prevailed, and the widow agreed.

"'Here we are, at home, lad,' the old woman said, showing him the dark cave. 'You'll see a lot and learn a lot. Be afraid of nothing, and don't be surprised by anything! Know that I am Death, for some a monster, for others a comforter, a messenger, or a carrier.'

"The lad was dumbfounded, but there was nothing he could do now. Reluctantly, he entered the cave. It was dark and damp. Through the entrance, the whole earth was visible, illuminated by the sun. And at night, the sky, dotted with stars as large as pears, stared at him with curiosity.

"The lad stayed with Death for some time. During his stay, she showed him different herbs and trained him to heal different diseases, revealing many secrets.

"When five years passed, it was time to say farewell. 'Remember well and obey,' Death said. 'I'll only show myself to you alone. When you see me standing at the feet of a sick person, treat them as I mentored you, and they will recover. If you see me standing at the patient's head, know that they're mine, and do not interfere. If you do, you'll lose your life.'

"The young man promised not to violate his master's will. Then he bowed to her and went out to help the world.

"He travelled to myriad lands, visiting crowded cities and quiet villages. At every stop, he treated the sick. Whether they were poor or rich, it made no difference. He would heal them when Death was at their feet and leave them be when she was at their heads.

"As the years passed, the boy, now a doctor, grew restless. He dreamed about having a family and building a home, but his work appeared to have no end. He met grief and suffering all around him. His heart bled each time he saw his master above a child's head or above young people who were desperate to live, and he could do nothing.

"One day in the middle of a cold winter, he visited a widow and her five little kids. The mother was dying, and the kids were fidgeting around a lifeless stove, snuggling with each other, scared and hungry. When the doctor saw his master above the woman's head, his heart pinged."

Koda paused to take a bite of an apple. Tyra listened to him, mesmerized. Koda took another bite, noticing dark, heavy clouds thickening above their heads.

"Koda? Do you want to continue? I'm dying here," Tyra said, filled with impatience.

"Hee-hee! For the last scene, will you join me inside the mirror? Whoo-hoo."

Koda's hooting made the story sound even spookier. He gestured at Tyra with his paws spread out like a fan. Then he laughed, tweaking her long pigtails.

Tyra smiled as she tidied her hair. "As a matter of fact, I will. The last scene is my favourite."

Koda giggled. "Okay, child. Long story short, the doctor disobeyed and saved the mother of five little ones. Sorry, sugar, can't wait to get to the last scene."

Tyra rolled her eyes, then continued the story. "Death was furious."

Koda raised his hands in disbelief. "Yeah, I mean, *obviously*."

"Well, what would you expect him to do?"

"I understand. The situation's controversial. But there are laws of nature that are beyond our comprehension. Life and death are indecipherable. My heart shrinks when I think about these little ones but mostly because I've known them, seen them, and grown attached to them. But how many others are out there, unseen and unnoticed?"

"I see what you mean, Koda. But I would never wish to take his place. I understand his dilemma and how this job shattered and eroded him from the inside."

"I know, sugar. I'm just saying some things are beyond our mundane perspective. Anyway, she forgave him that time but said, 'You cannot see further than your nose, boy, although I have revealed all secrets of life and death to you. This time, I forgive you because you did this out of a desire to do good, but next time, don't try to overpower me.' With that, Death disappeared into the darkness."

Koda rushed to finish the story. "The second time he disobeyed his master by saving his mother from a lethal disease. I mean, his own mother, right? I think Death understood his humane limitations very well, so she forgave him the second time."

"Wait, you missed the most interesting part!" Tyra said, her eyes brightening as a smile broke out. "'I feel so much better, son!' his mother said. The doctor kissed her forehead and held her hand for a long time as if saying goodbye forever. He knew Death was waiting for him outside, but he still went out, ready to face the consequences of his actions.

"'You violated my ban again,' Death whispered. 'I'm grieving for the lost five years. You turned out to be an unfaithful student.'

"'You never had parents or children,' the doctor replied, trying to justify his choice. 'I give up my life in exchange for my mother's.'"

"'Why? Have you forgotten your duty to those who suffer

across the world? You belong to them. I'll forgive you one last time. But you have no right to interfere with what you don't understand.'"

Tyra stopped, deep in thought. Koda picked up the story from there.

"He disobeyed his master a third and final time when he saved an entire town by healing their dying leader during a deadly battle. I know it was a hard choice. I guess it's impossible to sit still on two chairs at a time. You either stay human, or you become something else entirely to complete your duty according to the laws of nature. Can we enter the last scene now?" Koda stared at Tyra with puppy dog eyes and a mischievous sparkle on his face.

"Alright, let's go. Oh, wait. Death touched the mountain. Oy. Remember how she took him to her realm? Death touched the mountain, and it opened like a gate. Now we can go." Tyra rushed toward the mirror.

Before he jumped into it, Koda took off his red scarf, placed it on his bed with care, then put on the silver gloves that made him invisible, just in case. *I'm too young to meet her,* he thought.

Tyra had already disappeared under her invisibility cap.

On the other side of the shivering mirror, they found themselves in a spectacular cave filled with countless lucent bowls. Some of them shone brightly, spreading their vibrant glow all around. The others flickered with a dim flame, then drifted into darkness.

Death appeared as a beautiful young woman with green eyes —wise, bottomless, and unreachable. Her long, snow-white hair streamed across the floor. She glanced at Koda and Tyra, her eyes gleaming, almost smiling. She looked formidable yet relatable. Her indigo dress tickled the earth, and her entire figure spread a glowing multicoloured light and a profound acceptance of what is.

Tyra and Koda trembled in awe. The doctor, a tired man in his forties, looked guilty, scared, and curious but without regret.

"Where's mine?" he asked as he examined the illuminated space. His gaze moved fast and with apparent unease.

Death gestured toward a beautiful mosaic bowl in which the light barely flickered. The doctor came closer and stared at the feeble flame. It was smouldering and shuddering, as if short of air.

When they returned home, Koda smirked in delight. "Phew, that was dark! Shall we proceed with more darkness next time? One at a time?" He opened his mouth and threw in some berries, grinning. Then he yawned and stretched and settled in his brand-new rocking chair.

"Agreed. See ya tomorrow."

~

Tyra woke up early and rushed to get ready for another wonderful day.

She was responsible for cleaning the barn and folding the laundry. The kitchen and hallway needed cleaning each day too. She always managed to get it done before she went to the forest or, at worst, by late evening.

Tyra learned how to cook in the kitchen of her new neighbours, eager to surprise her parents with a homemade dinner or dessert. Each morning, Scarlett would send Tyra to buy raw milk from a nice old couple who treated their cow like it was their child. The milk lady would also help Tyra with recipes and suggestions. After each brief but pleasant visit, Tyra would stop and drink the milk on her way, returning home with a half-empty three-litre jar. Each time, Scarlett would sigh and smile, reassuring her that the challenge of bringing home a jar full of milk was an impossible feat. How could one resist rich, creamy milk, straight from the cow? The neighbour, a plump, smiling lady, made it even harder by offering Tyra a nice round loaf of crusty country bread she baked each morning for that exact occasion.

This time, Tyra poured half the milk into a smaller jar. Then she hid the jar and the loaf of bread inside some blackberry bushes and went home.

"Tyra, goodness, where are you heading this early?" Scarlett asked. "To the forest, again? God knows what you do there all day, all alone until dusk."

Tyra shrugged. "I read, picnic, walk, and build homes for small animals."

That was partly true.

Her mother looked out the window. "It's raining."

Tyra followed her gaze. "Just a drizzle. It'll pass soon."

"Wait. I made you sandwiches and orange juice for lunch. And look what Grandma sent for you. You might need it. It's getting cooler." Scarlett handed Tyra a hooded, cream-coloured poncho made from warm alpaca wool, soft and cozy. Tyra texted to thank her grandma, and then she retrieved the jar of milk and a loaf of bread, wrapped it in a linen towel, and headed to the forest.

"Koda, I have something for you!" Tyra yelled as she approached his tree house, sweating in anticipation of their next adventure.

Koda jumped down, and they settled under the mushroom. "Milk and bread! Holy Moley! Best breakfast on Earth!" He slurped and chomped in pure chillness. "So, what's the story you dread the most? I promise we'll never visit it. Pinkie promise." Koda offered Tyra his tiny finger.

She shook it with a faint smile. "'The Shadow' by Hans Christian Andersen."

"Oh-ho-ho, that one gives me goosebumps." Koda shivered. "When the learned man, kind-spirited and tender, absorbed in poetry and a romantic search for true love and beauty, dismissed his shadow?"

Tyra nodded as she felt an uninvited chill crawling down her spine.

Koda began to tell the story. "The man refused to see himself as he was and fell into the illusion that this world could be fixed, and perfection could be achieved. Perfection, mind you, creates shame. It manifests as an escape from criticism and fear of rejection. Anyway, the shadow, now free, enslaved the man!" Koda said it in a loud voice, making frantic gestures. "The *id* became bigger, stronger, as it built a life of its own, obtaining and fulfilling everything the learned man had ever dreamed of. The shadow had even deluded the princess, the love of his man's life, and attempted to marry her. The man tried to rebel, but it was too late. The shadow was already far more influential than its man. And then, afraid of being exposed, the *id* killed him. The horrible end." Koda cringed as he tried to pull himself together. "That's the most mortifying story, indeed."

The drizzle had escalated into a squall. Koda and Tyra scuttled under the giant mushroom, but it was no use.

Tyra looked gloomy. "I see. He ignored his shadow at first. I can understand why. And when it was small and pitiful, I felt sorry for it. You know? I did." She sighed. "When the man freed the shadow, it became everything the learned man rejected and everything he wished for but never dared to have."

"The shadow eventually filled the man's psyche, leaving no room for the light, the grains of which it destroyed easily," Koda said, offering his own interpretation as he slurped the frothy, creamy milk. "The *id* filled up not only the man's unconscious mind but also his consciousness. The man yielded to his instincts, unable to oppose them. Everything that had been cast out, lying dormant on the bottom of his mind, was eager to rush out."

Tyra became still, absorbed in her thoughts. Koda didn't interrupt.

The entire forest went silent.

Then Tyra sighed. "I wonder how many among us are not people but shadows? What if we live in the World of Shadows?"

"That would be dreadful, indeed," Koda said, checking himself for goosebumps but not finding any. Then he smirked. "Imagine, sugar. In some beings, deep down, the remnants of self-awareness, light, and kindness are still lurking. In others, these parts are buried under their shadows, too deep to be retrieved or recovered. These remnants are tucked inside their subconscious minds as a non-necessity. A dangerous mechanism. A weakness, undermining their survival in the realm of darkness." Koda tickled Tyra until she burst into laughter.

"Okay, okay, enough. I give up! No more creepy stories!" she cried.

Koda caught his breath and then turned serious. "Have you met yours?"

Tyra frowned, wringing and twisting her four-lemonade braids. "I'd rather not."

"Don't you think that by dismissing it, you might give it more power than you'd like? That way, you'll allow it to operate within you and *control* your narrative without you ever noticing."

Tyra scrunched her nose. "I don't know. I think I'm still too young. When I'm ready, I'll try to find it. I hope my shadow will forgive me one day. Can we skip this topic and just have fun?" Tyra felt an uneasy sensation in her gut. She gripped her arms. Her skin was pale, her mouth open, and her muscles tightened. She was scared. Her shadow moved and squeaked, unheard and unnoticed.

"As you wish, sugar. This is *your* tale. But beware of losing your balance. Light and darkness, life and death, are inseparable," Koda warned. "You wanna jump?" he asked, his eyes smiling.

"Yes, please!" Tyra perked up and ran after her friend.

They stood in the pouring rain, unsheltered, wet, and happy. Their faces were tilted upward, their eyes closed, and their tongues stretched out as they caught the fresh, cool drops. Barefoot, Koda and Tyra sank their feet into the soft, slushy soil and wiggled their toes. They lingered there, soaked and relaxed.

"Shall we climb?" Koda asked when the rain reverted to a drizzle. "But let's add some dry leaves. I have some in stock in my room."

Tyra smiled. "Of course. You knew in advance that the pile of dry leaves would come in handy, didn't you?"

They grabbed a huge wicker basket full of crinkled, veined, spotted leaves and piled them under a broad, sturdy branch.

Koda and Tyra climbed the tree and settled on a wide branch that looked like a bench or a bridge. They stayed there for a while in comfortable silence, swinging their legs back and forth as the rain faded. Then they jumped into a fluffy, rustling mass, screaming with joy.

Tyra and Koda lay on the pile of scattered leaves, touching the slushy soil, burying their toes, and talking. Relaxed. Untroubled. Connected.

CHAPTER 6
Equanimity

"If you can dream—and not make dreams your master;
If you can think—and not make thoughts your aim;
If you can meet with Triumph and Disaster
And treat those two impostors just the same . . ."
– Rudyard Kipling. "If"

Sitting under the tree, chilled and pleased, Koda crunched a cookie that Tyra had made with her mum the previous night. "How about a sleepover, sugar? Remember, time's irrelevant here."

"I haven't had sleepovers in a while. Not since Luke, my friend, disappeared."

"He hasn't. He's okay."

Tyra's eyes sparkled. "Thank you," she whispered. "And Zoe?"

"And Zoe."

Tyra smiled. "Thank you, Koda. A sleepover would be nice."

"Nice? Wait until midnight. Heh, heh, heh!"

The marvellous dining table served as a charcuterie board with cheese of all kinds, roasted and fresh veggies, dried fruits, nuts, crackers, cornbread, stuffed squash, and a tea tray with fruit tarts, edible flowers, and an elegant teapot.

After a bountiful feast, Koda and Tyra sat on the bench board and watched the night sky. The sky stretched out like a vast, inky canvas, strewn with tiny stars—vibrating, twinkling, smiling—as if they were blanketing the darkness like scattered brilliants.

Koda gave Tyra his bed, then settled on a pile of plush blankets on the mossy floor. They revealed their innermost secrets to each other and told stories until midnight.

Tyra told Koda about the monsters hiding under her bed when she was little, whispering in a foreign tongue. She also told him how scared she was, how fear would crawl and float in her veins, and how she would cover her head with a quilt and tremble until she fell asleep. She told him how vivid and tangible the tiptoeing sensation of freezing cold felt through her skin.

"Have you tried looking under the bed?" Koda asked, tapping Tyra on her back.

"Sure, my parents and I searched the room each night. But I could still feel them, still sense their presence in my room through the night, you know? No one believed me, of course." Tyra shrugged.

"How did you feel when you were asleep? Still afraid?"

"Weirdly, no. I felt safe, calm, and taken care of somehow. I don't know how to explain it. I thought some night fairies would drive the monsters away and protect me while I slept. Of course, there are no fairies or angels to protect us."

"True. But when I was little, my mama told me to try to befriend them. I was scared at first. The fact she believed me felt good and frightening at the same time. If she believed me, the monsters existed, you know? But I gathered courage, and I would make a cozy nest under my bed with some pillows, blankets, and a flashlight. Then I would crawl under the bed and have an herbal tea party with them each night with a book."

"That sounds fun. Do you still see them sometimes?"

"Rarely, but I see other monsters, and they aren't mine. They're *real* monsters, if you know what I mean. No boundaries, no shame, and no desire to get cozy," Koda said in an ominous voice.

Tyra shivered and laughed. "What's a sleepover without a scary story before bed, eh?" Happy and sleepy, she dozed off, falling into a sweet slumber.

Then, through her blissful napping, she heard hushed giggles and rustling sounds. Straining to listen, Tyra heard heavy, muffled footsteps. She felt as if she were shrinking. She touched her chilled skin, brushing off goosebumps. Panicking, she buried her head under her pillow, squeezing her eyes shut.

Koda chuckled, his eyes grinning with joy and affection.

Tyra rubbed her eyes in fearful anticipation. Then she got up and slinked around, tiptoeing so as not to spook any unsolicited guests.

Then she saw them, the beasties.

A dreamy monster was in the pantry, crunching on a butternut cookie. The crumbs fell from the monster's round belly and onto the moss carpet, causing the creature to look both ashamed and delighted. She resembled a plump, light-purple squishmallow covered in plush chick down. Her large rainbow eyes and tiny, round pupils looked shy and satisfied. The creature appeared timid with a charming, lopsided smile and aligned brows above her diagonal oval eyes. She seemed formidable yet super cute with her tiny limbs and fluffy bunny slippers. And she had funny turquoise freckles on her cheekbones.

Beside the monster was another one. He was climbing the ladder, searching for delicacies. "Yummy, yummy, yummy," he mumbled. His smooth coat was bluish-grey. His topaz eyes were enormous and a bit narrow. He had floppy bunny ears, puffy limbs, and a sad mouth that stretched from ear to ear, along with tiny white fans and horns covered by sleeping cups. He was super cute.

Tyra smiled. "Hello."

The monsters were startled, embarrassed, exposed.

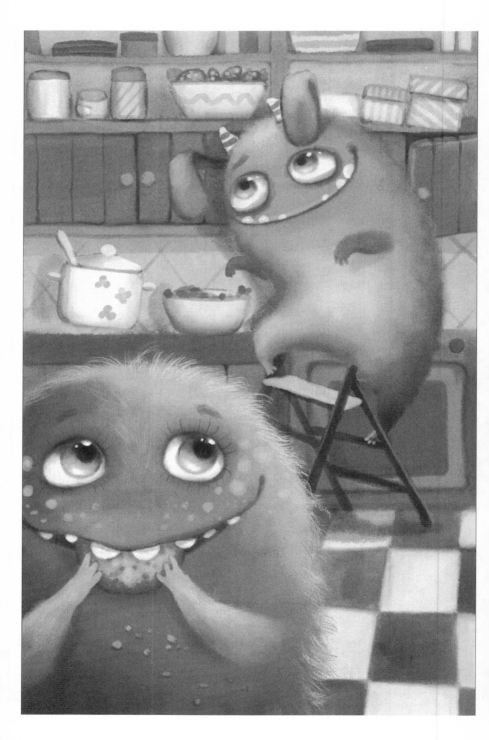

"Don't be afraid," she said. "You wanna be friends? I don't think Koda will mind sharing some goodies from his pantry, right?"

Koda rolled his eyes, grinning.

Tyra turned back to the monsters. "You wanna play or maybe read together? Can I sit beside you? We can have cookies with milk."

The purple monster looked at Koda with caution, curiosity, and an adorable smile. The other one froze on the ladder, unsure what to expect.

Koda nodded, giggling. "Alright, monsters, let's get acquainted. I'm Koda, the owner of this kingdom. This is Tyra. But you already know her. You can't fully speak, right? May I introduce you then?"

The monsters nodded eagerly.

"Koda, how can they fit in your home? They're gigantic."

Koda shrugged. "The same way you can, sugar. It's magic. My home is adaptive."

"It's odd. You both seemed to have jumped right out of my favourite picture book. To be precise, it's like a wordless comic or an unmoving cartoon with illustrations. One lady, a talented artist, can tell stories through her drawings. It's fantastic!"

The purple monster blushed, and the blue one smiled.

"This is Cami, and this is Kent," Koda said, pointing at the purple monster and the blue one in turn.

Kent changed his colour to milk coffee, then creamy white, then maroon, then back to garish blue. He swayed, giggling. Then he changed his size to a regular squishmallow then to a big one, before settling back into his regular form.

Cami laughed and clapped. Tyra was over the moon with happiness.

"I believe those are your monsters, sugar," Koda said. "Do you recognize their vibe? No idea how they got here, but a few months ago, well before we met, they appeared one night in my kitchen, munching, whispering, and wandering around until dawn. Over time I got used to falling asleep to their muffled sounds, pretending I'd never noticed them. They seem to value their privacy. Heh, heh!"

Cami and Kent gasped in disbelief. Then they tapped their arms on their hips and chuckled. Cami lowered her eyelids, blushing. Kent whirled, transforming from a gigantic squishmallow to a tiny one. Then he bounced around like a squishy ball.

"I recognize the vibe. I see now that they were frightened. Well, Cami certainly was. Kent probably was grumpy and displeased. Maybe our feelings got mixed up and had been amplified altogether. I don't know, just guessing." Koda smiled and then went outside to perch on the branch and observe the stars again, providing the trio with some privacy and time to bond.

Tyra and her beasties had a relaxing spa night, followed by reading. Cami pampered Tyra by polishing her nails and giving her a facial, head, and shoulder massage. Meanwhile, Kent prepared a bubble bath for Tyra, singing to her in a foreign language. The bath appeared out of thin air with a hammock, a swimsuit, and a wreath made of roses. Kent also sprinkled some rose petals on the moss carpet.

Tyra fell asleep in the hammock while Cami sang her a lullaby, and Kent watched her sleep as he drank fresh roasted coffee with a pinch of ginger and sprinkled with cacao powder. Koda slept peacefully with earplugs in his bed.

The following morning, Tyra woke up late to the horrible smell of fresh paint. She saw her mother bustling about with a bucket of light-purple liquid and a bunch of brushes.

"Good morning!" Scarlett said with excitement. "Look how pretty it is! I'm painting the whole hut! You're okay with this colour for your room, aren't you?"

"Sure. It's better than the peeling floral wallpaper. Do you need help, Mama?"

"I'm good. I'll put on the music you don't like, but I do. It'll be fun. But there's no lunch today."

Tyra smiled. She made her mother pan-fried golden potatoes and a salad with nuts and fresh veggies for lunch. She also grabbed the fancy herb flatbreads they'd baked the night before, cheese and avocado spread, greens, and fresh mini veggies from their neighbour's garden. Then she packed it all up and headed to the forest.

It was a sunny day. The air was chilly, accompanied by a stroking breeze and the smell of autumn's approach. Tyra was wearing skinny jeans, a lightweight shirt with a buttoned plaid flannel shirt and red sneakers—the usual. She had also wrapped an emerald cardigan around her waist due to the changing weather. Her long ponytail braid flowed and danced in the air while her linen backpack, full of food, flopped from side to side.

The forest was still full of greenery, but the fall colours were increasing.

"Greetings, my braided friend. What goodies did you bring this time?" Koda asked as he poked his head inside Tyra's bag, searching with both paws. "Oh, good, good, me *like* it!" With a wide smile, Koda took everything out.

Tyra smiled with pleasure. "Koda, do you know the tale about Frosty?"

Koda gaped at her. "Do I know Frosty? I've only visited her, like, a million times! You wanna? *Yes*, you wanna, oh yeah! You wanna visit Frosty, eh? Let me guess—the scene in the forest! Gosh, you're dark, my friend. Officially. I love it! Shall we?" He grinned, offering Tyra his hand like a gentleman.

Tyra giggled, then she took his hand, and they swayed around the room. "You know, it's an ancient tale," she said. "I loved it when I was a kid."

"Sure, it's like the story of Cinderella, only creepier. Much more so." Koda rubbed his paws together.

"Well, yes. It's a combination of Cinderella and Snow White, I think. The same narrative of a poor, motherless girl who's kind, beautiful, and handy. She lived with her weak, spineless father, a wicked stepmother, and a lazy, goofy stepsister. Basically, she was their maid. The father was their servant too. Frosty would always find support and comfort in nature; birds and animals were her friends and helpers.

"One cold winter night, her stepmother, as stupid as she was, insisted that her husband take Frosty to the forest and leave her there to die. No brains at all. How did she intend to survive without Frosty? She couldn't even warm up stew, let alone manage the house on her own. And the father? Oy vey, he only pretended to love her! He was such a nice man—who could kill.

"Well, nice men can destroy your well-being for sure. They'll do everything they're asked for to avoid rocking the boat. They'll shut down, turn away, and leave you to deal with hurtful situations, so *they* won't get hurt. Defending his daughter would have required confronting his wife, and I don't think he was capable of that."

Tyra shivered. "So, he harnessed the cart and took his 'beloved' daughter to die in the frost. Disgusting."

Koda gave her side braid a gentle tug. "Let's go, sugar."

They entered the shuddering, vibrating mirror.

Frosty was a young girl who was about sixteen years old. She was sitting under an old oak, wrapped in her mother's shawl and rubbing her hands together as she blew on them. She was pretty. Her long, dark-brown braid was covered with frost.

Suddenly, branches above her head began to crackle. Frosty lifted her head and saw an old man, Frost, dressed in a glittering, light-blue coat. He was also wearing a fluffy fur hat, black high boots, and a red belt. His beard was as white as snow, as was his shaggy hair.

"Are you warm, child? Are you warm, beauty?" he asked as he crept closer.

The temperature dropped, and the gust raged stronger, sneaking under Frosty's bones and into her heart. She trembled with uncontrollable intensity. "I'm warm, dear Frost."

Frost gloated. His eyes flashed with malevolence as he lowered the temperature even more. "Are you warm, child? Are you warm, cutie?"

"I'm warm, dear Frost. I'm okay," Frosty said as she leaned on the oak's trunk, her eyes closing. By then her body was covered by a thin white crust.

Frost got wild. His loud, echoing laughter shook the entire forest. He summoned a final smashing wind, and the cold air became unbearable.

Poor Frosty. Her nostrils became as hard as iron. They hurt so much that it felt as if someone were pulling them out with metal pliers. Her breath became weaker and weaker, and her eyelids fell shut.

"Are you warm, girl? *Are* you warm?" he roared.

Her frozen, alabaster lips moved with a final effort as she slid down the tree trunk, slumping to the ground. "I am."

Frost transformed in an instant, looking at Frosty with benevolence and admiration. He touched her chest, warming her still-beating heart, and then he touched her shoulders, filling her crusty body with warmth and love.

Frosty opened her eyes and flashed a weary smile. Her cheeks were rosier than ever, her lips a lush red, and her hands warm and soft.

"Well done, Frosty. I'm proud of you," the old man said.

The scene vanished, and Tyra and Koda returned to their reality.

"Whoo-hoo! What a scene, eh?" Koda said. "I'm glad Frost gave our friend a silver cart filled with gold and jewels and walked her home."

"Yes, Frosty earned her independence and can now live her own way. Yay!"

"Her stepmother was super jealous, remember? That same day, she sent her daughter to the same spot. But she came home much earlier in a rusty, rattling sled filled with acorns and pinecones. I wish I could have them. Dang it." Koda stomped his paw.

Tyra chuckled. "Sure. The girl was rude to Frost, impudent. She was lucky he took pity on her and sent her home, safe and sound. Well, stupidity and ignorance aren't exactly a person's fault, to some extent, right?"

Koda shrugged. "That's debatable. But, yeah, at times, it is what it is. What do you think about our Frosty?" he asked as he snacked on their delicious lunch.

"Sofia, my librarian friend, says it's about women's suppression and people-pleasing. I think she's right. But I appreciate Frosty's kindness, and I like her connection to nature. I'm furious with her father, though. What kind of love is that? Sending your daughter to die during the coldest night of the winter? And why isn't she allowed to voice her discomfort and fear?"

"That's what happened on the surface, yes. But I believe it's important to dig deeper and scrutinize what lies beneath the surface. I find it prudent never to be satisfied with obvious, easy answers. See, this tale was written in prehistoric times when people used an initiation ceremony as a passage into adulthood. They lived in a harsh natural environment, so it was vital for them to learn how to endure any circumstances. It's about their ancient philosophy of accepting what is. It's a test. They sent their teens into the cold forest as a coming-of-age ritual. Those who survived the night could join the society as adults, build a family of their own, vote, and have equal rights within the clan. Those who didn't, usually died."

"Brutal! But why?"

"Because they couldn't accept the law of nature—impermanence. They rejected and fought it, becoming angry and restless. Resentment brought tension and fear. I guess fear killed them even before the frost could. Anyway, Frosty accepted reality as it was, with equanimity. That's why nature helped her get through the night. There's a difference between giving up and surrendering, right?"

"This is wild, Koda. We've all been taught to fight for our happiness."

"Right, and what is happiness? Is it possible to pass through life without any crises, conflicts, and loss? I believe that happiness isn't the absence of suffering but the ability to get through it. The only way to overcome fear *is to allow it.* To feel fear frosting your bones, numbing your movements, silencing your voice, crushing your sense of grounding, crumbling your obsolete perceptions, and driving you out of comfort. That is an allowance. Childish dreams for eternal joy and the pursuit of constant ecstasy, what are they? It's better to find peace and harmony inwardly and stop seeking new experiences to feel alive again; or to see ourselves as we are, not too bad and not entirely good. Then we may see life *as it is.* Everything we hate, fear, reject, and hide creates misery. But if we notice it, observe it like waves, we'll get through. Misery, observed and felt, passes away rather quickly. Long-suppressed misery takes a solid amount of time to be felt and released. And . . . you zoned out, my friend," Koda giggled as he patted Tyra on her back. Then he yanked her braid, smirking.

"Ouch!"

~

When Tyra returned home, she sensed her mother was in a bad mood. She could tell by the sparkling kitchen, the polished floors, and the folded laundry.

"Mama, when did you have time to do all this? You've been painting all day! I'm sorry I didn't stay to help you. I thought you'd be painting until late evening, and I would clean the house and do the laundry tomorrow."

"Really? You spend your days with the neighbours and the milk lady! Or in the library with Sofia, talking for hours. And then you go to the forest for God knows why, making friends with chipmunks and squirrels like Moose!" As Scarlett raved, her beautiful raven hair whipped around, her brows furrowed, and her eyes narrowed.

Tyra stared at the worn, glossy floor. It was spotless, as if it had been scrubbed so hard that tiny holes might form at any moment—just like the repeated efforts within her to be better, kinder, and happier. "I'm sorry, Mama."

"You've clearly shown us that you're on your own! You do what suits you. And for you a family could always appear out of nowhere. Blood bonds are of little importance. You've always been strong-headed. Your own person, your own master. You're a rebel, and you can be so egocentric! You don't need anyone. You know that?"

"Am *I*? Why? Because I'm content with myself? Why am I egocentric, Mama?"

"I don't know." Scarlett looked uneasy, unsure if there were any grounds to her claims. "But I know this: you rejected my milk when you were born! You spat it out and turned away from my breasts and never nursed again."

"How was that my fault? You can never be truly accountable for your failures, Mum, or in this case, accept that things happen and it's nobody's fault. Not everything in life is under your control. And everything and everyone isn't against you. You, yourself, feel unloved, rejected, and abandoned. So, you soothe your wounds by hurting others!"

Immediately regretting her harsh words, Tyra went to her room and shut the door. *Oh, that was so rebellious!"* she thought. *Now she'll think she was right.*

Tyra grabbed Jenna, the huge squishy doll with a happy face that Logan had bought for her birthday when she was little. Then she collapsed onto her bed, buried her face in her pillow, covered herself with the plush blanket, and cried.

In a while, Scarlett calmed down and approached her daughter's room, knocking on the door.

"Come in," Tyra said.

Scarlett stayed in the doorway, feeling anxious. "I'm sorry, peanut. I overreacted and said things I didn't mean. I hurt you. Please forgive me."

"Okay, Mama."

Scarlett remained in the doorway, shuffling her bare feet on the scratchy, exhausted surface. Then she said goodnight with a hint of tenderness in her voice and went away.

"You have played (I think)
And broke the toys you were fondest of,
And are a little tired now.
Tired of things that break, and—just tired.
So am I."
E. E. Cummings. "You Are Tired, (I think)"

CHAPTER 7

Jerry

*"I shut my eyes, and all the world drops dead.
I lift my eyes, and all is born again."*
– Sylvia Plath

Tyra got up before dawn. She went for the milk, picked fresh veggies, berries, and fruits from the neighbour's garden, made coffee for the rest of her family, grabbed nuts for the chipmunks and seeds for the birds, then went to the forest, a coffee mug in hand.

"I should've made tea for myself. I hate coffee!"

Tyra didn't want to wake Koda so early, so she went to the river. There, she sat on a massive granite rock rooted in the ground and watched the sun being born again.

A while later, Tyra heard Koda's voice behind her. "Good morning, sugar. Tough night?"

Tyra didn't turn around. "That's an understatement."

Koda sat beside her. Together, they watched the sun show off nebulous shades of crimson and gold. They remained there in peace and quiet for some time.

In the morning light, when the river was fog-bound, the forest awakened slowly, bathed in the soft morning light. The

66

sound of rustling leaves was gentle, and the chirping of birds was subtle. The fog covered the ground like a soft, cool blanket. The air was refreshing and tender. Dewdrops clung to the spiderwebs and bushes, sparkling like tiny jewels. The taste of the foggy moisture was soothing, and the damp, plush soil was grounding.

"You wanna talk, sugar?"

Tyra hesitated, fiddling with her milkmaid braids. "It's hard to say out loud."

"Then there's even more reason to speak it aloud."

Tyra waited, marshaling courage. Koda didn't rush her.

"I hate her!" she said, vocalizing it for the first time. "And I love her."

Koda smiled proudly.

"It hurts," she added. "What's wrong with me?"

"Nothing. You're perfectly human. A mother wound is the hardest to bear, sugar. "

"Everybody has a mother wound."

"True, but not everyone is blamed for it."

Tyra and Koda had breakfast in cozy silence—egg-dipped, pan-fried toast with goat cream cheese and a cherry pie.

Koda broke the silence. "I wanna show you my favourite activity—well, my second favourite." He smiled toward the mirror as he slurped a strawberry milkshake.

The mirror snorted and trembled.

"I promise, you *are* the best," Koda assured it.

The mirror snorted again.

Koda put their lunch inside the linen bag. "Let's get to the boat, sugar. Take the bag, will you?"

Koda jumped down from the tree and sprinted toward the river. Tyra followed him, breathing heavily and full of excitement.

They retrieved a yellow two-seat boat from some purple lilac bushes and dragged it to the waltzing water. Then they climbed aboard and floated down the river.

The scenery was stunning. Blue lilies floated about on the water as if dancing, and birds sang in a harmonious choir. It was beautiful, but Tyra felt like crying.

"Is fun coming?" she asked after a while with a gloomy grin.

"You betcha! Look around. We're here," Koda said with the eyes of a youngster, full of joy and wonder.

Tyra stared at an enormous mountain, upon which were roses of all colours.

They sailed to the shore and ran toward the foot of the mountain. Tyra's heart was carefree and happy again.

"Now's the hardest part," Koda said, giggling. "We gotta get up."

"Up? Don't you have some kind of magic we can use?"

"I do, but I don't wanna, and I'm not gonna. Besides, what magic can replace a real journey with a friend, eh? Go, go up, Granny. You got this, girl! It'll be fun."

They climbed for long hours in complete silence, relishing every moment. The view of the lush green valley and sparkling, flowing water was astonishing. The mountain was covered with exquisite, fragrant flowers of all types. Koda's presence felt like *home*.

When they arrived at their destination, they both gaped in awe. The mountain was crowned in roses like a velvet, vibrant carpet with an enchanting, supernal smell. Small passages had been crafted by someone rather pedantic. Koda and Tyra inhaled deeply. They took each other's hands and closed their eyes as they stayed there for a brief, sweet moment until a chirping bird disturbed the silence.

"Hey, we're having a moment here!" Koda yelled at the yellow-throated sparrow.

The sparrow yelled right back at him. Then they spotted a beautiful eagle, flying high in the clouds, going down and up, down and up, chasing and teasing the sparrow. Tyra looked worried.

"No worries, sugar. They're friends, just like us. The sparrow says our ride is ready."

"What ride? Where?"

"Wait and see, child," Koda said, tickling her.

Tyra chuckled, protecting her belly with her hands.

The sky overflowed with puffy pink clouds, softer than cotton flowers, drifting gracefully—except for one cloud that moved much faster than the others. It was approaching Tyra and Koda with determination and a clear destination in mind.

Tyra shook her head. "I still find it difficult—well, recently even more difficult—to accept unusual occurrences with no explanation except a rather generic word—magic. Why can't I simply enjoy it without questioning everything?"

Koda smiled sadly. "I assume you're getting older, my friend. The gates of wonders need an accepting mind to remain open. Try to keep your mind free of judgment and doubts." He winked, then flicked Tyra's big bubble ponytail.

Tyra frowned as she fixed her hair. "I don't want to grow up yet. I don't think I'll like it." She stared at the approaching cloud with a mixture of suspicion and excitement.

"Growth is inevitable, yeah? But if you make it right, you'll enjoy it! Look at me! Growing up is great. It gives you freedom," Koda twitched his eyes, tilted his head, and smiled, showing off his shiny teeth. "Anyway, you'd better accept it. Otherwise, you might get stuck somewhere in between, as most adults do. Nasty business, I'd say. They just pretend to be grown-ups, right? As long as they manage to be on their own, pay the bills, and have a draining career, they think they've cracked the mystery of adulthood. Ha! Such people can be pretentious, and all puffed up. Cynical, sarcastic, and judgmental. These are fundamental masks of being a semi-grown-up. But beneath each mask hides a kid, a toddler who switches to a teen, and vice versa. It's all so messed up, sugar. Oh, great. Hello, dear. Great landing."

The cloud had arrived and landed in a safe distance from Tyra. It flashed a timid smile at Koda, then snorted and snickered at Tyra.

"I'm sorry for staring at you," Tyra said. "It's nice to meet you. I'm Tyra."

The cloud had a mouth that resembled a rushed drawing and big blue eyes. It looked funny but cute. "You can call me Mihi. Hop up. No worries. I'll remain silent during the ride, unlike the other drivers." Mihi snorted again, pointing his pinkish nose at his fluffy colleagues, who were gossiping in whispers. "Unlike the others who can't just keep their mouths shut and stop disturbing their passengers, I will give you a private experience, as if I wasn't here."

Koda sneered. "Oh, come on, Mihi. Long time no see. Tell us what you think about adults."

"I despise them. I have nothing to add."

Koda giggled. "Well, some are fun."

Mihi grunted. "Rare kinds. Hard to find. Most of them work with little kids or create cartoons and books, and not the heavy ones, mind you."

Koda gasped. "Well, heaviness is a part of life. Unfortunately, even for kids. Anyway, being a real adult frees you."

Tyra raised her eyebrows. "What do you mean by 'real'? I feel like childhood is a prison. I'd love to be my own master."

"Did you know that most people carry this prison within them for the rest of their lives? They recreate the same patterns they were exposed to when they were little. Even worse, they treat themselves the same way as they were treated. But most people never notice. That's the real tragedy. It's a trap. How can you get out if you're unaware you're in it?"

"What do you mean they treat themselves the same? If you have good parents, it sounds great, but if . . ."

"Exactly. If your parents didn't take care of you as they should have, you're destined to continue their legacy until you *choose* to break the cycle. We all know that being a good parent doesn't

JERRY

mean being perfect. But it requires a certain level of self-awareness and the ability to accept constant growth and change. I believe you might need to re-parent yourself when you grow up, sugar."

Mihi waited for them, getting restless.

Tyra gave Koda a puzzled look. "Reparent? How?"

"With kindness. We're all bound to seek the true self under piles of foreign opinions and forced perceptions of who we are and who we are not. It's important to recognize and address our needs, right? But most adults search for comfort and salvation from other sources. Real adults grieve and accept what was and what is, making cardinal changes in the present moment." Koda knew Tyra was too young to understand such concepts, but he was planting the seeds.

"Let's go up now," Mihi said, using the moment of silence.

"Let's!" Koda and Tyra replied in unison. Koda jumped up with no effort. Tyra hesitated, then started to climb but slipped. Then she slipped again and again and again. Koda giggled and held out his red scarf as a rope. Tyra grabbed it, pulled herself up, then settled down. They went up higher and higher. Tyra held her breath. Oh boy, so high, so scary! Such a majestic ride! The view of the mountain, the forest, the valley, and the dazzling river was breathtaking. The air sparkled and tickled. The flowers, like tiny, dressed-up dots, whirled as if floating beneath the clouds. Tyra felt free and ethereal.

Koda looked attuned to somewhere or someone. "Mihi, let's visit our friend, shall we? You'll see, Tyra. He's a good fellow, and he might need some help."

Tyra scratched her nose. "Sure, why not?"

Mihi floated for a couple of blissful moments, then sprinted north and landed with grace on a splendid hill covered with blue-purple forget-me-nots, delicate, whimsical blooms.

Tyra ran to examine and sniff them. "My favourite!"

A short distance away was a house made of acorns and shaped like a giant acorn, with a porch built of cones, pine branches, and spider webs. It was flooded with multicoloured potted flowers.

71

"Mihi, you coming, boy?" Koda asked.

"I wouldn't miss it!" Mihi said as he floated toward the house.

Beside the porch was a chubby, fluffy raccoon. He waved to them, a wide smile on his face.

"Hello, Jerry," Koda said.

"Hello, hello, my friends! Right on time for the tea party. Come on in. So happy to finally meet you, Tyra!"

"Hi, Jerry. It's nice to meet you too. What a wonderful, artistic home you've built! Such a great idea! It's my dream house, really."

"Oh, thank you, dear." Jerry looked pleased, as if he were blushing.

On the porch, a round wooden table had been set up. There was a beautiful, lacy porcelain tea set, a golden cupcake stand with creamy tarts on it, a massive plate of biscotti, macarons, fortune cookies, and a teapot with a candle beneath it.

Jerry ran up to Tyra and shook her hand with enthusiasm. He patted Mihi and gave Koda a slap on the back. "So happy to have you. A solitary tea party doesn't feel right," he said as he poured flavoured tea.

Tyra took a sip. "Gosh, the tea is delicious! The smell, the taste! Heaven."

Jerry smiled with delight.

Koda scratched his chin. "How're you doing, brother? I gather you've been having some troubles lately with—"

"Well, yes, the same. They come every night and steal my harvest! Shameless, shameless!" Jerry lowered his head and shook it from side to side.

Koda giggled. "I have an idea. How about we stay the night and help you get rid of them for once and for all, eh?"

Tyra tapped her fingers. "Koda, I can't stay the night."

"No worries, sugar. Time's irrelevant here, remember? You'll be back home by dinnertime, as usual. The question is: do you want to stay the night and participate in our little prank?" Koda rubbed his paws together, smirking.

"Well, perhaps. Fill me in."

Jerry turned to Tyra. "All righty, there're thieves who come to my hard-earned, well-cared-for garden and ravage it, ravage!" Jerry was devastated.

"Who? Who are they?"

"Obnoxious creatures, really," Jerry huffed. "Groundies."

"Groundies? I'm afraid I'm not familiar . . ."

"Sure, sure, dear. They're little mischievous creatures who live underground. They have pale alabaster skin, red button-like noses, and round, striking ears. They're fast and sneaky. Slim, about two chipmunks in size. They have bushy grey hair, like a halo moon with pine-like needles around their heads. They wear peculiar clothes, like grey glimmering pants and colourful button-up shirts. I'm telling you, they're nasty, nasty thieves."

"I'm in, definitely. What's the plan?"

Jerry shrugged. "I'm out of ideas."

Koda snickered. "I've got one. Do you have long sheets you don't need, you old hoarder?"

"I need them. I need them!" Jerry said, pouting.

"No, you don't. I'll make you other ones. Trust me; you must teach these guys a lesson."

"Alrighty, let's give these yucky thieves hot and strong! Let's do it!" Jerry agreed.

Koda lowered his voice. "So, we'll wait until midnight, and . . ." He filled the others in on his plan, cackling.

"It might work. Cowards, cowards, these two." Jerry clapped in delight and wrinkled his nose, giggling.

"Mihi, you can split in two, right?" Koda asked.

Mihi shivered. "Hmm . . . I hate it! Well, alright. Can't miss out on the fun."

Jerry was excited to have a sleepover. He turned to Koda and Tyra. "You can sleep in my tent, in the garden. It has yellow lights and long, puffy cushions. You'll love it. Love it!"

When the round moon turned red, the insects became quieter. The friends sneaked to the kitchen and made scary ghost costumes with huge, narrow eyes and big black smiles. Each of them put on a sheet, then went outside. Jerry perched in a wicker laundry basket, floating above the ground. Poor Mihi, split into two small clouds, accompanied Koda and Tyra. The four hid behind dense pine bushes and waited. In no time, they heard a rustling sound and saw two groundies sneaking into Jerry's garden. The creatures smirked, giggled, and gloated. One was wearing a maroon shirt with green floral buttons, the other a blue-sky shirt with silver moon buttons and a purple umbrella-like hat. They were as pale as alabaster, with big, round ears that stuck out and narrow, lush, pink ear-to-ear lips.

They look rather cute, Tyra thought.

Koda signalled his friends to launch the attack. The four left their ambush and floated above the petrified groundies. The ghosts howled, shrieked, rattled, and hissed. The red, smoky moon was dragging above the terrified thieves as if it had decided to participate in the show.

The poor, petrified fellows dashed out of the garden and dove under the ground, screaming like crazy monkeys.

The ghosts waited to make sure they were alone, and then they burst out laughing. Koda and Jerry tumbled in a happy-baby pose, trying to catch their breath. Mihi quaked so hard that it caused him to burst into rain.

"S-s-s-sorry," he said, blushing. Then he rained again.

Tyra hugged her belly, then leaned on her knees, trying not to choke on laughter. "Oy, my stomach hurts. I can't . . . can't anymore." She tried to make a serious face but failed. "You know, I like them. They're funny, these groundies. Pity and shame they caused you so much trouble, Jerry. Otherwise, we could've befriended them."

Jerry gave her his harshest look. "Uh-huh! I knew you liked them!" he pointed his finger at Tyra, offended.

"Sorry," Tyra said as she buried her feet in the grass.

"Sorry, she's sorry," Jerry grumbled. "Okay, let's go to bed. It was fun! I bet they won't dare come here again. Good for me, good for us." He winked at Tyra as if to forgive her.

"I think I'll be staying here tonight beside the tent. If you don't mind, Jerry," Mihi mumbled.

"Sure, sure. We'll have breakfast tomorrow, and you'll accompany us with the sound of rain. Will you, Mihi? I love having breakfast on the porch while it's raining."

"My pleasure," Mihi replied, blushing.

Tyra and Koda settled in the transparent, crystal-clear tent filled with warm dragonfly lights, comfy cushions, and knitted blankets. They looked at the night sky, powdered with sparkling stars around the marvelous red moon, until their eyelids grew heavy and closed on their own. It was a quiet, breezy night. Tyra and Koda slept safely and soundly, like beloved and nourished babies.

First thing in the morning, Tyra sat on the damp grass and watched the garden wake up. Dew on plush, silky flowers, a popping baby frog, a red cardinal chatting with a bluejay. The air was misty, fresh, and clean.

Koda emerged from the tent and stretched. "I smell *waffles*!" he said. "And omelets. Yummy. Jerry's omelets are the best of the best."

Tyra smiled from ear to ear in anticipation, then the two headed into the house.

It was a studio with a kitchen, a sleeping area, and a living room. The kitchen had an octagonal window overlooking the garden, a stone oven, wooden cabinets, and a round yellow table with four upholstered chairs. The sleeping area contained a loft bed, and beneath it a bean bag chair, a shaggy off-white carpet, warm lighting, and a desk with bookshelves. The living room was even more inviting. Beside the wall-size cathedral window, a soft off-white couch was covered with cushions and a green fleece blanket. On the left wall next to the window was a fireplace, surrounded by bookshelves on both sides and above. Wicker trays filled with candles and gemstones rested on a rectangular wooden coffee table. There was a column floor lamp, a few canvases, and beige side curtains.

Through the window, Tyra noticed Mihi floating back and forth across the porch. Jerry was bustling about in the kitchen. The smell was unbelievable.

"Mihi, Mihi, my friend! He's waiting and waiting. Oy. Hurry up, guys. Help me serve. We're eating outside."

When they were settled on the porch, Mihi sighed with relief and let out a pleasant drizzle. The breakfast was delicious, and the company was wonderful. There was a tapping rain, wet wood, and the view of the distant, hazy mountain with roses on top. It was terrific!

"'I have drunk deeply of joy, and I will taste no other wine tonight. Percy Bysshe Shelley," Koda said, tipsy with bliss.

CHAPTER 8
Anicca

"All is flux; nothing stays still."
– Heraclitus

The last month of summer flew by. Tyra dreaded the approaching school year and the fading away of the magic. She visited Jerry and Mihi every now and then. It was always fun, cozy, and unforgettable.

One rainy day while heading to the enchanted forest, Tyra noticed an uneasy tingling sensation in her stomach. Butterflies snuck in and made her body chill. She had never felt such a flurry before, at least not that she'd noticed.

The heavy rain turned into a sprinkle. Tyra closed her bubble umbrella and rushed to Koda's house. She looked cute in her yellow raincoat and glossy, raspberry-red rubber boots. Her slick, long fishtail braids were a bit clammy.

The post-rain air was refreshing, pure, and crisp. The scent of showered flowers, moist soil, and soaked pines was splendid. The sound of dripping water and the birds' chirping created a perfect outer ambiance.

Koda peeked through the window. "Morning, sugar! Wait, I'm coming. Look behind ya!"

Tyra turned around and spotted a timid stream of the rainbow washing over cranberry bushes. It was beautiful.

"Boo!" Koda said, having crept up behind her back.

Tyra jolted and screamed.

"Gotcha!" Koda nudged her and ruffled her hair, and they both laughed.

"I have an idea. Instead of swimming, how about puddling and splashing, eh?" Koda suggested, catching his breath.

"Marvelous idea!" Tyra exclaimed as she dashed to the nearest puddle.

Koda and Tyra embraced the spirit of wildness. They leaped, danced, and splashed, filling the forest with laughter.

Afterward, while sitting on the muddy ground under Koda's home tree with mugs of hot chocolate, feeling happy, tired, and cozy, Tyra couldn't help but wonder how long it would last. It was one of those perfect moments mixed with sadness. The type of moment where you panic that you'll miss it and then start craving it in advance instead of savouring it. Then, poof! It's gone.

Koda and Tyra climbed into the tree house to make lunch. Miraculously, a rich assortment of goat cheese and a round, boiling-hot loaf of sourdough bread appeared on the table. The bread had a crispy brownish crust and an earthy scent with a hint of nuts.

"Do you know—" Koda asked as he bit into the most delectable sandwich. "Mmm . . . yum-yum. Do you know about the Land of the Great Lakes?"

"I've heard about this legend here and there." Tyra paused and inhaled the fresh aroma of another slice of bread layered with soft cheese, spinach, olives, and ripe cherry tomatoes. "Some say there's a tree between a myriad of realms that, once in a while, awakens from a deep sleep. It shakes its leaves and sends them to different people across every realm on Earth as invitations. The tree has leaves of all types, colours, and shapes, but one leaf is the most desirable of all—the maple leaf. It's sent as an invitation to come and live in the Land of the Great Lakes. Many dream of receiving a leaf from that tree. But even more believe it is just another myth of hope in a land without a future." Tyra smiled, full of sarcastic pathos. "I never believed this story. But now it seems that everything might be possible."

Koda made a tinkling sound. "It is very possible, indeed. I mean, the realm exists, as do many, many others. They coexist on our beloved green planet as alternative realities, each within their personalized path of myriad choices. The Land of the Great Lakes is a gorgeous continent, but most importantly, it is *evolved*. I'm not talking about technology but as a society. They're at a pretty high stage, as humans. I wish you, my friend, could wake up one day and discover a maple leaf on your coffee table."

Tyra felt restless. Each fantasy tended to fade.

After lunch was over, Koda looked at Tyra and gasped. Tyra had felt it coming: 'the talk'. She scanned the room as if trying to carve every detail into her memory compartments and keep them there forever.

Koda stared at his muddy feet. "Tyra, I'm sorry. We only have a couple of days left."

Tyra flinched. "What do you mean? We can meet after school and on weekends and during holidays. School days start near the end of September. Anyway, we have a couple of weeks left." She shuffled her feet in apparent unease.

Koda sighed. "You're turning thirteen this week. See, you won't be a child anymore."

Tyra felt puzzled. "I don't understand. Why didn't you . . . Why didn't you come over earlier?"

"You've never voiced it before," Koda muttered, shuffling the withering leaves under his furry feet. "I wish we had more time, sugar." He sighed. "But even magic has its limitations."

"Why didn't you tell me earlier? I could've had more time to prepare." Tyra was disappointed, frustrated, and angry.

"I'm sorry, I didn't want to ruin your stay or our fun. Otherwise, it would be as if a gloomy grey cloud—forgive me, Mihi—

would've been hanging above us, spoiling the entire experience." Koda's words came out softly.

"I understand. You're right. Let's visit Jerry and Mihi today, can we? I wanna say goodbye." Tyra's heart ached, and her stomach cringed. Fear crept in and crawled from her head to her toes.

"Sure. They're already crying."

The goodbye was painful, as all goodbyes are.

On the way home, Tyra lingered by the edge of birch trees where slender white trunks made an arch above a tranquil brook. The sun's timid glow was melting away as a golden afterglow in the trickling water.

Life is about moments.

"Koda, you say time's irrelevant here," Tyra said on her last visit. "Why can't I stay here with you a little longer? Or maybe much longer?"

Hope tickled her belly, refusing to give up just yet.

"Sure, sugar, you can, but there're limitations. Four days in a row. That would be wonderful! I was just about to offer."

"Offer? Seriously?" Tyra rolled her eyes and shook her head.

Koda chuckled, ruffling her crown braid.

Tyra stayed in Koda's domain for four days and four nights. The monsters visited every evening, staying until the first tender blush awakened on the horizon. After dusk, sitting on the windowsill, Tyra enjoyed a book or herbal tea, dangling her legs from the sturdy tree branch. Cami perched beside her, holding a lamp for her braided friend to illuminate the night. Sometimes she would also read a book written in a foreign language. At night, Kent held Tyra in his gigantic, puffy arms as Cami surrounded her sleeping baby with bubbles. All the while, as Tyra slept, Cami was immersed in knitting a blanket.

Each morning, Tyra awoke in Kent's nurturing arms, feeling

well-rested, while Cami leaned over her with a timid, affectionate smile.

On the last night, Kent wrapped Tyra as if she were a precious bundle. Kent winked, nodded, and then darted through the window in his tiny form. Then he transformed into a towering figure and soared high into the sky, above the clouds. Tyra held her breath as she watched the sky around them, mesmerized, delighted, and relaxed. Her loose caramel hair swayed around, floating.

They soared above the mountains, the rivers, and the ocean, landing on a once beautiful but now deserted street in the City of Moss.

Tyra was in the City of Moss!

She struggled to breathe at first but took a deep breath and released her tension. Her heart was pounding, but her tummy felt loose as it rose and contracted.

Tyra looked around. The street had remained untouched by the horror, but it was dead.

The city looked like a rose or a grape after the first steps of vinification and distillation—crushing, pressing, and squeezing— before, *and if,* they were transformed into wine or essential oil.

After the first steps the streets looked like sore flowers. And they had been left in that ugly, agonizing state forever and ever. Fragmented and empty. A dark, raw mass with a dispirited remnant of the flavour of life. Vulnerable, unprotected, exposed.

The final steps of vinification, or extractions, were left for humans to endure.

One was maceration, which involved soaking and steeping to extract flavours. For grapes and flowers, the process was painless. For humans, it was excruciating. It forced them to dive into their innermost fearful, torturous emotions with no preparation or guidance. The process could create growth, but it could also crush people down for good.

The last step was fermentation. When intense emotions were

bottled up for a long time, they could trigger inner transformation through agonizing pain.

Maybe or maybe not. The wine could turn off, and oxidation could occur at any moment.

These last steps were burdened on people rather than the streets. Now, millions of souls, former citizens of the once vibrant city, were scattered all over the world. Some were fortunate to release the pain and grow while the others had become dead in a living, functioning flash. And it depended not only on their ability to cope but rather on their exposure to horror. It was that simple.

Some said, "I've been through difficult times. I've overcome my struggles. Why can't others?"

Because everyone had their own unique combination of final breaking points. Their unique mixture of catalysts. Often an array of them.

But there was a bottle of dead water for each person on Earth.

As she stared at her childhood mirage, Tyra realized that her home, for which she had longed for so long, was no longer there or anywhere.

She looked around and saw a black cat sitting on the roof of a bleak, forsaken building. It flicked its tail as if it were waltzing in the subtle breeze.

Tyra and Kent settled on top of the only bright building with a blue roof and weathered light-pink façade. Tyra's home in Moss.

Mournful, orphaned buildings surrounded the oasis of love and care, the oasis of two. Tyra was tucked in Kent's warm arms, covered with a quilt, snuggled and safe. The black cat turned around and stared at her with affection and sorrow. Her big emerald eyes gleamed like two lanterns in the night.

So, they sat there for a long time—the monster, the girl in his arms, and the black cat with emerald eyes.

Tyra's gaze wandered along the withered street and fixed on one window. Her heart pinched. Once upon a time, that window had been radiant. It brimmed with light, boisterous laughter, and the rhythmic patter of tiny feet—then with blood.

It was Tyra's favourite window on Blue Daisy Street.

Her childhood friend, Aksana, had lived there. They were like sisters, their hearts and minds entwined with invisible rays. Tyra was two years old when Aksana was born, and she carried her in a stroller as her first live treasure, covering her with a soft blanket to shield her from the bothersome breeze. Tyra watched her nursing and watched her grow. It was a majestic transformation, a baby turning into a person.

They grew up side by side and spent all their evenings together, telling each other fairy tales from illustrated books, acting out their favourite scenes, and soaking their feet in the nearby stream. On rare snowy days, they made snowballs and built funny snowmen. On summer evenings, they sprawled on the soft grass, powdered with forget-me-nots, and had breakfast in a nearby oak tree.

On cold evenings they savoured hot chocolate with cookies by a crackling fire as the frost cracked and hissed outside the window. They would write notes to each other, leave them in a cardboard box decorated with colourful postcards, ring the doorbell, and then run away, giggling with tickling anticipation.

At dusk, Tyra loved to sit on her windowsill with hot tea and a slice of pie, looking at her favourite dazzling Blue Daisy Street window. Before long, Aksana would show up on her windowsill and wave. The girls would communicate using gestures and grimaces. An alley was between them, illuminated by flickering lanterns and lined with young trees. The girls would settle down to read, facing each other by the frosted windows that were warmed by their breath and decorated with funny faces drawn in the haze.

Aksana had a little brother, a lively, funny boy who loved participating in their games and was happy to play any part, even the most ridiculous ones. They loved him and nursed him, and he worshipped them. Sometimes they would make fun of him, dressing him in peculiar outfits. They felt guilty about it afterward, but they were unable to resist.

Aksana's mother made the most delicious soups in the world, along with boiled yellow potatoes from the farmer's market and crispy fried cauliflower, and her grandmother baked extraordinary cottage-cheese pancakes and delicious pies. Their rear balcony was full of flowerpots and decorated with cozy lights around a sofa and two rocking chairs. The girls loved to sit there together, whispering their secrets, giggling, and watching passers-by stroll down the beautiful alley. Under the balcony was a lush green willow tree, sprawling and whispering in the breeze.

The beasts had entered through that balcony, extinguishing the light and the children's laughter forever, replacing them with eternal darkness and chilling silence. Their death had been quick. They were lucky.

Tyra shuddered as repressed memories flooded to the surface, almost crashing her soul into tiny pieces. But Kent held her close, his touch tender. Tyra cried without effort. Her heart bled unrestrained as her body released intense pain and sorrow in her monster's embrace.

On the last morning, a moment before dawn, Tyra woke up in her hammock. She opened her eyes and saw Cami and Kent bending over her with wide smiles and holding balloons. "Happy birthday, our little bundle!" Tyra heard a subtle whisper in her head, and then her monsters vanished into the light.

Tyra covered her face with a soft pillow as she lay on her belly. She fell asleep again on a damp, salty pillowcase covered with yellow roses. When she woke up, she found a teal knitted blanket at her feet. It was the softest, warmest blanket on Earth. It was a weighted shelter and a comforter all in one.

That afternoon, Koda and Tyra visited their other friends through the mirror. They were the only ones who could see Tyra with or without her invisible form. Koda and Tyra entered their favourite scene, where the Little Prince met the Fox.

No words needed to be said. The Fox and the boy knew it was a farewell visit. They waved and shared a blue smile. Tyra waved back, then returned to Koda's room.

She was sad, very much so.

Koda sighed. "I'm sorry, my friend. Farewells are the hardest. But I think you're now well rested and ready to face reality."

"I don't feel like I'm nearly strong enough."

"You *are* strong, Tyra. You'll discover that along the way. But there's no need to be *always* strong. Trying to be strong no matter what makes us rigid. When the storm comes, the formidable oak breaks easily, but the flowing willow bends and sways in the wind. When the storm's over, the willow straightens up again and regenerates. It sheds its damaged branches and leaves to reduce its overall burden and recover. Recovery takes time, and the willow allows it."

Tyra tried not to cry, but tears have their natural rhythm. So, they dribbled down her chilly cheeks, secretly and in silence. Her hands and lips were shaking. Letting go of happiness was painful, but there was nothing she could do to keep it.

Life had its path.

"Now, we have to part ways, sugar. Life is about change. Embrace it, and you'll be good. For now, let's savour what's left, shall we?" Koda smiled with tenderness.

"Life is about moments," Tyra whispered as she stared at the green plush carpet.

"Yes, and moments fade. They also never repeat."

Tyra swept her tears aside in resentment.

Then two gigantic cats appeared out of the blue. One was white, the other black. They walked beside each other with royal grace, almost snuggling. The tips of their tails touched in a hug. In the blink of an eye, Tyra saw her monsters instead of cats. She shook her head, closed her eyes, and then opened them again, but no one was there.

"I wanna give you a present, sugar. Anything you need. There're no limitations. What do you need, Tyra Tara?"

"How do you know my middle name?" Tyra asked as if it was her innermost secret.

He shrugged. "I just know stuff."

"You certainly do." Tyra smiled, deep in thought. "I need to be invisible in school."

"Very well." Koda fetched a scarf from his green ragbag and passed it to Tyra. It was soft and sheltering. "When you wear it, you'll be visible and nonvisible. They'll just pass along or beside you as if you're just a leaf slipping in the air. The best thing is that it changes colour, size, shape, and texture. It'll be different each time, as if you were wearing a different model every day. Isn't it cool? My design." Koda smiled proudly. "I also grabbed some goodies for you." He handed her a woven basket filled with delicious food and sunflowers.

"Thank you, Koda. For the scarf—for everything. I wish this could last forever." Tyra sighed, gesturing around her.

"There's no such thing, sugar. There's only *anicca*." Koda drawled the last word. He smiled with apparent seriousness. "It means impermanence."

Tyra sighed.

"I'll remember you for eternity," he said, hugging her. Then he vanished in a puff of smoke.

Tyra shook her head and observed the environment. She was in her garden. The sky was red, the frogs were croaking, and the daisies were already closing.

"I shouldn't have eaten these "edible" flowers. Or maybe I hit my head or something. I can't recall it. Perhaps I've been lying in a coma for the past month. If so, how did I get there?" she mumbled, baffled.

Then Tyra noticed a basket in her right hand, filled with mini pies, goat milk, crunchy oval bread, cheese pastries, baked chestnuts, which were soft and warm, sunflowers, and berries. In her left hand she gripped a scarf. Tyra felt an ache in her chest and a cool hollowness in her belly. Fear crawled down to her feet.

"How can I carry on now?" she wondered.

But sadness overcame fear and settled.

CHAPTER 9
Alone, Facing Reality as It Is

"I know you're tired but come, this is the way."
– Jalal-din Rumi

Weeks later, the trees had already changed their outfits. The forest was stunning, radiant and full of whispers. It was beautifully dressed as if a gifted artist had just painted it with playful crayons of vibrant colours, never the same, always exclusive. It was a cheerful celebration of nature's beauty before the inevitable change: winter.

"Mama, I have a drawing of two monsters to show you. I also want to ask you a favour."

Scarlett frowned and trembled.

"No, no! Other monsters. They're sweet. I'll show you. Here." Tyra retrieved Koda's drawing from her bookshelf. "See? They're super cute."

"Oh, they're adorable! Where did you get this drawing? It's fantastic."

"Don't ask. Could you please, please, please make me two squishy pillows like that?"

"I can try."

"Come on, you're very artistic. You crochet, sew, and design

89

clothes. You decorate. You make bouquets from autumn leaves. You're super talented, Mama. I've told you that, like, a million times. You should've made it your career. Each piece you make is original and authentic."

"People here, or in any other part of Azure except Moss, won't buy it. And Moss is no longer with us," Scarlett said. "They prefer mass-produced, dispirited, copy-and-paste homes and clothes with no character. Even the architecture here is boring. Home decor or shop design is a foreign concept for them. Look at these stores' windows. So pitiful and lifeless. Everyone here is almost identical. Bleak, spiritless, and dull. God forbid anyone is different from or, worse, seen as inferior to anyone else."

Tyra chuckled. "You don't believe in God."

"I was blessed by God's will to be born an atheist."

Tyra laughed. "But you do believe in something, right?"

"Sure, in family, in the universe at large, and in myself."

"Olivia believes we can manifest everything we wish for. That we can visualize it, and then the universe will unravel her secrets, taking good care of our wishes. Olivia often says, 'Improve and fix yourself. Design your thoughts, emotions, and beliefs.' But isn't that a bit . . . I don't know. Unnatural? Unrealistic? I mean, maybe there's more. Maybe it isn't the way. I love nature, and I like observing its cycles. A friend of mine said. 'It doesn't matter what you do or don't do; winter will come and bring frost, storms, and isolation. There'll always be earthquakes, tsunamis, and hurricanes. And then stillness will come and the time to recover, rebuild, and grow. You can't fight or beat nature. You can only allow yourself to flow with the stream of life. Life inside of us is the same as outside, always flowing and never repeating. It's a constant torrent. I doubt we can control it. All we can do is enter the flux and surrender.' I think that makes sense. Nature works that way."

"Where did you read such things? You speak like a wise, old man. I close my eyes . . ." Scarlett closed her eyes in a dramatic gesture. "And I picture you. Here it comes, the vision. A petite braided creature with a white beard, sturdy boots, and a gown of bliss."

Tyra raised her eyes, her cheeks like puffy apples and her teeth twinkling. She bent over, clapped her hands on her knees, and chuckled, letting out a long breath.

Scarlett laughed through her tears. "What's the name of your ancient, silent, immortal friend? Let me guess. He's a mysterious creature. Oh, let's make it a quiz! Does he have aged, yellow skin and a creaking spine adorned with fading letters? Oh! Tattoos of ancient letters and peculiar illustrations? Oy, wait!" She stopped Tyra, who rolled her eyes and opened her mouth to speak but was interrupted by Scarlett. "He shuffles with a crisp, rustling sound or a crackling noise. And he smells like old, earthy parchment." Scarlett mimicked the gait of an old man.

Tyra laughed. "Mama!"

"Oh, don't tell me! It's better to stay in the bliss of ignorance." Scarlett giggled. "And voila, his name is Sage!" She bowed and chuckled in a solemn manner. "Okay, peanut, I'll make you your pillow monsters, but after I return from vacation, okay?"

The following weekend, Scarlett left to visit her family for two weeks. Her heart was heavy, and she didn't understand why. "He's a good father. He'll take care of our girl. He hasn't been drinking for a while. It's all good, relax," she repeated to herself.

Scarlett had been waiting for the visit for far too long. She missed her mother so much, as if inside her heart was a deep hole in urgent need of care and nourishment. Scarlett adored her mother. When she was honest with herself, she glimpsed an unhealthy attachment. She ached for her mother's presence in her life. But she tucked away that thought, noticing a hint of embarrassment and an uneasy sensation in her gut.

When Scarlett returned home, she found Tyra in an unstable emotional state. She was curled up on a windowsill with a weary, prickly cushion on top. The maroon and brownish stripes had almost faded, and the cushion itself was cold and nonchalant. The window displayed tiny cracks through which a diamond-like ornament sparkled like a snowy blanket.

Scarlett moved closer to her daughter and took a deep breath of the frosty air drifting in through the window. It's snowing, she thought; her gaze fixed on the freshly frozen snowflakes clinging to the glass. "What happened? Tyra, tell me. Please tell me!"

But Tyra refused to communicate. She remained silent no matter what her mother tried or said.

Scarlett felt helpless. "Look what I've got for you," she said, giving Tyra two squishy pillow monsters. The softest, the funniest, and the cutest. Tyra took them with gratitude and squeezed them.

"Tyra, I know something is wrong. You looked like that once when you were a toddler. We were worried sick about you. Remember when I hired a nanny with impeccable recommendations? You turned into a scared, indifferent doll instead of a cheerful child, full of life."

Tyra sniffled, pressed her head to her knees, and wrapped her arms around her shoulders, still silent.

"We struggled to understand what happened to you until one day your granny came over the stove, holding you in her arms. You were petrified. You screeched and wrapped your arms around your tiny body, pointing at the fire. You made sure we'd know that something terrible had happened to you.

"Olivia spied on her and saw the nanny alone on the street. 'Where's Tyra?' she asked.

"'She's sleeping on the couch,' the woman replied. 'Oy, don't make a fuss, girl. I put some pillows around her.'

"Olivia was in shock, picturing you waking up all alone. It turned out that the 'impeccable' nanny was neglecting the babies in her charge. She also used atrocious strategies to implement discipline, leaving no marks on their bodies. She was clever, but you were even smarter. Despite your young age, you communicated and got our attention. I was so proud of you. In that instant, I knew that whatever happened, you'd be okay. But now I know something is off. I need you to tell me. Talk to me, Tyra, please!"

Tyra began to shake.

"Tyra, what did he do?" Scarlett asked, feeling desperate.

Tyra groaned and clenched her legs closer to her tummy.

Scarlett left the room, returning a moment later with a fuzzy blanket with yellow daisies on a lush green grassy field, Tyra's favourite from a distant part of her childhood. Scarlett covered her baby with unusual softness. "Tyra, how long have you been alone in this place?"

Tyra raised her eyes and looked at her mother with gratitude. "Maybe a week. But each night he'd come home late and enter my room, smelling like a broken bottle of vodka. He never harmed me, but he looked like a hungry monster, seeking blood. Each time, he'd growl like a wounded animal and turn away. I've never seen him like this. So much rage, Mama. Barely controlled. Monstrous grimaces. I was so scared, Mama."

Tyra cried in her mother's arms for a long time. Scarlett remained silent. She was horrified—and furious. Mostly with herself.

Tyra woke up at night and noticed a halo moon outside her cracked window. She went to the kitchen, poured a glass of foamy milk, grabbed some oatmeal cookies, then went to the garden to sit on the birch stump and watch the moon. It looked as if it were dressed in a dreamy, surreal outfit with a silver glow and a hazy tint of lavender.

As she munched the cookies and nursed the comforting milk, Tyra listened to the whispers of the night. The hushed rustle of leaves, a serenade of elusive crickets, and the gentle breeze brushing the branches of the wild apple trees.

Then, out of the blue, she heard an eerie, crispy voice. "Eating cookies, alone, smacking and scrunching as if nobody's here craving comfort goodies. Grr . . ."

Tyra searched for the cranky visitor and saw a whimsical creature that resembled a tarsier. It had a round, flat face and enormous amber eyes shaped like peaches. It was about the size of a large cat with earthy-coloured fur, big, round, pointy ears, a leafy belly, and a feline mouth with long whiskers.

"Well, I don't mind sharing. Suit yourself." Tyra pushed the bowl of cookies toward the creature, examining him with a hidden smile. "I'm Tyra. And you are?"

"Aye. I'm Aye," he said as he snatched a cookie with his long, thin fingers. "So, you cried your eyes out today. Good. It helps. Stillness helps too. It's my favourite comfort, besides cookies."

"Who are you?"

"Does it matter? I gave up on finding out, and now I feel free. No need to put a label on me. Heh, heh. I'm a nocturnal creature who likes cookies, stillness, and friends. I'm grumpy but cute. Am I? I am. That's me. Here's my bestie." Aye pointed toward an owl with the face of a cat, hiding behind another birch stump. "That's Duplex. My brother, my friend. He's suspicious, not shy. Don't be fooled. Heh, heh. And who are you besides your name?'

"Hmm . . . I'm a girl, a human. I'm a daughter and granddaughter. A friend."

"*Boring.* Besides the friend part, which I get, it's ho-ho. Who are you as you?"

"I don't know. I guess I've never thought about it in depth."

"You should. Don't give up. Don't listen to me. Not now. Listen now, then don't."

"I just know I want a different life. I wanna find my sense of home again. With my dad, making butternut cookies, eating chocolate ice cream, picking autumn leaves with my mum. I wanna find my people like you've found Duplex, people who won't vanish when I grow older. But I like me, although I'm not sure I'm familiar enough with myself."

Duplex purred, then rumbled with a soft yet firm voice. "So, figure it out first. How can you create a different life and find your people if you don't know who you are? Then, each day, do yourself a favour and check for updates. Besides, some friendships are destined to last for only a certain amount of time. It doesn't make them any less valuable." Duplex licked his wings. "Milk for me? Yum, yum."

"Sure. Sorry, I thought cats were intolerant to milk." Tyra handed her irregular half-full mug to Duplex.

"I'm not a cat, and I'm not an owl. I'm both and beyond," he said as he slurped, his whiskers smudged with delicious ambrosia.

Aye hooted, then mewed with a grumpy face. "Besides, your memories are just memories. They're irreplaceable—one. It's true. They're nice to have—two. They're useless for what's to come—three. Think big, Ty-Ty. Think flux."

Duplex came closer to Aye and nuzzled his face into Aye's belly, wiping his mouth. "Thanks, friend."

"Anytime, brother." Aye snapped his fingers, and a lavender cloud appeared, pouring out a stream of silver water. Aye washed his belly, then touched the cloud with his finger. The cloud burst into uncontrollable laughter, changing its colours and creating a kaleidoscope of joy and rain as it poured out a memory.

In front of Tyra appeared a young Aye and Duplex as an owlet-kitty, chasing each other on the sunflower field, chuckling and creating memories.

Tyra gasped in awe. "Can I touch it? It's beautiful. Thank you for sharing."

Duplex and Aye nodded in unison, and the cloud blushed as it came closer to Tyra, as if smiling. Tyra touched it, and the cloud giggled, attuned to Tyra's mood and memory. Like a scene from a long-forgotten movie, the Blair family appeared before their eyes, laughing through their tears. Logan and Scarlett held Tyra's tiny hands and swayed, humming a roundelay until they got dizzy and dropped onto the lush grass, hugging their daughter and smiling at each other with affection. Then the cloud burst into tears, dissolving into a colourful puddle of mixed emotions.

"So, we're crying again then," Aye grumbled.

"Don't rush her, amigo. Don't shame her. Remember, it wasn't easy for us to let go of memories of our old tree house. These humans cut it down. No shame."

"Yeah, right. We cried and cried until we could cry no more."

"And then we realized we *are* our home. We can live anywhere as long as—"

"Terrible timing, bro," Aye grumbled. "Terrible timing."

Tyra stopped crying, but she still looked gloomy.

Duplex purred. "Oy vey. Sorry, Ty-Ty. Moose, Koda, now your dad. Too many transitions, ah? Seek your personal sense of home within you. We're also trying."

"Ah?" Aye raised his eyebrows.

"Right, but we *are* trying," Duplex rumbled. "That's the best we can do for now. And sticking tight to memories prevents us from creating new ones."

"Right. And hugs?" Aye jumped up and wrapped Tyra in a heartfelt hug. Duplex chuckled, then they melted into the air as if they were lavender puddles of Tyra's tears adsorbed in the dry soil beneath her. Beside her bare feet, Tyra saw a bouquet of purple asters. She picked them up and sniffed their balsam-like scent. Then the flowers melted in her hands like a silky haze.

In the morning, Tyra woke up and mulled over her peculiar dream. Behind the birch stump in the garden lay a bowl with the crumbled remains of a cookie and a dried mug with milk residue and two whiskers.

～

The next day, her father came home to say goodbye.

"Your mother kicked me out. I deserve it. I'll never forgive myself for what I did, Tyra. I have loved you from the minute you were born. I was the happiest dad alive. I'd always dreamed about having a daughter, you know? I . . . I don't know. I hate myself. I'm a weak man, turned into a beast."

Tyra remained silent.

"There's no excuse, Tyra. No repair. I'm not the father you deserve or need. I'm leaving to see my aunt and uncle tonight." He said it all quickly, in one breath. "Actually, I'm going to stay there for a while. No." He hesitated, struggling to find the right words, or better, just to be honest.

Tyra waited in silence.

"I won't be coming back," he said.

Tyra waited. Logan couldn't bring himself to look at his daughter. Nervous, he tried to find a spot to stare at. His gaze fixed on a deep scratch that Moose had made on the squeaky wooden floor.

Tyra looked straight into his eyes. Her harsh stare made him feel even more uncomfortable.

"But they live on another continent, don't they?"

"Yes," he whispered.

"Why don't you find a job here? Find a place, settle down?" Tyra struggled to understand what was happening and why. Her head was spinning, and she felt confused. Robbed.

"I can't, Tyra. I'm not well. We'll talk about it someday when you're older."

"Will you come back to me when you sort things out?" she asked, still refusing to abandon hope.

He didn't answer.

And he never returned.

"In the pain of my loss, I gave you the pain of absence."
– Alix E. Harrow

CHAPTER 10
Black and White

"A ship in harbor is safe,
but that is not what ships are built for."
– John Shedd

Just before the winter solstice, Scarlett secured a project manager position at a respected IT company in a grey city with no forest but a central park. They rented a three-bedroom townhome with a garden full of walnut trees and clover instead of grass. Tyra's grandparents and aunt lived in the same neighbourhood. Nothing could have made Scarlett happier. Living next to her mother had always been her greatest wish, second only to getting married again, hopefully with better luck.

The city of Moonvine was ordinary and grim, filled with dull, prosaic townhomes and high-rise buildings, under-decorated window displays, and a lack of greenery. People on the streets of Moonvine passed one another like solitary strangers. They never stopped or paused to chat or take in the air of the changing seasons. Instead, they rushed to complete their long to-do lists, their minds trapped in a constant whirl, never stopping and never resting. They often walked with their heads bent down and their eyes focused on their smartphones. They moved at a monotonous pace, engaged in their artificial world and fixated on success and outer beauty. They lived in relentless pursuit of constant comparison, absorbed in a race that had no end. Who had achieved more? Whose milestones shown in made-up photos were more desirable? Whose lifestyle and experiences were more to die for? In short, who was happier?

It was total nonsense, under which hid the deepest needs of validation: love, connection, self-realization, and acceptance, covered up by meticulously fabricated personas.

On a cold, gusty afternoon, Alma entered their home, followed by two gigantic cats. One was white and fluffy and had enormous round eyes. The left eye was ocean blue, and the right was yellow. The other cat, black with silky, glittering fur, stared at Tyra with its deep, elliptical emerald eyes.

Tyra dashed into the hallway, amazed. "Grandma, what are these cuties? I can't believe it! I saw them in the woods near Marigold!"

At age fourteen, Tyra looked like a well-shaped, pretty young lady, with her caramel bubble side-braid growing longer and becoming lighter.

"This is Tom Sawyer," Alma said, gesturing to the white cat. "And this is Calla. They appeared on my doorstep the other day, and I invited them to come inside. Since then, they have decided to stay. Ethan agreed, and I'm happy. They're cute indeed, these little monsters." Alma frowned with affection as she petted them with both hands, one for each.

Tyra and Alma entered the living room, which was designed in an eclectic style. It featured a mixture of vintage and contemporary furniture, including a plush, beige, faux-leather sofa with a potent assortment of throw pillows in different fabrics and patterns and a soft cotton mustard blanket dropped over. Next to the sofa was a large, square wooden coffee table, a maroon shag carpet, and a reclining armchair. Sheer curtains swayed with grace on the floor-to-ceiling windows. The walls were decorated with canvases that Scarlett had discovered at a local art studio, painted by a talented but underappreciated artist. One canvas featured a red-headed woman. Her short, curly hair fluttered around her face like a protective shield. She was sitting on the ground, her legs forming a ring, and surrounded by darkness. She was holding an umbrella above her head with one hand as she hugged a black cat with the other. A second cat was resting beside her, wearing a striped cotton baby hat. A third cat, this one white and black, was sprawled across her legs with a blissful smile. There was light, warmth, and love under that tiny shelter. It was small but just enough to get through difficult times.

Alma's cats entered the room, their tails intertwined in a mischievous hug.

"These beasties woke me up around five a.m. Tom was standing on my chest, staring at me with his enormous, tipsy eyes. Then he started kneading in a rapid, unsteady rhythm. Faster, then softer, then faster, purring with authority. And then he got crazy. He turned around, jumped on my belly, and tried to retrieve my hands from under the downy blanket. The usual routine, mind you. He's bonkers but fun! Calla is cleverer. At first, she snuggles, purring like an overexcited tractor. Then she gets up, rubs my face with hers, and starts grooming me as if I were her kitty. I say, 'Too early for breakfast, monsters.' After some time, they give up and play, chasing each other. Calla hides behind the door or under the furniture and then jumps out without warning. Tom screams, does somersaults, then chases her while mewing with a happy voice. He's quite talkative, this round furball."

Scarlett dashed into the room in a slim, ruby-red dress and turquoise high heels, with a matching satchel. "God, I despise my boss! Yesterday, he lectured me about my project for so long that I zoned out. This from the guy who gets confused when the phone rings while staring at some spilled coffee with the helpless expression of a toddler!"

Tyra chuckled. "Poor fellow. He's getting on your nerves."

"And when I lashed out," Scarlett continued, "he said, 'That's why we broke up! You're crazy! You can't decide whether you're happy or not. One day you're a delight; another day you drive me nuts.' So, *I* said, 'Middle-aged men believe women are all the same. The younger ones say we're unpredictable and, therefore, crazy. But the truth is we can share ordinariness with craziness, and no woman could *ever* be one or the other on schedule to make your life easier! Lack of maturity is why wisdom keeps chasing you, with no luck!' Oh, he loves me! And he's a beauty. Too bad we're both so stubborn. Gotta go, bye!" She rushed out to her car with two cups of steaming coffee and two raspberry scones.

Alma looked at Tyra. "Your mama's in a good mood." She chuckled. "How're you really, my girls?"

"I don't know. Mum's happy you live nearby, and she loves her job. You know, she has an active dating life—she's on a quest for *love*." Tyra smiled. "We're settled in and getting used to our new life. The city's bearable. At least they decorate it properly once a year for the winter festival. There's no forest, but the park is beautiful. Still, it's not the same. I miss Moss, and I miss Willow, Moose, Aksana, Dad, and Luke.

"You know, I see Luke in my dreams sometimes. Last night I had a lucid dream again. I was in a lush, luminous lavender field. The light-blue sky was clear and unclouded. It looked like a canvas with a tint of peach and turquoise. The air was invigorating, and the smell was divine. I was standing barefoot on the moist soil, wiggling my toes in the lavish, squishy earth. I could feel the cool flow from the ground and a tickling breeze on my face. The breeze played with my loose hair while I was licking lavender ice cream. Yes, lavender! It was delicious. Not too sweet. Then I saw Luke from a distance, walking away. His hair became darker, and his waves swayed slightly. He was tall and toned. Zoe was hovering above him, as usual. And . . . it's weird, but a giant beaver was walking beside him. He was wearing a green jacket and a brown scarf! I knew it was a beaver by his distinct webbed hind feet and large, flat tail. I called out to Luke, but he didn't hear me. I panicked, tried to race him, but no matter how fast I ran, he remained at the same distance."

"I'm sorry, little one. I hope you'll meet him again someday. You two were inseparable. Such friendship is hard to find and even harder to keep. But life can be mischievous. Wait and live, darling."

"I don't see how it's possible. Anyway, the kids here are indifferent, which is great. I'm on my own, but no one bothers me. I'm glad I've started dancing. I read and I walk. The house is lovely, and I'm happy to have you just around the corner. This is such a gift and a relief. But it's like night and day, compared to Moss. I want to travel the world and meet people who aren't afraid of living. I feel like we live in a different realm, you know?"

Alma nodded. "Yes, dear. I hear you. The rest of Azure is grim, cold, and lifeless. People are distant. They hurry to finish their day and never stop to notice life. They're loners. Tolerance, connection, and kinship are foreign words to them. No wonder there's a rise in depression, anxiety, and conflicts. Financial success is the most important goal, even on behalf of others. Social media is only making things worse."

"Yes, and it's funny how you can win the lottery or make a lucky investment, and voila! It puts you in a position of high status, which seems ridiculous. Or you can work for ten years and earn a decent living not only because you've worked hard but also because you happened to be in the right place at the right time. Then you can retire without accomplishing or creating anything significant, but people will leave you alone and even worship you."

Alma sighed. "Right. This type of hierarchy is absurd and pure ignorance! And their social structure is inhuman and wrong. There are no communities. People avoid each other. At work everyone acts formally. No mutual lunches, birthdays, or coffee afterward. But they appear content with their boring lives, or so it seems. And the turmoil around 'my faith, your faith,' which one is better or more correct, has gotten out of proportion. So many pointless battles and senseless victims."

"I'm happy to be agnostic and that I was born into a family that allows freedom of belief. Well, Mama considers herself an atheist, but she believes in this New-Age distortion against the real laws of nature. At least she doesn't worship or believe in any god or goddess. Oy, the other day she took me to this lady with this New-Age chic, who *positions* herself as a holistic witch and claims she can heal *any* ailments and predict the future. She has a spooky vibe and wears odd clothes. Her entire body is covered with glittering charms and crystals, and her room looks like a realm of modern enchantment, full of candles. Gosh, it smells horrible with some kind of smoking thing. She said you don't need vaccinations or pills. Oh, great, what a relief. She declared, 'I can heal you with my elixirs! It's all completely natural.' Yeah, and completely useless. And then she said in an alluring voice as if she were purring, 'No antibiotics, and no antidepressants.' Then she screamed, 'Oh, these products of demonic energies in this world!' After that she returned to her melodious tone. 'No, oh, no! No toxins whatsoever. I'll heal you in no time. But do not interfere with skepticism. Ever.' Sure, an easy way out when nothing works. And, of course, she has shelves stuffed with dozens of bottles filled with noxious liquids and random powders mixed with regular water from the sink. She said her home is charged with cosmic energy. Ha! And then she purred again, 'Everything I say is proven by underappreciated scientists. Don't allow doubts to enter your mind; otherwise, it won't work.' Then she screamed like a spooked cat that had been stung by the wasp, 'Open your mind, girl! Believe!' Oy, Grandma, I couldn't restrain my laughter. Then she gave me a look as if I had fallen too deep into the darkness to be saved. She pressed her hands against her chest in a praying gesture. 'May the mother universe guide you in your next life toward freedom and shield your little soul from false beliefs! *Namaste*, dear, *namaste*.'" Tyra laughed.

Alma giggled. "Did it help?"

"Sure, a week later my flu was gone, heh, heh. Honestly, I got lost in all the numerous variations of sectarian doctrines. It's super confusing."

"Me too. I believe the gods, goddesses, and demons are inside us. Of course, the government encourages these developments. It's the easiest way to control the masses. It always has been instead of promoting mental health and providing free therapy sessions or giving people tools to cope with the changing nature of life and its struggles. But here, people rarely question anything. Instead, they just follow the system that the government provides. And there's no need to punish free spirits like us. Our voices will drown in the waters of blissful ignorance. I hope you'll find a way to find your oasis again. It's a vast world. Somewhere out there are people like us who long for a different life. Like our ancestors who built a beautiful bubble in Moss. It lasted for a while, and it was beautiful."

Alma hugged her granddaughter. As Tyra stood there in her grandmother's arms, she stared at another canvas by the same artist. It was the head of a woman with branches and autumn leaves instead of hair. The tiny yellow-orange leaves around her closed eyes resembled freckles. Between the branches was a house. Between the branches was a *home*.

"How about you, Grandma? How are you holding up?"

Alma looked at her black-and-white besties and then at Tyra. "Where love and joy remain, I can live there too. My sense of home is in people—and cats." She chuckled.

Tyra sighed. "This world is everything *but* normal. I wish we lived in a more stable realm without all these abnormalities. I just wanna feel at home again and be an ordinary girl with a simple life."

"I know, little one, but within this chaos is so much beauty, excitement, and wonder." Alma looked at the canvases. "You know, I read a post by this artist. It said, 'I'm hovering between two worlds. The old one is no longer mine, and I haven't taken root yet in the new one. The feeling of home is gone. Home is no longer there, and it's not here yet. I believe, from all our tears, rain will fall. The planet will absorb the moisture, and beautiful flowers will grow.'"

CHAPTER 11
The Shoes on the Table

"The rose that once had bloomed."
forever dies.
– Omar Khayyam

Two uneventful years went by, marked by a monotonous routine.

Scarlett enjoyed her new job, but she continued to complain about her mansplaining boss. She was excellent at her job and had no doubt she could supervise *him* instead. Besides, Scarlett was a free spirit, and she despised the patriarchal society in which they lived. Her dad treated her and her sister as equals, and she expected the same from other men.

Tyra was happy to be invisible. She wore her scarf every day at school, spending most of her free time reading, studying, and dancing. Dancing became her new passion and her ultimate escape from lingering loneliness. She made passing friends along the way and was almost ready to feel content with her colourless life.

Tom and Calla visited often, becoming her faithful companions and active participants in her joys and struggles. Ethan installed a cat door in their entry, so they could come and go as they wished, as all cats do anyway, making their owners jump out of their chair dozens of times an hour, rumbling like offended gods.

Logan wrote short letters and called from time to time. For the most part they engaged in small talk about their day-to-day lives. Every call ended with Tyra sobbing in her room. Scarlett had a hard time listening to her daughter crying. But she also rejected her right to miss him. Scarlett felt betrayed and hurt. She was angry with Tyra for showing such strong affection toward someone who had left her while she, her mother, was always there, no matter what.

Scarlett *hadn't* run away. How could she? How could he?

Tyra struggled to deal with frustration and loss.

When she was little, she seldom had the chance to investigate and process her feelings.

"Oh, Tyra's crying!" Alma would exclaim, and everyone would rush to calm her down by offering toys or showing her the passing birds. Alma and Tyra's parents never allowed Tyra to cry for long. They did everything possible to hush her outbursts and cover them with pleasurable distractions.

Weekend evenings were pretty much the same.

Guests and strangers bustled and hustled around, engaged in never-ending chatter and laughing like horses. So many people. Too many. Little Tyra was bored. She needed attention. Someone to be with, to share memories with. To play outside with sparkling water in a splash pad, to chase a neighbour's dog and feed chipmunks.

They offered her a meringue cookie, then a new doll, then a book filled with artistic illustrations. All of it was prepared in advance, with thorough consideration for that exact occasion. It was hard to resist. She accepted it.

Tyra became quiet and busy—for a while. Long hours dragged by with no interruptions. Tyra felt lonely. She went to her mother's workshop to play with fancy fabrics, baroque lace, and luxurious yarns of silk, cashmere, and alpaca wool.

They had a small TV. She turned it on and watched cartoons. And more cartoons.

She was bored again and restless.

"Here's my phone, Tyra."

Tyra scrolled through it with no interest. She dumped the phone, drew abstract figures, and almost fell asleep.

She was tired. It was midnight, but she was *too* tired to sleep. Little Tyra rubbed her droopy, shiny eyes. Her brows furrowed, and her lips formed a pout. Her cheeks were flushed. She began to cry. They brought her chocolate, dark and creamy, with orange peels, her favourite. It was so hard to resist.

She dashed it on the floor, crying harder.

At first, her parents felt confused, even embarrassed. Then they got upset and then irritated, feeling helpless. "Why are you so capricious? What's wrong?"

Olivia shrugged. "We spoiled her. Well, *you* spoiled her." She was but a child herself, but she noticed. "Tyra, you're tired, girl. Let me put you to bed. Yes, I'll stay with you until you fall asleep. Let's go, cupcake." Olivia picked Tyra up in a tender hug.

Since then, little had changed. *Now* Tyra was the kind of person who treated herself the same way. She was tired, hurt, and lonely, but she never stayed still long enough to notice.

Tyra missed her dad dearly. Whatever he did or didn't do made no difference at that point. She couldn't understand why he had left her and never returned. The feeling of abandonment arose and cracked and then disappeared inside her body.

The shadow squeezed and became denser.

Tyra was too young to understand that a man who had left his most precious treasure could not turn back. A failed father, an unloved son, and a despised husband, he sank into clinical depression and fear.

Fear of being unwanted in this world.

His aunt and uncle were simple but kind and fair people who did their best to heal his wounds. In time, Logan found a great job as a transportation carrier. He visited the realm of Terra and shared some of the stories with his daughter. Adventures became his refuge from the emptiness and sorrow of his wasted life.

The job was unlike any other. It was the most desirable of all in the realm of Azure.

The main difference between Azure and many other realms on Earth was its closed borders. No one could enter that realm, and no one could get out. Well, almost no one. The truck drivers were the only people who could cross. All information about other existing realms was prohibited. It was meticulously secured by the government as part of a worldwide system in Azure's realm. There had been rumours and speculations about other realms, but only one was officially known to the masses—Terra. It was said that Terra played a significant role in an array of worlds that coexisted in harmony. Terra was the bridge. However, her people believed they were the only humans on the planet. Ironically, her gates were wide open for almost everyone but her people.

Any type of production in Azure was a rare exception, and even their books and art were mainly borrowed. They traded their rich natural resources of precious stones with Terra's massive production in every possible domain.

This trade was carried out by secret organizations that spared no effort to conceal the truth. However, the people of Azure knew about the trading system. Terrans, except for politicians and their wealthiest people, were unaware of it all. Besides, the only interest Terrans had in Azure was the gems. It was a win-win situation for two isolated systems. A fair trade.

The path between the two realms was dangerous, populated by the beasts.

One day when Tyra was sixteen, Logan disappeared. On that day, Tyra received his last letter in a pale blue-grey envelope scented with blooming violet mums. Inside the envelope was a flawless white-gold ring with a radiant, astonishing emerald gemstone. The letter said: "Good day, kiddo. I miss you. I love you. I made this ring for you. Look closely. I'm preparing for your upcoming visit. There is so much I want to show you. There's an ice cream shop nearby with exquisite flavours. I hope you'll find your favourite. Mine is still dark chocolate."

The letter ended with a cheerful, silly smiley and happy hands holding two types of ice cream.

When Tyra received a phone call from her dad's uncle, her bubble of sanity collapsed once more.

"They got him. His death was quick, almost painless," Logan's uncle said, sobbing. "The funeral will be held today. Cremation. They said the beasts might be infectious. I'm sorry, Tyra. There's no time for you to get here for the funeral. I'm so sorry, my dear."

Tyra wept for four days and four nights. She lay on her bed, nuzzling her red, puffy nose into her soaked pillow as she hugged her squishy doll with the cheerful face, a present from Logan.

Tyra's grief was unbearable. She needed it to stop. On the fifth day, she called her semi-friend. Her shadow squeaked, cringed, and grew chubbier.

"Let's get together," she said. "I'm tired of crying."

"Sure!" her friend replied in a merry voice. "I'm grounded, but I'll let my parents know you, like, need a shoulder to cry on. They won't be able to resist showing kindness to someone in need." She giggled. "Then we can go to the party! Oh, gosh, I was dying to get there. I'm glad you're done with your grief stuff. I hate it when people share their feelings. It makes me uncomfortable. What's not my problem isn't my problem, right?"

"'Sorrow is too great to exist in small hearts,'" Logan had said often, a quote from Kahlil Gibran.

Tyra hung up and put on her scarf. Then she heard a hushed male voice in her head for the first time, melodious and mellow. Here's what it said:

Get cozy with your sorrow,
Cuddle with your grief.
Float with your fears,
And melt within your anger.
Stroll through your frustrations,

Your disappointments,
And your regrets.
Dive into your doubts,
Your powerlessness,
Your hopelessness.
Surrender, child!

"I can't!" Tyra replied. "I'm drowning, freezing, burning, falling."

"That's okay. Let it be."

"You don't understand. Nobody can."

"That's true. It's your grief, and it's unique, as each person's grief is. But try to listen, child. When you're having a good moment, savour it, but know it won't last forever." The voice paused to allow the words to sink in. "When you're having a hard time, let it be. But keep in mind, this too shall pass."

Then there was a long silence.

Tyra squeezed the emerald ring and caught the thought before it slipped away. She tilted her head and looked at the flimsy, lonely desk in the corner of her spacious, off-white room, decorated in pastel colours in a simple but cozy style. She reread Logan's letter, which was lying on the desk's birch surface. Tyra scratched her head and then examined the ring. She found a tiny, faint word carved on the inner side of the ring: "Anicca."

"What does it mean? I've heard it before." She mulled it over, recalling her conversation with Koda. "Anicca. Anicca. Anicca. Oh! Impermanence."

Tyra dropped the letter, threw on her coat and boots, and dashed out into the dazzling white street as a blizzard squeaked in her ears. Her frozen cheeks burned and ached. She took a deep breath of icy air. It hurt. Her broken heart was still beating. How come? Buses were running, buzzing, humming. People were smiling.

Birds' chatter and kids' laughter rang in her ears, causing her pain. The streets with fancy boutiques, ready for the winter festival, were nonchalant to her sorrow. And the coffee shops served croissants.

"Life has its way of going on and on, never slowing down, each moment restarting," the voice whispered.

Tyra fled to the central park. *Piles of snow.* She fell, sat down, and dove deeper into the sparkling white hole, and then she stopped moving. No thoughts, only a blank space. Her head throbbed, pulsing in a frantic rhythm.

Can't feel it . . . too painful. Can't bear it.

Tyra's heart was soft and tender.

Snap. Flip. Her neck blocked all her anguish, fears, and anger. It clicked.

Ouch! She felt a sharp pain. Her head pinged, threatening to explode, but from then on, her heart had its own space and her head its own domain. There was no connection between the two. Convenient.

Tyra stood up and went home. Back in her room, on her bed, at age sixteen, Tyra acquainted herself with her melancholy and chronic pain for the first time. Her entire body was aching, burning, itching. Penetrating pain and acute tension. Brain fog, itchy eyes, exhaustion. General heaviness and malaise all over. No joy. Life was dull, colourless, and senseless. It felt as if she were wading through a dense swamp.

The shadow was trembling on the dark corner, frozen, isolated, and trapped. *Powerless.* Who else, if not Tyra, could set it free?

But Tyra was absorbed in denial and resentment.

The shadow felt neglected, rejected, and abandoned. And it cried, voiceless. Then it got angry, furious even.

"Get cozy with your pain. Merge with it. Dissolve in it," the voice murmured.

"I can't," she replied.

There is love, and there is fear. Fear is often stronger.

≈

The next seasons were almost identical. Tyra felt better. Denial helped, for the moment.

Tyra would dance, read, walk, garden, and study. Scarlett was worried sick, but she felt powerless and confounded by such intense feelings boiling inside her daughter. As a family, they weren't good with emotions or hugs.

Little by little, Tyra found comfort in her grandmother's kitchen where she felt safe, seen, and loved. It was enough to heal her visible wounds, little by little. The subtle whispers of delicious food being cooked in Alma's kitchen was soothing. The searing sound of onions getting caramelized in the skillet, the smell of crispy golden potatoes and freshly baked homemade bread with butter. Alma's apple gem and fried pastries with eggs and chives were divine. It was all that Tyra needed to feel at home again. Alma's cooking, filled with warmth and love, rekindled her aching heart, bit by bit. Alma's quiet presence, her softness, felt safe and nourishing.

Tyra often wondered how, one day, she'd be able to carry on without her grandmother's presence in that frosty world. Whenever her mind glimpsed that terrifying future, Tyra felt an ache that was almost unbearable. Such a vast hole was preparing itself to be created inside her heart, far in advance.

As is often the case, a series of unfortunate events occurred one after another, shooting forth like a high-speed train in front of her eyes. When her heart was still hurting, still fighting, another strike was already on the way.

No time to feel, no time to notice, no time to heal.

Alma sat in her kitchen on a wooden rocking chair that Ethan had made for her birthday the previous year. It had a soft purple velvet cushion and lotus flowers carved into its arms. Alma rocked back and forth, holding a cup of hot chocolate in her left hand and a porcelain saucer in her right. She scrutinized her granddaughter, who was sitting behind the oval white kitchen table next to the open window, immersed in a book. The apple pie they had made together was still steaming. Tyra's wet, loose hair was frizzled into cute curls around her face. She looked so cozy in her jersey pants and a cotton shirt with Minnie-Mouse on it. So fragile. Alma took a crunchy nut cookie from the pale green saucer and dipped it into the boiling-hot beverage Tyra had made from pure dark chocolate.

Waves of sadness washed over Alma, tingling her stomach as she looked at Tyra with loving kindness. *Such hard times for my little one*, she thought.

Tyra noticed her grandmother's look and flinched. "Granny, what's wrong?"

"I'm so sorry, my little one. It's cancer."

They sat there, staring at the apple pie in complete silence.

No words felt right, and no thoughts came in handy. Only waves of pulsating sensations all over their bodies. They rose and flashed by with astronomical rapidity. Tyra could barely feel her own breath. The air in the room felt dense. Smothering.

Tyra hugged her granny as if trying to freeze that moment, to create a time loop where nothing would ever change. She hugged her for everlasting moments in a desperate attempt to shield and protect her.

"Only you can hug me like this, little one," Alma said, smiling. "I want you to have something." She went to her room and returned with a massive figure of a cow made of amber gemstone. Inside the cow was a beautiful dragonfly, trapped in amber.

"In our family, we have some abilities unknown to this realm. Not each generation. But it has passed to you, my dear. When you need my help, speak into the cow's ear, and you'll get it. The cow contains a part of me, a part of our ancestors, and the power to connect to the source of wisdom beyond this realm. I will leave you soon, but remember, nothing really goes away. It only transforms. I will love you for eternity. You'll always have my guidance because I live inside of you, as all essential parts of our childhood do. And I want you to find your way out of this realm. You don't belong here." Alma rubbed her beige pencil skirt. She was only fifty-five, still young and beautiful. "Or, probably, the way will be found."

"I don't understand. We're all trapped here. The only way out is through the job Dad had. I'll never work there. As much as I wish to escape this place, that option is out of the question." Tyra put her feet on a cushioned chair and hugged her knees, pressing her legs to her tummy. She completely dismissed the cow.

"Have you heard about the Land of the Great Lakes?"

"Sure, but that's just a fantasy. I don't live in fantasies anymore."

"They say it's a land full of wonder and a true chance of real happiness. Every decade or so, some fortunate people receive invitations to come live there. This is your chance to build your new life. The portal is getting closer to being opened again. I don't know for certain when it'll happen, but it will. There's a tree between the realms on the other end of the deep, dark forest where no one dares to go. The forest exists, but only some can find it. When the time comes, you'll be instructed. The tree sends its leaves as an invitation. The key to the portal will be waiting for you when you find the tree. I want you to have a different life, my little one."

Tyra's head was swirling. Everything she had just heard felt surreal.

The wind from an open window got wild, the windows thundered, and the garden grew dimmer. The heavy, oppressive air was preparing to be rescued. Rain was on the way.

"I promise I'll do as you say, Grandma."

Six months passed in the blink of an eye. Tyra's heart cringed each time she saw a grimace of pain on her grandmother's freckled, youthful face. She watched Alma disappear, slowly and inevitably.

Tyra cried on her way to school and on her way home. She cried while she cooked, cleaned, made her bed, and walked in the park. Mute and sad, her eyes were pricked by drops of salty water. Tyra's anguish was profound and deep. It attempted to merge with other losses, but its strength was too prevalent, too grasping, too unique.

The winter overstayed its welcome that year, slipping through spring's rightful season with the inconsiderateness of an impudent child. One day after a snowfall, when nature was resting, Tyra went to the central park. The piles of sparkling snow looked fluffy, warm, and inviting. She started sculpting hug-sized hands on the ground. After she finished, she took off her long, puffy navy jacket and nestled into those welcoming arms in a silly anticipation of warmth and comfort. The snow arms were firm and frosty. Tyra got up, exasperated. She wiped away the lukewarm drops flowing down her flushed cheeks.

Feeling stupid, she headed home.

On her way there, she stopped by a cozy café with unexpected charm and wall-to-floor arched windows. She ordered a chamomile tea and an avocado sandwich with cherry tomatoes on top. Tyra looked out the windows at the winter paradise and sighed. The view was spectacular. Pine trees were burdened with sparkling snow, the streetlights were already on, and the poorly decorated shops reminded her of the upcoming festival. It was beautiful.

Days before Alma passed away, she asked Tyra to open a closet made of walnut. One door had an asymmetrical oval mirror on it, and the other was made of translucent, polished amazonite, a greenish-blue gemstone with a pearly luster. Inside, Tyra found a wicker linen basket containing one pair of black and white flats, a pair of casual ginger sneakers with frail white soles, two pairs of Crocs—one pink and the other green—and a pair of tiny crochet lilac shoes, one with a squirrel on it and the other decorated with a chipmunk.

Alma was curled up in her bed. She looked so fragile.

"There's a custom I like," she whispered, each word an effort. "When someone passes away, a family member puts their shoes on the table to honour their memory. I want you to have mine, your dad's, Aksana's, and her little brother's. Here, I crocheted a pair in memory of your doggy. Take them to your new life and pile them up on a side table. One day, they'll come in handy."

"How?"

"You'll see."

When Alma died peacefully in her sleep, Tyra bought a round side table and placed the five pairs of shoes on top. She also printed and framed a poster of a famous artistic work called "Melancholy," created by Albert György. It portrayed the massive void that grief leaves in our hearts—a copper figure slumped over on a bench with a giant hole in the centre.

Tyra's fear of a rebroken heart was almost in vain. This time, her grief was deeply felt. Alma had given her granddaughter as much as a mother could ever give her child, so Tyra's heart felt full and at peace, although she missed her grandmother very much.

Scarlett felt broken. Throughout her adult life, she had dreamed of getting closer to her mother. She worshipped her and craved her love, warmth and softness like a hungry infant longed for her mother's milk. Scarlett felt abandoned. Empty. Struggling for comfort in the wake of the immense loss, she dove deep into her childhood memories and told Tyra all the stories she could recall. Spinning in circles, Scarlett stayed in the past.

Tyra was struggling too. Saving others is a nebulous virtue. Saving a loved one from their grief is unattainable. Volatile. To hold onto the belief that one can rescue someone other than oneself is a treacherous trap.

Tyra would sit beside her mother for hours, reading a book, her head resting on her mother's weakening shoulder and listening to the perpetual echoes of sweet memories until her mind wandered. But she tried the best she could to comfort her mother. Grief requires silent company.

CHAPTER 12
The Instructions

"To be nobody but yourself in a world
which is doing its best day and night to make you like
everybody else means to fight the hardest battle
which any human being can fight and never stop fighting."
– E. E. Cummings

Each day Tyra missed her grandma more and more. She missed her presence in this world. But she found comfort in her cow, whose amber ears were always attentive. The cow spread a peculiar and almost sensible warmth. Tyra wasn't sure what powers it possessed. Still, she sensed her grandmother's presence, which was just enough. Like when she touched Alma's spider-web-like cashmere shawl, when she hugged it in her sleep, or when she sniffed the fading residue of her perfume. Tyra would tell the cow about her innermost desires and troubles while sitting on the windowsill and watching strangers pass by through the white hoarfrost-covered window, holding a cup of cardamom tea and a slice of carrot cake with cream-cheese icing on top.

The cow was always beside her bed. Tom and Calla visited more often.

Winter lingered, withholding awakening and renewal.

On a Saturday morning when April was still crystal powdered and the smell of mint behind the slightly open window met the whistling sound of the north wind and the muffled sounds of napping nature, Tyra woke up and followed the aroma of freshly baked cookies. She petted the black-and-white monsters lying in the hallway next to the entrance, still grieving, still waiting.

"You miss your mama, my little beasties. I feel for you. But it's time to get out of bed. She's not coming back. Death is always final. I'm sorry."

Tyra stroked them both, one cat with her right hand and the other with her left, as Alma used to, and then she entered the kitchen.

She found her mother cleaning up a mess on the wooden countertop of the turquoise island. Her hands were covered in flour. Scarlett was wearing Alma's favourite apron with lily valley flowers on a blurry green field. The downward-facing, bell-shaped blooms were pure, white lace-edged petals. The red kettle was hooting on the hissing stove, the water purring as it bubbled.

Scarlett gestured toward an open jar, causing a spicy, grounding, uplifting aroma to waft out of it. "Tea for you and coffee for me. I made a new blend of herbs and flowers. Check it out."

Tyra was a tea person in a family of coffee lovers. She poured tea for herself and lavender coffee for her mother. Scarlett pulled a burning-hot tray of steaming rose meringues out of the oven and put them on an elegant aqua-lacy porcelain plate. Then she and Tyra settled around the square maple dining table in front of the icy window and dove into the warm, fancy cookies and hot beverages.

As they ate, Tyra spotted a creature hiding behind the turquoise-and-yellow pantry beside the kitchen island.

"Mama, did you see that?" Tyra asked in surprise.

"It's Zeus. He's shy," Scarlett replied as she crunched a cookie.

A tiny white lizard stuck its head out, sharing a timid ear-to-ear smile as his black-goggled eyes stared at Tyra with cautious curiosity.

"He showed up in the kitchen the day Mama passed away. He was suspicious at first but slowly got to trust me."

"And you never told me? Why? He's a cutie."

Zeus's smile widened even further.

"I don't know. I guess we needed some alone time to bond." Scarlett smiled, though she looked a bit guilty.

"Mama, how's your new boyfriend? Do you like him?"

Scarlett nodded. "I think we have a chance. His name's Neil. The other day, we were getting ready for work in his apartment, and I found myself in this indecisive state. You know, when I can't quite grasp my mood and choose the right outfit. So, I wore this mustard sweater I made last week with plaid navy-green pants and a matching puffy red bag. I asked him what he thought, and he said, 'Sorry, darling, I'm in a hurry.'

"'It'll only take a minute,' I replied. 'What do you think?' I spun around, looking for his approval. He gave me a suspicious look and said, 'I'm too short on time for trouble, woman. Let me go. I beg you.' He keeps me grounded. I like it." She chuckled. "I hope it'll last. Yesterday, I asked if I'd gained some weight. He said, 'No, you're good.'

"'But it wouldn't hurt to lose some, right?' I pushed.

He said, 'Rubbish, I like you as you are.'

"'But I'm not inspiring delight, am I?' I asked.

"'Why, you certainly do,' he said. But I wasn't ready to give up just yet.

"'But not the crazy kind, right?' I asked.

"'Are you trying to pick a fight?' he grumbled. 'If so, I'm all yours. Let it all out.' Then he smiled. I think I'm in love." Scarlett giggled.

"Good. A man with life behind him," Tyra said. "Uh-oh, a great basis for a healthy relationship." She chuckled as she took another cookie. "I want you to be happy."

"Thank you. I *am* happy. At last."

"Oh, Mama, these cookies are heaven!" Tyra declared, her mouth sticky and gleaming.

"Thanks. I wonder sometimes why you never liked my cooking as much as you loved Mama's," Scarlett said with a hint of caution, afraid of spoiling the moment.

"Well, you're an excellent cook, Mama. No doubt. But you're like a gourmet chef, and kids prefer simple dishes, you know? You're also fond of spices, which is great. I'm learning to appreciate it now that I'm older. Still, as a kid, ugh, sorry, it wasn't my cup of tea." Tyra smiled. "I also appreciate your attempts to simplify your recipes for me. Like the bow-shaped pasta you made from scratch. It was delicious."

Scarlett's face lit up with amusement. "I'm happy you remember. Your grandmother was impossible to compete with. She never had to set boundaries or do the harsh side of parenting, you know."

Scarlett went to the pantry and fetched a box filled with mixed leaves, cloves, and dandelions. She chopped up some fruits and fed Zeus by hand while continuing to talk. "I know you were escaping me then for a reason. But I feel like I've never had the chance to build a close relationship with you. You had your grandmother, whom you adored. She was your safe place. I know that. And you had this clique group with your dad. I wanted to be invited into your cozy, carefree bubbles to spend more time with you, but I guess I didn't know how. I feel like you've always rejected me. But I'm sorry for how I behaved when your dad left. I felt robbed. Twice."

"Well, Mum, I was just a kid," Tyra said, feeling uneasy. "It wasn't my fault. I can't be held responsible for bonding or the lack thereof."

So close. They had been so close to having a nice moment and then . . . poof!

"No, it was my parents," Scarlett said. "They decided I was too young to be a mum. They steered and stirred the boat. Look, Zeus is getting closer. He's examining you. He's so funny. I love him." Scarlett smiled with affection.

Growing bolder, Zeus settled beside Scarlett's chair, not far from Tyra. Scarlett leaned over and stroked him.

"He's a cutie," Tyra said. "Hey, you wanna stroll in the park? Oops! I keep forgetting spring refuses to come and rescue. Every time in March, let alone April, I feel like it's unfair, and I lose my patience. Enough is enough. And these 'plus one' promises are a scam. The weather forecasters are definitely having some fun, huh?" She chuckled.

"I know!" Scarlett laughed. "Let's watch *Home Alone* again!"

"Yes, let's!"

Tom and Calla entered the kitchen and spotted Zeus, but he didn't notice. In a flash, Calla sprinted and caught him with her paw. It looked as if she were smirking. Her eyes lit up and then narrowed. Tom dashed, then stopped, preparing to strike. He lowered his body to the floor in a fluid, controlled movement. His ears pricked forward, fully alert, and his eyes became wider as his pupils dilated while he fixed his gaze on Zeus. His whiskers twitched as he let out a haunting sound. Soft and lyrical. Alluring.

"Leave him alone, beasties!" Tyra cried. She grabbed Tom and hugged him. "Calm down. You, little troublemaker."

Meanwhile, Scarlett took Calla away and lectured her as she petted and comforted Zeus on her knees.

"Okay, hooligans. Let's make acquaintances," Tyra said as she brought the two cats closer to Zeus, though she was careful to remain at a safe distance. "This is Zeus. You can't hurt him. No, you can't. He lives here now too. Sniff him. Good. Good kitties."

Zeus shivered, frozen and unable to move. Tom and Calla sniffed him, and Tyra gave them treats, praising their composure. Zeus finally revived, then bolted away and hid behind the kitchen cabinets. Tyra and Scarlett sighed in relief.

Scarlett giggled. "I'm happy they're back."

Tyra nodded, tittering.

Tom and Calla lost interest and invented a new game. Tom found a pencil under a woven cream rug and crawled under it, confident that no one could see or find him. The pen rolled farther. Tom stretched out his puffy snow-white paw in slow motion and hid it again. Then he stretched and hid. Calla watched him with contempt. Then she jumped above the rug with all her might, meowing and hissing.

Tyra chuckled. "Let's watch *Home Alone*! Did you know *all* the movies and cartoons are also borrowed from Terra? And they've been telling us that artists like privacy. Aha. They live on their own isolated island, blah, blah. Dad told me." Tyra rolled her eyes.

Scarlett shrugged. "Shock has lost its sting for me. But this world is all we've got."

They settled in their neat living room in front of the flat-screen TV with two bowls of caramel popcorn, ready to get crazy and laugh, as they always did when watching that hilarious movie.

When spring eventually strolled in, Tyra felt restless. It seemed as if her life was refusing to start. Final exams were approaching fast. Twelve years of school had flown by. Tyra was a good student, but she was never good enough for her grandfather, who was a decent, good-hearted, but fearsome man. Ethan wanted her to have a good life—from his perspective. He cared for his girls and did what he could to keep them safe, though he often overstepped his boundaries.

"I want you to be grounded, Tyra. Strong-spirited," he'd say. It was his way of protecting her and preparing her to be self-sufficient in adulthood. Every person expresses their love differently. Ethan demanded hard work and diligence. "No time for dance, books, or foolishness. Grades must be excellent," he reminded her.

Tyra was drowning in homework, part-time tutoring, and housework, while Scarlett worked long hours and spent her evenings out with Neil, diving headfirst into an active social life. In quiet moments, she devoted her remaining free time to crocheting stuffed toys for the children at a local orphanage.

Tyra felt drained. One day, when she was at her breaking point, she heard a strange sound from the cow. Intrigued, Tyra approached it. When it didn't move, she pressed her ear against the cow's ear and listened. To her disbelief, Tyra heard a soft voice, like a distant, echoing record.

"At last, child. I'm happy you can hear me now."

"Is it real?"

"Sure. Reality is ever-changing. Before you could hear me, it wasn't real, but now it is. Perfectly logical, eh? Do you need help, Tyra?"

"I don't even know. I'm so tired. I can't think of anything."

"What do you need? Pause and listen. Your body knows."

Tyra pondered. *What do I need? Such a bizarre question. What do I feel? Mmhmm, probably tension, irritation, and exhaustion. Pain all over. It never goes away.*

"I miss my walks, my books, and dancing. But it makes no difference what I need or want." She shrugged and then saluted like an obedient soldier. "I must provide perfection; otherwise, I'm doomed. My grandfather gets so mad that it scares me. A lot. He's impossible to be around. Every spoon must be on the exact spot! Yes, sir. Make the countertop sparkle! Done. My clothes must be in precise order and my desk empty. Eh, there's a struggle, sir. Can't help it. Oh, and my bed needs to be made with the precision of a hotel maid, like I'm auditioning for a five-star rating every morning. It's ridiculous. Or, God forbid, I spill something in the kitchen or forget where he put the milk in the fridge. He yells like a mad Doberman. I don't know why Mum tolerates it. It's our house, after all, and we should be able to live our own way. I feel so pissed off sometimes but wait a minute! I'm not allowed to be mad or sad, let alone protest. I get yelled at for having a tantrum."

Tyra stopped and calmed herself down. It felt good to let the steam out at last. "Who would've known it could be *so* draining to live next door to your extended family?" She smirked. "And Olivia, she's just like him. She comes to visit and rustles in our kitchen, cleaning the fridge and the drawers with all the enthu-siasm of a ghostbuster. She hunts down missed spots with the kind of determination I wish *I'd* had in school. Of course, her swift movements are accompanied by loud, never-ending complaints about how messy we are, asking how we can live in such chaos, and why there's a basket of laundry in the room still unfolded. Well, a few baskets. But the rest of the house is well-maintained. Hmm . . . except the dishes." Tyra chuckled. "Any-way, it's driving me nuts. *I hate it* when she nags and scolds us like little kids. And she doesn't even live here!"

"Thank God for that. Heh, heh."

"Thank God, indeed." Tyra laughed. "I'm glad Mum changed. She was just like that when I was little. It was awful. I was petrified to step into our living room, knowing I'd probably mess something up. But I did anyway. Tiptoeing around like a thief, trying not to leave any trace of my sneaky candy hunt."

The cow chuckled. Tyra felt much better.

"Your grandma's early departure changed her," the cow said in a serious voice.

"Well, yeah. But she kind of became like a child. It feels like I'm living with a teen sister. It's probably safer and easier this way, eh?" Tyra snorted.

"Perhaps. Heh, heh, heh."

"You know, it really gets on my nerves when people try to take on the role of my teacher or parent. I already have enough authority figures to deal with. I don't need any more people telling me what to do. What I need is a friend." Tyra rolled her eyes, snorting.

"I hear you, child. But, hmm . . . do I sense boundaries issues?"

"Well, yeah, guilty." Tyra smirked.

"Okay, what do you think I can help you with, little one?"

"I don't know. If only I could have enough hours to sleep and spend time as I wish. I already have my finals and so many completely useless chores! It's like never-ending torture, especially the dishwasher and laundry. Each day it appears miraculously, as if some mischievous groundies have been working day and night to create piles of filthy clothes and dishes. *After* they steal our socks, one sock from each pair. How else? Now all I have are mismatched socks. Mama gets cranky when I wear them like that, but what's the point in buying new ones? They'll vanish by the end of the week anyway. Ha! Oh, I *hate* dishes and laundry! Gosh, we're only two people living in this house! Holy cow! Oy, sorry. Where does it all come from every day?"

The cow chuckled. "I can help you with that, little one. Don't worry. Time's irrelevant to me. As for your feelings, you should allow yourself to feel them to the brim. Otherwise, they'll get trapped in your body and destroy your health. Locate them in your body. Sense them. There's no need to act out in a harmful way, but you're allowed to feel and think whatever comes. Focus on your sensations and observe them with no judgment as they are. Anger is just an emotion. It manifests as heat, perspiration, and an increased heart rate and respiration. Observe it as it naturally comes and goes. The same goes for sadness, fear, frustration, guilt, shame, hatred, and anxiety. Never repress, suppress, or get agitated by such feelings. They're just signals that something is wrong *for* you, not *with* you. Listen to your body, child. Don't dismiss its methods of communication. It's better to get yelled at, punished, or rejected than to deal with the consequences of suppressed emotions.

"Depression often stems from repressed emotions, much like chronic pain or anxiety. When feelings are bottled up, they find their way out, seeking relief and space to breathe. It's advisable to take your inner witch for a walk on the leash every now and then. Heh, heh."

Tyra chuckled. "I like it. My witch is certainly in need of air." She scratched her ear. "This is a whole new concept for me. Well, Koda and Voice mentioned it, but Grandma never talked to me about such things."

"She had a hard time applying this knowledge, so there was no point in discussing something theoretical."

"I'm probably going to have a hard time doing it too."

"Let it sink in. The first few times hearing new words of wisdom are enough only to plant the seeds. For now, try to notice when you tuck your feelings into your psyche. One day, it will help you get them out."

"And then they'll drown me."

"They will—for a while. But sooner or later, they'll pass away. Nothing lasts forever, right?" It seemed as if the cow winked. "And, Tyra, you might want to consider wearing your scarf less often, dear. Trying too hard to fit in is a tricky game."

Tyra cringed.

"It's a dangerous business to abandon your true self," the voice whispered. Then it sighed. "I know, Tyra. Those kids are jerks. But we can't change them. They are what they choose or *can* be. Marigold is an exception. Try not to judge others by this horrible experience. Most places are a mixture of all types of people. And all people are different, even the ones who hide it. There's nothing wrong with you, and there never has been—ever. These types of wounded souls are everywhere. There's no escaping them. But Marigold *will* stay in the past. Mourn and let it go. You'll find *your* people. You'll find your sense of home again. Give it time."

Tyra whispered, "Thank you. I appreciate it."

"Voice is right. You'll see, little one," the cow said. "As for additional time, no worries. When you need to study, sit beside me, and greet me in my right ear. No time will pass for your body. No time will pass at all. When you have chores, say them to my left ear. It'll be enough."

Tyra did as she was told. Against all odds, her chores were done. The cow never intervened in Tyra's preparation for her exams, but as she said, no time passed when Tyra was studying beside her. It was an excellent system.

Meanwhile, Tom had formed a whimsical friendship with

Zeus, and the two spent hours playing. Calla adopted Zeus and groomed his skin until it gleamed. Sometimes she would chase him with a tireless effort, pouncing on him with her soft paws. She'd grab him, swatting and tickling him with maternal tenderness and filling the air with calming purrs. Once, Calla brought a bundle of fragrant lavender and tiny bells in a small basket and sprinkled them all over Zeus. The room was filled with a soothing aroma. Zeus stretched out his head, his eyes smiling. Tom went crazy. Zeus escaped. And the goofy white-as-snow kitty wallowed in the scattered blue-purple paradise. Later, Calla showered Zeus with affection, licking and purring in a hasty manner.

Tyra began to read again. It felt fantastic. Sometimes she wondered what it took for a child to fall in love with reading. Some said kids needed to be encouraged and motivated to read books. Others believed it came naturally or not at all, and all a person could do was set an example. Tyra believed it was better to foster the love of reading in children as a relaxing, mutual ritual. No pressure and no lectures.

Olivia and Tyra used to read to each other aloud, making proper gestures and grimaces. They would mimic postures and intonations like pros. They would act out their favourite scenes like artists on the stage of a local theatre. It was hilarious. Fun *and* bonding. Alma had read to Tyra while they cuddled on the sofa in front of the fireplace, covered by a fleece blanket and wearing matching plush socks. Tyra loved reading next to her mother as she watched the movement of her crochet hook.

She was born into a family of people who didn't read very often. They had never tried to motivate her to become a good reader. They lectured her about sports, though they never showed her any examples or created any opportunity to pursue them. As one might expect, she hated sports until she found a great contemporary ballet teacher. Trudy kindled Tyra's passion for dancing. She was in her mid-twenties, too old to be friends with a teen girl, but the two had become very close as if they were related.

Trudy was a beautiful woman with long, silky black hair that shimmered with hints of blue and purple in the midday sun. She had a sylphlike figure, smooth skin, and deep-set black eyes with epicanthic folds.

The girls often lingered in the dance studio and talked.

One lazy afternoon, Tyra shared her thoughts about books. "I think the most important ingredient in the recipe for becoming a reader was my exposure to the bookish world. And not only the popular and easy reads you could find on the bookshelves of Azure's libraries or regular bookshops. The others, the scarcer ones. The hardest to find and the forbidden."

"I know what you mean. It's the same for me with dancing. My mama taught me to focus not only on the technique but also on the natural fluid of body movements, connected to my emotions."

Tyra nodded, indicating a perfect understanding. By chance, Ethan worked as the CEO of a printing house in Moss. He was more of a collector of books than a reader of them, but his home was overloaded with priceless, exquisite treasures. And each month, he would bring Tyra piles of the most interesting and valuable books, those that held within them the ancient, archetypical knowledge of the entire human race, those that preserved the wisdom of millions of souls, and the most engaging stories of mundane life on the planet Earth with bold adventures or day-to-day joys and troubles.

The forbidden books in Azure were controlled by the government using thorough surveillance. The reason for the censorship was simple—to control the masses and tame free-thinking minds. The perfect replacement for books was faith, which came in myriad forms, some of which were ridiculous. Like the God of Pasta or the Flat Earth movement or the promised paradise for the chosen ones.

Such absurd notions in the theatre of oblivion.

It was an easy way to create a desirable societal split to dull the minds, encourage isolation, and boost rigid perceptions.

The constant stimulation to drown in social networks,

emphasizing the outer shell and bravado, was another way to keep people away from the subtler whispers of their minds, which, God forbid, could provoke mutiny. "Oh, look how happy I am! Join my group, follow me, and I'll show you where real happiness lies."

The contrast between social-media accounts and the grey lines of people walking the streets absorbed in their smartphones was remarkable. The censorship worked with eminent success. It had been preventing critical thinking and numbing the awakening of the masses for centuries.

Tyra fell asleep in her bedroom, thinking about the enormous, good fortune of her circumstances, which had led to her becoming a reader. She entered the lucid dream again, which was more like a memory.

Tyra was in the apple orchard in Willow. She and Luke were sitting in an apple tree, crunching crisp, juicy, bittersweet apples as they talked about books and their early memories. Both of them looked much older than in her real memory, and they were wearing fancy, fairy-tale-like clothes. Tyra was dressed in an emerald dress that fluttered down her slender figure. An infinite headband braid encircled her head, and the rest of her hair swayed in the wind. Luke was a handsome young man with short, wavy hair, a charming smile, and soft green eyes.

"I feel like a bird!" Tyra said, spreading her arms.

"What kind of bird?"

"A bald eagle!"

"Come on," Luke said, chuckling. "You're an owl; I'm an eagle."

Tyra giggled in return. "True. Do you remember our daily reading hours in the kindergarten and elementary-school library?"

"Sure. We would create a circle of excitement around the librarian and listen to her soft, deep voice. I can't recall her name or appearance, but I liked her voice."

"Yeah. She would gesticulate and make funny or creepy faces with a full range of emotions and expressions."

"Which even I could grasp and understand."

Tyra laughed. "And her assistant would play music and sounds selected in advance! The rustling of leaves and the hum of seagulls, the splash of waves, the flutter of air in the summer breeze, or a draft slamming the window shutters. It was phenomenal! The most interactive."

"We all were totally absorbed in the tangible world of sounds and visual effects instead of computer games. Much better."

"Obviously. Who could resist continuing to read those stories, right? Remember how all the kids were rushing to get the available copies afterward? We would get in line and wait in sweet anticipation, mixed with worry. Those who had to wait for a week were super upset. But not me." Tyra smiled. "You'd always be the first one in line, holding a spot for me."

Luke smiled.

"I miss you so much," Tyra said in a receding voice. Her words echoed.

"I know! I miss you like hell!"

Then there she was, all alone again, in the apple tree, feeling like a solitary bird. Tyra pictured Luke in her mind at age eleven, finding a forbidden book in his parents' locked bookcase. When Tyra came to visit, she found him sitting on the tip of a chair reading *The Master and Margarita* by M. Bulgakov for the first time, his favourite. For two long days, she was left alone until he read and reread it. Tyra smiled at the memory and then woke up.

The moment Ethan noticed a strange change in Tyra's behaviour, everything went sideways. Tyra spent more time reading, walking, and dancing than doing chores. Everything was done in a perfect manner. Her grades were excellent. She was happy and well rested. Each day, Ethan grew more suspicious.

Ethan was the kind of man who valued impeccable clothes with strong, angular features. He had a prominent jawline and piercing eyes. His rigid posture and solid, well-defined physique reflected an inner tension, strength, and resilience. And as good and dedicated to his family as he was, he couldn't restrain his anger. When his beloved wife was alive, he'd spent countless hours begging for her forgiveness after he snapped, yelled at her, or dismissed her. He was a difficult man to live with, and he knew it. He loved her more than anything in this world, but at times he would become jealous for no apparent reason. After a wave of restrained rage, Ethan would calm down. Remorse was painful, yet he bore it. But he never knew how to prevent or confine the next one. And he despised all fantasies, considering unproven realities to be misleading.

"No time should be wasted on nonsense," he often said. "Make practical, rational choices in life that you can rely on. It's a good way to avoid disappointments."

Each time, Tyra would become anxious. And each time the voice would say, "Notice five things you can see, four things you can hear, three things you can touch—touch it—two things you can feel—feel it—and one thing you can taste—taste it."

Tyra saw, heard, and felt whatever was available. She would often touch her belly, arms, and shoulders, creating a safe bubble of a self-hug. Tyra would also taste her tears or her sweat.

The day Ethan discovered the truth about the cow, he lost it. Cognitive dissonance between what was seen and what was believed had driven him mad. His grief for his wife, combined with his fear for his granddaughter, who lived in a made-up world, drove him insane. Fury arose and captured his humanity again.

Olivia was disappointed, and when she was disappointed, she lectured. Full of zeal, she berated Tyra about her poor choices. She pushed and pushed and pushed. Her fair-haired curls, with a yellow tint, flew about in every direction.

"Tyra, hard work is the most important ingredient for survival, no matter how hard it is for you or what you want. You must work *and* study. This is all that matters." Being short, she looked somewhat formidable.

"So, I have no value other than my grades and the work I do? And how can you say that? You often work part-time, and you travel a lot!"

"My work is hard; I travel *for* work and make enough money for a decent life! You're too sheltered. Dad gave everything to us *and* to you, his favourite baby. He sacrificed everything to protect and provide for us, *for you*, when your father failed. You must honour his will and obey. It's not enough that you're a good student and do your chores. You should work and make a financial contribution to the family. And now it turns out that this cow even does your chores for you! Outrageous! How can you get a good education and succeed in life if you rely on such ephemeral sources? Do you want to live your life with no money and no achievements? Why did Mama give it to you? I'll never understand. You're just a granddaughter!" Every word she spoke added oil to the fire of Ethan's rage.

"Stop it! Stop it!" Tyra screamed, struggling to set boundaries. Then, exasperated, the next minute, she burst. Couldn't help it. "So, I'm an object? I mustn't defend myself; I can't pursue my dreams or fulfill my needs? I have to be obedient until I die? Who cares if I was exhausted from all the relentless work and the grief and stress I endured? I barely slept, only two to four hours a night. That's how drained I was! And I'm in constant pain every single moment. The pain is still there when I smile. And it's *still* there when I don't talk about it. When I say I'm fine, it only means I can function. I'm so exhausted from this cloak I'm destined to wear with no breaks! You've never noticed or cared! The only way you would have noticed is if I had gotten deadly ill, because you *do* care about me in your twisted, crazy way! And you think you have the right to yell at me, to scold and criticize me all the time! As if I'm a little kid or worse, a wooden doll with no feelings, needs, or opinions of my own! You smash me with your judgment, with your constant disapproval, and then you *lecture* me? Why do you think you're allowed to treat a human being like this? Just because I'm not an adult yet? Because I don't have a respectable job, and I don't pay taxes? Do you think that gives you this privilege to shape me as you wish, to break me when it suits you? Because in your eyes, with no real job, a person has no value! But Dad was happy driving his truck across the realm. Happy! Who's to establish what success is? Being happy is the greatest achievement of all and the hardest one to accomplish! What's wrong with simple endeavors? Life is in the little moments, slipping through your fingers while you race for ephemeral approval of your worth! You can never find it outwardly, Olivia! You numb your misery with another goal and then another one, never stopping to savour any of them. Is that what you want for me? No, thanks. I'll figure out my own way of living. My way!" Tyra unleashed her anger, and it gushed all over.

Scarlett was shaking in anxiety. What would Ethan do? Scarlett knew she was supposed to protect her daughter, but she always transformed into a fearful child when her father was in this smoky, clouded state of mind. Scarlett couldn't help it. All she could see, hear, and feel were the slaps on her face. Bad grades, dirty dishes. Too loud, too needy, and too dreamy. Scarlett's only hope was that Tyra would somehow get away with it, as she always did. The cow could intervene any minute now. But in all the commotion, no one asked her to do so.

What happened next was like a slow-motion scene from a movie. Scarlett and Tyra watched in horror as Ethan took a hammer and darted to Tyra's room.

"No!" Tyra screamed. Then she heard her cow's voice.

"It's already happening, Tyra. I'm sorry. It's inevitable. I'll be giving you instructions now. Listen with great concentration and memorize my words."

Time paused. Olivia, Scarlett, and Ethan froze in place.

"Don't use the broken pieces when he smashes me. Take only one piece, the one with the snowflake ornament, and hide it. Make a powder out of it afterward and put it in an amethyst bottle. Carry it with you wherever you go. One day it will help you when you need it the most. Plant the dragonfly's exoskeleton in your garden. An apple tree will grow. When the time is right, gather the apples in the bag I left beside your bed. Don't worry; all the apples will fit into it. Use one apple to show you the way. Bring the bag of apples to your new homeland and plant the seeds in your garden. Remember the shoes. They will also fit perfectly in my weightless bag. Take nothing more than what's absolutely needed. Be free of burdens, and try to forgive your mother, little one. She's not herself in those moments. She's also wounded. She never managed to break free, b*ut you can.* I treasure the moments spent with you, little one. Nothing goes away; it only transforms. I'm sorry for your loss, child. Too many losses. I wish we had more time together. Remember, time is irrelevant to me. I am okay."

A crash was followed by silence. Afterward, Tyra gathered the snowflake piece. Her hands shook, and her breathing was shallow and wheezy. She turned it into a powder, poured it into the amethyst bottle, put it in the weightless bag, and hid it. Then she planted the dragonfly in her garden.

Trembling, Tyra entered her room, locked the door, and crashed beside her bed where, only an hour ago, her cow had been standing. Tyra sat there in silence, holding her knees against her crying belly and trying to make the pain in her chest stop until she fell asleep in a fetal position on her shaggy, worn grey carpet.

She found herself in Koda's home. The room was dark, musty, and empty. The mirror was calling. It made an eerie rustling noise. Ominous, muted music emanated from the inside. The mirror bubbled, stretched, and glimmered. Tyra pushed her hand forward, and then she melted into the mirror.

Am I inside a dream? she wondered. She wasn't sure, but she couldn't wake up. She felt as if she were losing her mind. As if she were losing herself. Tyra was desperate.

"Darkness and light are inseparable in human nature," the voice said. "Deny the darkness, and it will consume you."

Then Tyra heard a beautiful, lyrical song in a foreign language. She saw a woman of heavenly beauty with long blue hair. Her hair was sprawled around her head as if she were underwater, and tiny golden fish were floating around her. She stared at Tyra through the mirror and then slapped her fingers. Two monsters, Kent and Cami, but as black and white as yin and yang, appeared out of nowhere. They bent over the mirror with wide smiles, sniffing and licking its surface.

Tyra woke up and saw Tom and Calla above her face, grooming her heartily.

She looked around. It was still dark. She was afraid to fall asleep again, but Tom and Calla sprawled on her chest and belly, intertwined in a white-and-black circle, purring with a soft rumble. She petted them and fell asleep.

No dreams and no nightmares this time. Tyra slept like a baby.

Only a silver, plasmic drop was drying up and evaporating from her forehead.

By dawn, an apple tree had grown, but nobody except Tyra could reach or use the apples. The tree was beautiful, flourishing, and filled with fruit. No one, not even Ethan, dared to cut it down. He had crossed the line and felt sorry, as usual.

The next day, Scarlett crocheted a pair of shoes that could fit the cow's legs and gave them to Tyra with timid tenderness. Tyra touched the soft alpaca wool and then placed the shoes on the pile of others. A malachite vase with purple hyacinths, the flowers of sorrow, was placed in the middle of the table with care, surrounded by six pairs of shoes.

"There was a door to which I found no key:
There was the veil through which I might not see."
– Omar Khayyam

CHAPTER 13
Kai and Tyra

"Your fingers on mine—
I gasp once, and in that breath,
I accept you in."
– Kate Miller-Wilson

After finals were over and graduation had been endured, Tyra felt a mixture of anxiety and relief.

What's next? University? No, not yet. Anxious thoughts shrouded her mind like thick clouds with no clarity or refuge.

Uncertainty is one of the hardest challenges of being human.

Ruminating about her fogyish, eluding future, Tyra found part-time jobs as a dance teacher and an editor in the local magazine. She was almost eighteen, a difficult age in every realm. Vague, blurry, and full of expectations.

The summer stretched with repetitive monotony.

Each day dragged on without purpose or destination. Anxiety about her future dwelled in Tyra's head, making her fear that nothing would ever change.

Even books didn't bring comfort anymore, and nature showed indifference toward her mundane endeavors. She had no hope, no direction, and no purpose.

Tyra yearned for change.

She started having dreams about her father. Almost every night they met in the kitchen, the kettle humming on the stove, and the maple tree outside the window changing its colours.

Butternut cookies and brief conversations.

He was sorry. And she was lonely. A crackling blue flame smouldered inside the rustic, white-brick fireplace.

"Tyra, hold on. I know you're ready for a change. I'll help you."

"How? You're dead, and we're in my dream. It isn't real."

"What *is* real? Start writing, kiddo. You've been journaling, reading, and creating stories in your head your whole life. It's time to let them out."

Tyra woke up. Forgiveness felt good.

Following her dad's advice, Tyra began writing. Stories poured out with uninhibited force, like water bursting through the gates of a broken dam.

Tyra started publishing, but there was little money, and she feared asking for a raise. Self-doubt tormented her, and it felt odd.

"Who am I? Why would I become a writer?"

The age-old question echoed in her mind. "What do you want to become when you grow up?" This question always created uneasy sensations in her belly because she couldn't unravel the mystery of her talents slipping away. *Is there any for me?* she wondered. From an early age, Tyra came up with the idea to call herself "the Appreciator" because she valued art in all forms.

"You write good stories. You deserve a raise," her inner voice whispered.

It feels weird to expect money for sharing my vulnerability, she replied.

"You've put in hard work. Your stories are detailed and well-researched."

I don't know.

Then Tyra heard *the* voice. "You've opened your guts and your chest to create them. You dove into your psyche to retrieve your visions, your pain, and your struggles. It must've been torturous. Your stories are the backwash of your blood, sweat, and tears."

"Who are you?" Tyra asked.

"I'm the rustle of leaves under your feet.

I'm the quiet whisper inside your heart.

I'm the wind on your cheeks.

I'm the fog in your hands.

I'm the yellow dust on the tip of your nose.

I'm the purring of your milk on your lips.

I'm the tickling sensation inside your belly.

I'm your power, and I'm your doubts.

I'm your conscience, and I'm your shame.

I'm your fear, and I'm your love.

I'm your strength, and I'm your weakness.

I'm your pain, and I'm your joy.

I'm your shield and your destruction.

I'm your oblivion, and I'm your awareness.

I'm the darkness and the light of your underworld.

I'm the birth and the withering whisper.

I'm the breath of life and the sigh of death."

Tyra listened to her gut rather than her fears. She asked for a raise and received it. She would briefly eat and shower, spending days and nights typing on her computer, playing with the monsters, and then returning to the bottomless ocean of her psyche.

These days she talked to Tom and Calla more than humans, and even her braids looked wild, untidy, and uncared for. She seemed happily insane, with that sparkle in the eyes that everyone who opens the chasm of their creativity possesses. Tom was puzzled and upset by the locked door. He despised them, the closed doors. So, he would travel back and forth with rapid stupidity.

Tyra rose from her comfy chair, piled high with cushions and squishy monsters, for the fifth time in a row! "Gosh, Tom! Every time you change your mind and insist on coming in or going out, I'm forced to get up. The cushions go flying all over, and then I need to make the nest again! Can't you just decide whether you're in or out?"

Tom looked at her with an innocent expression of total confusion, as if it was that easy to choose.

"If you want to keep your sanity intact, you shouldn't keep yourself shut in your room all by yourself!" Olivia yelled from the kitchen.

Tyra chuckled and then petted Tom, trying to convince him to make a choice.

Uh-huh, sure.

~

I need a break. My body's crying for movement, longing for care, Tyra thought as she put on her black leotard and leggings. She grabbed a bag with a change of clothes in it, went outside, and paused for a moment, inhaling the fresh, post-rain air.

Tyra had grown into a beautiful woman with subtle charm and dormant power.

She danced with no effort in her studio behind glass walls as if nobody was watching. Her eyes closed, she swirled, twirled, and swayed around as if she were floating in a desperate attempt to soothe her loneliness. Then she felt a soft, penetrating glance. Kai was standing in the doorway, mesmerized by her.

He looked exactly like Trudy, only masculine. Kai was tall, robust, and attractive. His dark eyes were smiling as he stared at Tyra, feeling like the ground beneath him was moving. He didn't like it, but he couldn't help it.

Tyra paused as a wave of unease tingled along her spine.

Kai smiled with amusement. "I like your style. It's raw. You're like the goddess of wild nature under a thick, timid layer of darkness." He flashed a grin. "You're Tyra, right? I've heard a lot about you. My sister's obsessed with your performance and your personality. I thought I'd check it out. I'm Kai."

Tyra nodded, still unsure what to expect. She couldn't quite pinpoint what about him had touched her. Certainly not his appearance, although he was beautiful. There was something else underneath his confident bubble, beneath his sarcasm and mischief. Tyra sensed that he was sensitive but unaware of it or just dismissive of his true nature. She felt a light dizziness in her chest, attributing it to the swaying and twirling.

"Let's get coffee," he said.

Tyra hesitated, then nodded. "I'll go change first."

"Sure. I'll be outside."

Tyra took a brief shower, put on black skinny jeans, an ocean-blue shirt, and a necklace with an amber-drop pendant she found in her bag. She adjusted her braided bun and then went outside.

Kai was standing there, smiling. As Tyra looked at him, a strange sensation of déjà vu swept over her as if they had shared that moment before. It was a mixture of caution, excitement, and familiarity. Tyra rubbed her nose and smiled and then they headed to the nearest coffee shop, the only one that was nice and warm in the dreadful city of Moonvine.

Tyra buttoned up her red, knee-length wool coat and adjusted her navy flats. "The weather this year's rather indecisive, just like my grandma's cat. Closed doors freak him out, and he's driving me nuts."

He smiled as he pulled up his dark green hoodie. "Did you move here recently?"

"Four years ago."

"Oh, crap. I guess my sister has kept you hostage for a while."

Tyra chuckled. "She changed my life. I never knew I could dance. It's a great feeling."

"Yeah, I know what you mean. I've been dancing my whole life. It's great. But recently, I've switched to boxing. It's even better for me. I never knew I could do it."

Boxing? she thought. Tyra sensed rage, craftily suppressed yet acknowledged.

They sat at the same table where Tyra had sat not long ago when her grandmother was dying. Walnut floors stretched across the room, wooden walls hosted framed local art, and bookshelves overflowed with well-worn novels. The place was filled with plush armchairs and deep-cushioned corduroy sofas. Soft light from vintage pendant lights cast a gentle glow over the round tables. The rich aroma of freshly brewed coffee mingled with the scent of baked pastries. The soft hum of conversation and the clink of cups accompanied the soft music, classic favourites from every era.

They ordered tea and black espresso, mozzarella sandwiches, and pies.

Kai was different now. Clearly, he felt safe in that place. He opened up a little, telling jokes and stories with apparent ease. There were no games and no flirting. It was natural and nice.

"Do you like to read?" Tyra asked.

"Depends." He shrugged as his eyes grinned.

"What would you prefer, to be feared or loved?" she asked, smiling in amusement.

"To be loved. When people love you, they fear losing you. What qualities do you appreciate most in people?" he asked.

"There's one that's most important to me—kindness."

"And what are your favorite books?"

"It's hard to choose. Right now, I'm obsessed with Oscar Wilde and Carl Jung. But my all-time favorites? Definitely Ray Bradbury, the Strugatsky brothers, the Brontë family, and Shakespeare. I also love Three Comrades, The Story of San Michele by Axel Munthe, Faust, A Wizard of Earthsea, The Old Man and the Sea, Tess of the d'Urbervilles, Fathers and Sons, and Anna

Karenina. And yes, I still have a soft spot for Uncle Tom's Cabin. Can you believe it? Gosh, please stop me, Kai!"

They both laughed.

"You can tell a lot about a person by the books they read, right?" He grinned.

"Right. So, what are your favorites?" she asked, smiling.

Kai hesitated, as if sharing his list was like revealing something vulnerable. "Well . . . let's say One Hundred Years of Solitude, Catch-22, Orwell's 1984 and Animal Farm, The Hitchhiker's Guide to the Galaxy, Ecclesiastes, and Master and Margarita."

They talked and laughed for hours like old friends, and then he walked her home.

That was it. Tyra fell in love for the first time.

And Kai? Kai was *struck* by love, but this time he didn't resent it. He was seen, heard, and touched.

The feeling of belonging was simple and effortless.

Tyra and Kai sat on the floor in the dance studio, nestled in each other's arms.

"Let's get dinner," he said. "I know a place you'll fall in love with."

"Okay, show me. But let me get changed first."

A short while later, they entered a fancy seafood restaurant downtown and sat by the window, overlooking a slender evergreen tree. Tyra looked beautiful in a slim, sleeveless black dress with a high neckline and red shoes.

"So, the only nice and cozy café in the city belongs to your mum? Trudy never told me. This place is amazing, by the way. I never knew such places existed here."

"Trudy's the master of keeping secrets," he said, smiling. "For unknown reasons, she chooses to keep the strangest ones."

"Do you get along?"

"Oh, yeah. We're like besties. Although she's older than me, we've been friends forever. Besides, four years is a small gap. Especially now. Dancing always kept us close, and we share our parents equally. She's a daddy's girl, and I'm my mother's son. Come with me tomorrow. I want you to meet my mom. She's the best. You'll see. We can go to the secret jazz club afterward."

She smiled. "I'd love to. I didn't know there were secret clubs in Azure."

"Oh, there are many. Next time we'll go to the underground dance competition, if you don't mind."

"What? I'll only mind if we don't." She laughed. "Secret clubs? What kind? And how's that possible? I mean, aren't people afraid of the government finding out? I thought people here would never be interested in such things."

"Yeah, I know. Moss was different. But across the realm, some people yearn for a better life and long for the freedom to express their creativity. The government's interested in suppression and submission, but creativity can hardly be suppressed. It makes you unhappy, right? When people are too miserable, there's a chance they'll protest. Our authorities excel at creating the right amount of misery here." He grinned. "Anyway, once you unleash your creativity, you become close to waking up and wanting more or longing for a change. The government mostly turns a blind eye to such clubs spread all over the realm. But once they become too prevalent in one place, the government deals with it quickly and quietly. I'm going to leave this smouldering place someday."

"I hear you. I'm going to leave it too. I don't know when or where, but I will."

"'I've heard that in Terra there's more freedom for creative people and just more freedom in general. They appreciate photography and authentic art far more than here. I've been trying to move there illegally. I'm not a truck driver; I'm a photographer, but I would become a truck driver if it would help."

"Why? Isn't it an option?"

"Not really. They'd track me down if I quit and stayed there for good. I need to leave quietly. I've had offers to do my own exhibitions, but I'm staying below the radar for now. I don't want them to notice me. Once I figure out how to cross the border and change my identity afterward, I'll leave. Will you come with me?"

"I think it's too early to discuss our future together." She giggled. "But if . . . well, I don't know. I haven't thought about Terra. I guess I'm not ready for that yet. And now I understand why you work in the shadows. You're incredibly talented, Kai."

Kai shifted uneasily. Accepting compliments wasn't his thing. "What about your new book? What did your editor say?"

"He said I struggle to create main characters who are significant and that my side characters are more interesting. I guess it's because *I* feel insignificant."

"I'm fascinated by you, Diana. I can't relate. And I love your writing."

He called her Diana, referring to the goddess of wilderness. She didn't mind. It was their thing.

"That's because you're in love," she said, smiling.

Kai hugged her in a playful manner, then stared at her with concealed adoration. His gaze always held a mixture of unspoken emotions.

"I am, but it has nothing to do with my feelings," he said. "You're special."

Then they danced to the Leonard Cohen song, *Dance Me to the End of Love.*

Tyra felt as if she were melting. It was such an intense, deep feeling that she had never experienced before. It was soothing but also frightening.

The next day, Tyra met Kai's mother. She was small and pretty, warm and smart. Tyra formed an instant attachment to her. Mrs. Kato was a motherly woman who created a safe and charming nest for her children and her beloved husband. The Kato family was the rarest kind in Moonvine and in Azure in general.

Kai's relationship with his father was more distant. Mr. Kato dedicated his limited range of affection to his wife and daughter, whom he adored. He wasn't good with structure or boundaries, and neither was his wife. They led a freestyle bohemian life within their cozy family bubble. Kai had been raised by two people who loved each other, and he had wondered if he would ever be that lucky.

They ordered miso soup with chocolate chiffon cake for dessert and then chatted, enjoying a light, delicious dinner.

Afterward, Tyra and Kai thanked Mrs. Kato and then went to the street, catching a navy cab.

In no time, they entered the secret bar and found a place to sit. A quartet was playing jazz music. The man playing the double bass looked comfortable in his black T-shirt and unbuttoned blue cotton jacket, paired with well-worn jeans and milk-and-coffee suede boots.

Tyra stared at his fancy red glasses and smiled. He was six foot five, slim and bold—a man in his sixties. All the musicians were in their sixties.

Tyra thought how wonderful it must be to experience such freedom and make magic happen with music, evoking feelings and touching others with it. She wondered if she would ever be as happy and full of life at such a respectable age.

Another musician, a trombone player with white hair and black glasses, listened to his companions with his eyes closed, mouthing the lyrics during the brief breaks in his playing. They played ballads and tunes with peculiar names like "Embraceable You," "Lover, Come Back to Me," "Whisper Not," "Easy Living," and "Ill Wind."

The drummer was fantastic, creating absolute exaltation across the room. Kai and Tyra sat in silence, absorbed in the music. During breaks, they chatted with ease.

"Music talks," he said.

"Yes, just like kitchens and nature. Houses and streets."

"Touch talks."

"Dreams and sadness, anger and fear."

"Bodies talk. Lips and eyes."

"Tongues often hide intentions and dismiss meanings. Words distort. Delude. Redirect and hurt. And all we've just mentioned can say more than written words ever could, except poetry."

"People talk, but they rarely say anything," Kai said. Then he smiled and offered her his hand. They danced to the flowing sounds of jazz.

Tyra felt like she was soaring.

"Genuine, authentic art can heal this world," she said as they returned to their seats.

"Agreed."

"Because it opens hearts and removes barriers."

"Yes! But it isn't enough. There's something else, though I can't grasp it."

"Me too, at least not yet."

"Do you hate the human race?" he asked.

"People fascinate me, but I'm an observer. Interaction may cause people to drift away, so I stick to my comfort zone." She giggled. "But I'm human."

"Is that another reason to hate?" he asked, chuckling.

"Who are we without other people? Just an empty book. People are like moments. Never the same, always exclusive. Sometimes horrible, sometimes wonderful. There's beauty in complicity. It's more interesting. More in-depth."

"I see everything as black and white or grey," he said.

"Do you? But we all carry darkness within us. Choice is what matters."

"What about constant joy? We can create a life that allows us to sit in our backyard, drinking coffee and eating waffles," he said in a teasing voice.

"I don't believe in nirvana as an abyss of bliss," she replied, smiling.

"What about what we've done?"

"It's nothing but a wind that passes by and leaves scars but

150

never determines who we are or what we choose to become next. It never determines our final destination. It's a constant flow, undeniable and inevitable."

"I would certainly choose the blue pill," Kai said, referring to *The Matrix*.

Tyra smiled. Then she settled on his lap, snuggled and relaxed. Immersed in the precious moment of happiness.

Kai held her hand, feeling her fingers tap to the beat of the music. He was also happy. Too happy. It felt uncomfortable.

When the show was over, they sat on the stairs, hugging each other as they watched strangers passing by. An old man in a floral shirt and navy jacket stopped in the middle of the road with two heavy bags.

"Do you need help?" Kai asked, standing up.

The man strolled toward them. "Thank you. That's very kind of you. Very kind. I was just trying to remember a poem." He closed his eyes and recited it in a foreign language. "It's about how flirting may be dangerous. It implies cheating or betrayal that comes in many forms. What are you doing here?"

"Just enjoying jazz and the autumn evening," Kai said with a respectful smile.

"I've lived on this dazzling street for sixty years," the man said.

Tyra sighed. "It sounds like a dream."

"And it was yesterday," the man replied.

"I can relate," she said. "What's that language? It sounded like music. I never knew there were languages other than English."

"It's French. It can talk to your heart."

Kai nodded. "There are many families who have managed to maintain their ancient languages. It's prohibited, but people keep their heritage and culture this way. I find it beautiful. The government attempts to make us identical and bleak. Another way to suppress our identities."

"I'm too old to care what they allow us to do. I'm ninety-three years old." His eyes sparkled like a ten-year-old's.

Tyra smiled. "It *is* beautiful."

On their way to the car, Tyra and Kai strolled down the sleeping street until they heard loud music and cheerful singing. They entered a room stuffed with people of all ages, colours, and beliefs, dancing with joy and excitement. The people jumped, squatted, and swayed with closed eyes, moving every part of their bodies. They sang in a foreign, melodious, and rhythmic language. Tyra got wild too. She danced, smiled, and laughed while Kai watched her.

Then Tyra noticed that people's faces had become over-exhilarated, almost hypnotized. When she asked a boy what the language they were singing in, he said they were praising the god Osiris in Spanish.

Tyra and Kai stepped outside. When they were at a safe distance away, they burst into laughter.

"If there has to be a religion, let it be like this," Tyra said.

"Agreed." Kai giggled, then he hugged her, giving her rapid kisses on her nose, cheeks, and lips.

"But when I saw their glassy, hypnotized eyes, I couldn't help but wonder how close they were to excessive exaltation, to chaos and horror in the name of their god. Frantic minds are easily controlled. But it was fun to see their happy faces, their crazy, free, delightful movements, and their twinkling eyes." She chuckled, then hugged him around his waist. "It was beautiful."

"How can pure joy and the potential seeds for horror reside in the same place? People struggle to deal with life, so they invent all sorts of sectarian groups. I get it. It might be helpful, but beware, right?"

"It may even save you from falling into the abyss of grief or existential crisis. People need guidance and a sense of purpose. We all do. But the ice between ecstatic devotion and dangerous fanaticism can be thin, indeed."

～

Shortly after, Kai's mother invited Tyra to their family dinner on a Saturday night. It was casual and, therefore, more enjoyable. The food was delicious—freshly made ravioli with chestnuts served in a creamy coconut sauce and accompanied by green salad, burrata with yellow, red, black, and purple cherry tomatoes, and balsamic bruschetta.

"Thank you so much, Mrs. Kato. It was a fantastic feast!"

"Oh dear, it's all Kai. I haven't been cooking since I opened the café. All my efforts and resources are put into my little paradise. I've been dreaming about this my whole life. Now my family barely sees me."

"We're happy to see you happy, darling," Mr. Kato said.

Tyra raised an eyebrow at Kai. "You cook? Wow. This is splendid. I love food!" She chuckled.

"Well, Mum started teaching me cooking when I was a toddler. So, it's not a big accomplishment. It just came to me naturally." He shrugged and then began to clear the table. Kai turned to his sister, who was sitting in a burnt orange corduroy chair with her legs on the seat and her arms by her sides. "Hello, princess! Do you want to contribute?"

Trudy reluctantly got up. "Okie, dokie. If you insist, you ugly monster. I was *so* cozy, party pooper!"

"I look like Mum, you silly girl."

"What are you talking about? Are you crazy? Mum's beautiful!"

"Exactly my point. Your arguments are falling apart, my lady. Besides, you and I look alike!" Kai chuckled. "Come on, get up, you lazy chair slug!"

"I've handed you the chestnuts." Trudy rolled her eyes, then pouted her lips.

"I appreciate your input, woman. Now, get your bum up."

Trudy snorted and then dragged herself to the kitchen. Tyra attempted to join her, but Trudy and Kai protested, exclaiming, "No, don't even try! You're our guest."

"Next time I'm making sushi," Kai said.

Trudy licked her lips. "His sushi is to die for. You won't want to eat any other sushi after you try it."

After dinner, Kai showed Tyra his old bedroom, which had been maintained since he moved out. It was huge and stuffed with bookshelves full of books.

"Wow! That's what you meant by 'depends'? You're like a book devourer!" Tyra exclaimed, referring to their first date when she asked him if he liked reading. "It's like the House of Wisdom in here."

Kai and Tyra met almost every day. They talked about books and music, watched movies, and strolled in the park for hours. They discussed movies like pros, debating with passion and fooling about. They made dinners and hustled in the kitchen, practicing Master Chef recipes.

"Smell it! You must! It's a 'wow'! We did it!" Kai handed her a red spatula with steaming tomato sauce on it.

Haddock was waiting to dive in and soak. Tyra tasted the sauce and licked her lips with an exclamation of admiration. He lifted her up and then slowly set her down. Tyra looked straight into his eyes like a cat.

"You're so beautiful. Do you know how beautiful you are?" He touched the loose hair resting in her headband braid, hugged her waist, then kissed her nose.

Tyra chuckled. She touched his neck and then his arms as she nuzzled into his shirt, pressing her forehead to his chest. She was so happy.

She had retired her scarf, which now rested behind the garnet doors of her new closet.

Almost every day, Kai met her at the dance studio after work and watched her write and fall asleep behind her desk. Then he would cover her with her soft teal blanket, fearing sometimes she might disappear from his life as if she were just a bittersweet mirage, a summer bird who had come to visit but who would fly away for the long winter, never to return.

Kai helped her with heavy groceries and laundry. They would unpack the bags and fold her clothes together, goofing off and throwing mismatched socks and scarves at each other. Then he would tickle and hug her, kissing her lips.

On their three-month anniversary, they made sushi and then settled in together in the basement of his parents' home.

"Movie night?" Kai asked.

"Yes, please."

"Which movie? You decide."

"Let's choose something together this time."

He laughed. "Oh, no, it's a trap! You know we'll spend all night scrolling until we fall asleep. I don't care, really. Just choose and then we'll cuddle."

Kai liked holding her slender body against his chest and stomach, inhaling the subtle aroma of her lavender shampoo, and sensing her soft skin.

Tyra felt safe, cozy, and loved. She felt *at home*.

The first few months were blissful, as all honeymoon stages are.

Then, slowly but inevitably, Kai began to close off and drift away. The closer they became, the more distant Kai grew. Tyra became upset and restless.

~

One rainy morning, Tyra was cleaning her house. The floors sparkled with fresh lavender liquid. Kai entered the kitchen with soiled boots, leaving muddy footprints all over.

"Kai, look!" Tyra pointed to the muddy footprints.

"It's just mud," he said, sounding annoyed. "No need to get upset."

What? No oops or sorry? Tyra thought. *Nothing?* She was angry.

"Why would you do this?" she yelled.

"Oy, it's just a floor. Relax."

Tyra was puzzled. "I washed, I scrubbed it! How did it even occur to you to wear your shoes inside in such weather? I don't understand."

"Why are you yelling at me? That's the real question. Control yourself, woman!"

"You're accusing *me* of being unreasonable?"

Kai went out into the pouring rain, irritated and offended.

Tyra was furious. But even more so, she felt guilty.

Am I turning into a witch? What's happening to me? Why am I acting like this? Am I going crazy? After Tyra calmed down, she apologized.

Tyra worked hard on her communication skills, but it made no difference. Kai dismissed her no matter what she said or how she said it. Tyra felt as if there were worn-out hollows inside her, scrubbed bare from trying too hard to be spotless—like a flawless floor with no trace of imperfection. She felt sore.

Kai couldn't bear any critiques, not even if they were delivered with consideration and care. It was his raw, aching spot.

"What am I doing wrong?" she asked Trudy one day. "We were so happy."

"Tyra, I love my brother. He's a good man and an amazing brother and son. But he's not easy to live with. He's definitely not boyfriend material. He can get defensive, and when that happens, well, he's not nice and funny anymore. He restrains his anger, but boundaries are a foreign concept to him. He maintains his own boundaries fiercely, though. Be careful, buttercup. I warned you, remember? But you were too deeply in love. I don't want you to get hurt. I love you too, you know."

"I'm even more deeply in love now," Tyra whispered.

Trudy sighed. "It's a bummer."

~

Kai and Tyra woke up at night and went to the kitchen to warm up fresh milk. To their surprise, they heard a rustling sound coming from the kitchen cabinet. They spotted Zeus, smiling with unease. The cabinet had transformed into a vast shimmering hole. Zeus turned and disappeared through the trembling portal. Kai and Tyra followed him, dazed, as they entered a peculiar scene of an animated forest with whispering flowers and arguing trees.

"What the . . . Tyra! What just happened?"

Kai looked at his diminished body in shock. He was fifteen again, and Tyra was ten.

"Oh, at last, our dear Tyra! Come with us!" a female voice rumbled.

Tyra looked back and saw a small woman in her forties with a face like a sunflower. Her nose, lips, eyes, and brows resembled a weak sketch of a cartoon character. Her vibe reminded Tyra of Jerry. Weird.

The sunflower woman waved to someone with glowing yellow eyes who was hiding behind some deep, dark bushes. "Let's take her. Oh, poor girl. She's shrinking, hurting, vanishing. She's in an urgent need of care and safety. Quickly, come on, you!"

Kai roared in a frantic attempt to free himself from squeezing the branches of a wooden wall behind him.

"Let him go!" Tyra yelled.

"We don't make the rules here, honey. Everyone gets exactly what they brought in," the sunflower woman said with a shrug.

Woolly brown-grey creatures with yellow eyes bounced and hooted around Tyra.

"Okay, behemoths," the sunflower lady shouted, "lift her up! Get her away from this boy! Mama's making a pie from snap-dragon flowers!"

"No!" Tyra protested. "I won't come with you until you release him!"

"It's not up to us, dear."

The behemoths lifted Tyra and dashed to the nearest field, where a picnic table had been set. They prodded Tyra like gigantic puppies, buzzing and humming and babbling in a foreign language. There was another sunflower woman. She was ginormous, the size of an olive tree. And she was smiling. Her facial features were well-developed and gleamed with warmth and empathy. Her entire figure exuded sincere love and a nourishing nature.

"Come, child. Sit with us," she said. "You're tired, girl, so tired. Your soul needs a break from pain, growth, and battles. Be cozy, be weak, be a melting chocolate in my arms. Drink the water of oblivion and eat the flowers of illusion. Rest, darling. You're free to go whenever you want."

"Will I want to go?" Tyra mumbled.

"Of course. No one will be forever satisfied with the same state of never-changing happiness. Each soul will awaken on its own clock."

The daughter-sunflower stroked Tyra's bedtime braid. "You need this, Tyra. We'll take care of you. Stay with us for as long as you need. Oh, poor baby of ours. She's hurting, drowning. She's fighting too hard."

"I can't. Kai's trapped. At least let him go home. Leave him out of this."

"We're not the ones who are holding him hostage here, dear," the daughter said.

Tyra's eyes circled around the picnic table, which was filled with delectable goods. It was aromatic, inviting, intoxicating. She stared at the mother and then at the behemoths for a moment, then she sprinted away.

"Don't rush her, daughter," the sunflower woman said. "She'll be back. For now, this is the way. She can't let him go, and he doesn't feel safe here or anywhere in this sliver of time. Their stars have spoken, and we're just passengers on a train we cannot steer."

Tyra freed Kai, and they slipped through the closing portal at the last moment.

Zeus was sleeping safe and sound on his fluff cushion inside an open cabinet.

Kai and Tyra returned to their regular forms.

"Can we just agree this never happened?" he asked.

"Sure."

Tyra surrendered to the night, drifting into ephemeral dreams under a soft blanket of wonder. Kai tossed and turned in bed all night, forcing himself to forget.

～

When Kai's mother died in a car accident, he was lost.

Tyra would sit by his side, keeping him company in his sorrow, but Kai became even more distant. Strong feelings of loss, abandonment, and disappointment about the path his life had taken flooded him, and he struggled to keep his temper restrained. He was difficult to be around, but Tyra bore it.

Months passed, and as their seventh-month anniversary approached, Tyra got an idea. "How about we buy a mutual present this time, a membership at the Arts Centre? That way we'll have to go and watch shows and plays with no excuses. You said we don't spend as much time together as we used to. I mean, obviously, right? This isn't the right time for fun. It's time to grieve. But I think it might be a good idea for you to go out once a month. What do you think? Only if you're ready."

"I'd love to." He smiled and hugged her, squeezing her tight.

"I can't breathe!" she said, laughing. "Anyway, I can dive so deep into the world I'm creating, and you're immersed in boxing and work, which is great, but we've barely been able to match our schedules lately. Let's make it an unshakable commitment. That way we'll have a date night at least once a month. We can go to our place downtown, have dinner, and stroll in the park afterward. Early spring is so beautiful this year. I fear we'll miss it."

"Okay, as you wish, Diana. Good idea. I like it."

"But let's also give each other small presents, something cute and inexpensive. Just a gift of attention." She smiled. "And, Kai, remember I put the gifts Trudy might like in the cart? Have you checked it?"

Tyra put a great deal of effort into finding the best presents for Trudy, asking Kai to look not once but twice.

"Yeah, okay," he grumbled.

The next day, Tyra reminded him again, getting restless. "Kai? I need to make an order. I can't wait any longer. I'm waiting for you. I fear it won't arrive in time for Trudy's birthday."

"I checked," Kai said, rolling his eyes in irritation.

Tyra was offended by his reply, his tone, and his attitude. It was as if she were nagging him. "But I didn't know that."

"Well, you've been busy, and I've been waiting for you."

She tried to explain, but it didn't go well. "Couldn't you have at least texted me to notify me you were ready to discuss it? Now I'm the one who's bugging you and unavailable. Great."

On their anniversary day, they ordered the membership, and Tyra gave him her present. Her eyes gleamed with joy and fire, and she smiled from ear to ear in anticipation of his reaction. She had bought him a T-shirt with a Cheshire Cat on it and the saying "We're all mad here."

His gaze became gloomy and angry. "It's unfair! You said no personal presents this time!" Kai started fighting, saying hurtful things one after another, making absurd accusations, and completely redirecting from the topic of conflict.

Tyra was stunned. "Wait, it's okay if you didn't hear me say we should give each other a small personal gift, but claiming I never said it and distorting my reality like this is not okay. I almost believed you! Thankfully, this time I *vividly* remember saying that. I was already planning what to give you. You can't just delete what happened to convince yourself and me that *I'm* the bad guy here and that I made that up to hurt you. This is ridiculous!"

"I'm not saying you're the bad guy. I'm saying you never said it. You might have implied it, or more likely, you thought it was obvious we would buy another present for each other. It's not okay to put me in such a position!"

"No, that's not what happened. You deny it because you feel uncomfortable receiving a present when you don't have one to give. You never believe me or anyone. That way, you can say whatever suits you if I have no tangible evidence, like a text. I know you never manipulate me on purpose, only to defend yourself, but you won't hesitate to hurt me. Is it that hard to allow yourself to mess up? Is it really a catastrophe to make mistakes, especially ones you can easily fix? You made me feel as if I set a trap for you or gave you a test. What's the big deal in doing something wrong? I'm telling you, it's not the end of the world that you didn't hear me! *It's okay.*"

"If you point out my mistakes, what do you expect?" Kai asked, irritated.

"Why can't I voice my frustration and disappointment? Does everything always have to be rainbows and ponies? It's not possible, Kai. Misunderstandings are inevitable. What hurts me the most is that afterward, you become distant and wait until things get sorted out on their own!"

"Why are you nagging me? Why aren't you happy with what I can give?"

"I'm not nagging you, Kai. I'm just upset, and I need time to cool off. We'll talk about it later, okay?"

"No! We'll resolve it now or never. You can't just leave me like this. Let's solve it."

Tyra sighed. "Okay."

Kai went silent *again.*

Tyra was losing her patience. "I hate this silence. It makes me feel horrible."

"What do you want me to say?"

She stood up. "I'm going home, Kai."

"No, I said I can't leave it like this. Let's end it now."

"Another breakup after a simple conflict? I can't do this anymore. My heart isn't made of plastic."

Kai looked down at his feet, waiting for her to make a move.

"I don't know what you expect me to do, Kai. Are you waiting for me to fix it, as usual? You're not a child, and I feel hurt right now. Bye. I have to go."

The next day, they met and started arguing again.

"Nobody's perfect, Kai, and that's okay. We all need to try to communicate more effectively. It's perfectly natural to share our concerns and emotions in a non-harmful way. What's wrong with that?" Tyra was getting tired of hearing herself repeat the same thing. She felt as if she were forcing him to make it work. It didn't feel good. Tyra felt guilty and not entirely herself.

"It always leads to conflicts," Kai grumbled.

"It doesn't have to. Most of the time, a simple clarification will do. Or empathy. You fight because you're uncomfortable with your emotions, and you're afraid that my feelings will make *you* uncomfortable. You know how to be a good friend—attentive, caring, uplifting, and fun! If I'm upset with someone else, you're all ears and super supportive. But if it has something to do with you, oy vey. You never allow yourself to be wrong or express your needs and feelings. That's why you make me feel ashamed of *mine.* And then you shush me. But I refuse to be shushed! And then you get crazy. In those moments, you can't see clearly. You're too focused on protecting your vulnerability. You don't see me."

Tyra lowered her voice. "Will you look at me? Please look at me."

Kai turned away with a grimace of pain.

"You refuse to look at me because you'll have to face the fact that you've hurt me. But you can't. It's too painful. I'm alive. I'm not a puppet. I have feelings. I get hurt."

Stillness.

"Please look at me," she asked again.

"I hate conflicts," he said, staring at his phone.

Tyra adjusted her Viking braid. "Nobody likes them. But they're unavoidable. Life is about learning how to fight and reconcile *properly*. It's about healthy communication. That's it."

"What do you even mean?" Kai felt lost. It was as if her words were a combination of foreign sounds, creating elusive meanings and a potential yet unsettling value.

Tyra frowned. "It's simple. When I'm wrong, I'm wrong. It's no big deal. When you're wrong, you're wrong. Once again, no big deal. We take responsibility for our words and actions, make amends, and fix what needs fixing."

"I can't. I'll crumble. I feel like I'm losing you, but I can't help it."

"I love you through the conflicts. I'm mad at you, and I don't like you right now, but I love you."

"I can't see it or feel it."

"Because love has different shapes."

"I hate it when we fight."

"That's a strange thing to say for someone who will never stop fighting to keep their chest from hurting. We could've been done ten minutes after we listened, reflected, and talked openly."

Kai went silent again, scrolling on his phone.

"I don't see how we can make it work. We both need to heal our wounds, Kai. But I don't think you're ready, and I can't force it or demand it. It isn't right."

"I can do it for you."

"No, you can't. It doesn't work that way."

"I'm lost."

"I know, and that's okay. This is your path. If our ways part, so be it. It happens."

"Not with love. Love is unshakable."

164

"Yes, but it must come from within. We have to face our wounds first. Most people are too afraid to do that, including me. But I want to try."

"I want you. That's all that matters."

"We can't get what we want until we get what we need."

Kai got up and left the room, as he often did when things got too uncomfortable. He struggled to understand what he was doing wrong. On rare occasions he initiated reconciliations but not because he realized *why* Tyra was offended, only because he didn't like it when she or anyone else was angry with him. It never went well either. His frustration only made things worse.

When Kai came home, Trudy tried her best to help. "Kai, you hide who you are. You reject sides of yourself you don't like, are afraid of, or find useless. You try to be nice and restrained so people either like you or leave you alone. But, gosh, isn't it draining?"

"If I let my guard down, what will remain?"

"It'll be you, just you. Not perfect, not good or bad, but both. Just a regular human being. There's no need to be extraordinary, Kai. We're all quite similar in how our psyches work; no one is special in this regard. Look at the people around us who pretend to be so perfect! They lose their authenticity. I vote for authenticity rather than unreachable, pretentious perfection. For God's sake, we're not almighty. None of us are. And it's not worth losing yourself and the love of your life to prove something to Dad. He loves you the only way he can."

Kai shook his head, dismissing the last two sentences. "If I let my guard down, what's to like?"

"There's tons to like, but it doesn't matter. She loves you, *all* of you."

∿

Kai came to visit Tyra after his boxing class. She was stretching in the dance studio, looking tense and adrift.

Kai stood in the doorway, unsure of what to say so he wouldn't hurt her. He felt as if his words often betrayed his intentions. The conscious ones.

"Let's make it work, Diana. I don't wanna fight. Let's talk. I've been asking for a ceasefire, but you won't negotiate. You're drifting away. Nothing I do is good or just enough. Tell me what you want me to do, and let's get it over with."

Tyra cringed and sighed. "I'm tired, Kai. I've tried so hard to tell you what I need, but you won't listen. You pretend you do it, only to create a blissful break, but lately, I haven't been able to relax in these happy moments because I fear the break will end abruptly. I can never tell what will trigger you. I always get caught unprepared, and then it hurts even more. I don't know what I'm doing wrong. Will you tell me? Will you share your needs and fears with me? Will you ever open up to me again?"

"I came here, and I want a ceasefire. That's all. Let's negotiate."

"Negotiate? I'm not ready to negotiate. You want a ceasefire? Fine. How about you remove your troops from my territory first?"

Tyra was furious. She took a moment to calm down and then continued in a playful, theatrical manner. "I'll explain how I see it, how *I feel*. It's not about us, not even close. We're both good people, just a little broken. I believe that inside each person resides a tyrant of the age of two or four who controls our actions, choice of words, and intonations. They're in charge of verbal and non-verbal communication. If left unnoticed and untreated, these tyrants attempt to determine our behaviour, contradicting our conscious intentions. For example, we both get lost in these conflicts, projecting our innermost wounds onto each other. When you hurt me, I make you miserable by demanding change and growth. I become pressing, and you become tense and even more lost. It doesn't feel right. Anyway, I think you'll get the point, right?"

He nodded and put his phone away, ready to listen.

"It's like two countries. Through hidden underground tunnels, under the cover of night, one invades, driven by stealth and malicious plans to attack peaceful villagers who are sleeping safely and soundly in their beds, unaware of the darkness creeping upon their unconscious bodies. The attackers, stoned and distraught, perform a bloody massacre. They cling to the illusory idea of self-defence from those who chose to live their path, free of religious lunacy and childish, medieval values of conquest and domination. The aggressors are brainwashed by their cultivated, unleashed shadows, and they numb their conscience with drugs. They need an excuse to be at peace with their actions to justify unthinkable cruelty. Otherwise, how could anyone perform such atrocities?

"They invade their neighbour's territory, rejecting the simplest and the most humane idea: the idea of harmonious coexistence. They shut down their minds and numb their hearts. Blinded and deaf to the screams of parents to show mercy, to the bleeding wounds inside small bodies, and to the pitiful whines of dogs and cats, they shoot ruthlessly and leave their victims to die in agony. They bomb, and they inflict inhumane violence with abandon.

"And then they cry like babies who smashed their siblings with pure terror and complain about themselves being hurt *by their victims* who had no choice but to raise their weapons and defend their families, friends, and homes. Their victims are now fearless soldiers, defenders of justice. Women, men, youngsters, and the elderly, alike. They're unstoppable because they're protecting what matters most—the lives of their loved ones and their freedom.

"The aggressors whine about restrictions. 'Oh, it's unfair! There's no Internet! Our bank accounts are blocked, and our enemies have cut us off.' They complain that their victims refuse to accept their 'generous' offer of a ceasefire while their victims—kids, teens, and the elderly—are still being held hostage and tortured. These monsters, who sold their souls to the devil, justify their murders by God's will or by claiming this territory as their own. *God's will or territory!* How do such absurd reasons help them justify their crimes against humanity? What happened inside their psyche to make it possible?

"They had resources in abundance to build their empire on humanitarian values and coexist with their neighbours in kinship, mutual respect, and security. But, no! Creating and maintaining such societies is too complicated. Instead, they use all available resources to make more weapons, more bombs, and more tunnels. Some even dare to threaten with atomic power if the world won't comply with their medieval, vicious claims and demands, behaving like undisciplined toddlers who chose tyranny over mutual well-being.

"They bombard hospitals, kindergartens, and animal shelters. They *aim* for the vulnerable. And when the soldiers, the defenders of homes, accidentally kill civilians and mourn the dead and their own broken hearts—because no humane person would ever rejoice in taking a life, even during a war—the aggressors shout, 'Voila! Look what our enemies have done! See what we're dealing with? They're the real monsters!'

"The villains react like offended, puffed-up children. Pure gaslighting, in which the world might even believe that the attackers, who represent themselves so skillfully as innocent, are the victims.

"And who suffers the most, besides their victims? Civilians. Regular people with unfulfilled fundamental needs for clean air and water, food and shelter, schools and health care. Safety, love, belonging, and the other essentials.

"I believe they also strive for peace and quiet. No one in their right mind would ever choose war and destruction. I think that inside our psyche reside wounded fragments of our souls. Like neglected civilians, they suffer, unable to escape the trap of their leaders in toddler form. How desperate and abandoned they must feel! But what else can we expect from them if their basic needs are neglected and their cries for help are shushed with cold brutality by their leaders? How can they behave better if they're gasping for air in their smouldering dungeons with no nourishment, love, or care? They're so lonely, scared, and helpless.

"Or suppose you're a country that has chosen a more straightforward approach to show the world who's in charge. In that case, you fall under the illusion of superiority. Beneath this illusion is your fear of being exposed, the subtle whisper of disappointment, self-depreciation, and frantic denial of your own insignificance. But we're all unique and insignificant at the same time in this vast universe, which will continue to exist with or without us, right?"

Tyra sighed. "Those types of wars, while less atrocious, are still damaging and often happen between people who are stuck in unhealed trauma. The conflicts between nations or people are based on futile attempts to hush the nagging whispers of damaged souls. They think they can achieve greatness by obtaining more power to sustain their crumbling illusion of supremacy. It's so absurd.

"You want a ceasefire? You say you're ready to negotiate and put aside the defenses you've been clinging to for no reason. Open your eyes and see; your opponents stopped fighting ages ago. They want to build a better world that can accommodate any differences. You want a ceasefire? You want to negotiate? Then wake up! Acknowledge what you've done, no matter how painful and scary it might be. It will never make you weaker, only stronger, because it takes immense courage to face your pain and animosity. Even more so, it requires outstanding strength to see the pain of your victims.

"Take responsibility, annul your terrorist organizations, and drop your weapons! Stop this madness. Accept your limitations. Accept your darkness, your fear of rejection, and there will be no need to destroy others or defend yourself from made-up enemies."

Kai laughed in unease. "I see your point, Diana. You've pictured it vividly. I'm sorry. It must've been torturous to go through all of this in your childhood and now again with me. I don't know what's wrong with me."

"Nothing's wrong with you, Kai. None of us are easy to live with. As humans, we all have our weaknesses, fears, and trauma. But we can heal. I forgive you because I love you no matter what."

"And what about both sides defending their beliefs or sectarian values?"

Tyra raised an eyebrow and shared in his uneasy laughter. "I'm afraid they're doomed. No logic can penetrate fanaticism of any kind."

Kai smirked with a sense of fear. "True. But using your analogy, sectarian values and false beliefs are as strong as our problematic patterns, created as a trauma response."

"We all carry heavy baggage that weighs us down, but I'm willing to share yours."

Tyra was too young and idealistic to understand that none of her well-formed, theoretical tools about healthy relationships were simple or easy to apply.

She heard the voice. "If change were as easy for human nature to accept or endure, Earth would be a paradise. But it's not. And that's okay. It's natural for humans to stick to a familiar hell."

Tyra sighed, deep in thought.

"I can't forgive myself, goddess of the wilderness. You've been sitting all closed off, hugging your knees, protecting your heart, and sleeping in the fetal position lately," Kai said. "Is it because of me?"

"I don't feel safe, Kai. I feel like a cornered, wounded animal."

He sighed. "I'm so sorry, Tyra. Come, I got you."

He hugged her with warmth and strength, his arms providing quiet shelter as she released her tears.

Tyra tried her best to make it work, but she felt drained. She danced in her studio every night in the moonlight to the soft sound of *Storm* by Vivaldi. It helped. Her body and emotions moved in unison, crafting a long-anticipated reunion.

One hazy afternoon when Tyra zoned out after a long and weary conflict with Kai and fell asleep for a few blissful moments, she heard a soft voice through her nap. "Dear Ty-Ty, so happy to meet you. Finally. It seems I'm the only one who missed you."

Tyra looked around, and there she was, the Venezuelan poodle moth. The fluffy, alien-looking insect had a woolly white coat covering her entire body, large, feathery antennae that looked like bunny ears, and wide, dark, bulging obsidian eyes. Its delicate wings, also covered in fluffy white fur, gave it an almost magical appearance. She resembled a tiny flying poodle. "Koda, Jerry, Mihi, Kent, Cami, the sunflower mother, her daughter, and the behemoths, Aye and Duplex, say hi and pass hugs. We're worried about you, Ty-Ty. You're so unhappy."

"We love each other. We're best friends, and he makes me laugh."

"Yes, but he also makes you cry. Oh, Ty-Ty, I know you want to be properly loved, but, my dear, it's only possible for those who love and cherish themselves."

"I do love myself."

"All parts, Tyra, including the most dismissed, wounded, and ugly. But know we all love you so, so much. Hugs." The moth fluttered her wings and made a clicking sound.

Tyra woke up as she heard the diminishing echo. "Oy, Aye asked me to remind you that truth can never be found in conflicts but in stillness."

Tyra shook her head. "Sorry, I zoned out."

"I can relate to that," Kai said, giggling. "It's okay."

Kai and Tyra sat in her kitchen, eating Caprese omelets and waffles.

"You don't love me anymore," Kai said.

"I do love you. This has nothing to do with love. I need to be respected, appreciated, and cherished. You dismiss me, and then you get offended or mad when I protect my boundaries and defend myself."

Silence.

"I feel like I'm talking to a wall. A cold, indifferent, impenetrable wall."

Nothing.

"I can't be in this relationship anymore, not like this. I wanna be with you. I wanna be beside you when you need me, but you reject me and then punish me for not trying harder."

Not a word.

"I feel like I'm going crazy. I'm losing myself fighting for us. Do you hear me? Kai? Do you even listen to me?"

Kai became stiff and exhausted during such monologues. His arms would lock across his chest, and he would look down or sideways. His skin turned red, his jaw tensed, and his pupils widened. It seemed as if only black elliptical jewels, two onyxes trapped inside his eyeballs, recognized the void around him. After a while, he would become pale, his body loose and his eyes glassy and indifferent. His entire body was rigid and unresponsive.

Tyra was puzzled. *Who is this man? How can a person be so ambivalent about his behaviour?* It was as if two different personalities existed inside him, happily unaware of each other.

Tyra feared that she had given away her heart too quickly. Should one even consider such a thing? Perhaps not.

Opening one's heart was a different matter. Merging with another was a complex, unhealthy, and unnatural process. Yet, walking through life, hand in hand as two independent, self-sufficient, and healed entities was beautiful. It was liberating and fulfilling in its own right. Neither Tyra nor Kai were ready for that step, though. Their journey had just begun, and like every human being in every realm, this step would be the most challenging of all.

~

Tyra needed to make a decision, but she struggled to make a choice.

She took time off, rented a yurt in the closest village, and drove toward the untamed forest outside the city.

Surprisingly, it turned out to be a lovely place with lovely people.

Grandma was right, she thought. *Some areas in this dreary realm are different.* Perhaps it was the magic of nature around it, untouched by greed and the endless race to dominate over other species and other humans.

Tyra noticed that people who inhabited the bosom of nature near mountains, forests, and water were endowed with natural wisdom and open hearts. They didn't read abstruse books and knew little about the wisdom stored in ancient archives. Still, they sensed in their gut how to live in harmony with themselves and others, learning instinctively from the best master—nature. At times *she* was nursing and loving, caring and protective, and at other times, destructive and absorbing.

Tyra concluded that Marigold was an exception, an anomaly.

The yurt was cozy and romantic. It had a rustic charm, nestled in a beautiful meadow with wildflowers and an azurite brook next to the dense forest.

"A perfect solo getaway," she mumbled.

Plush, cheerful rugs covered the wooden floor, and a vast window framed the brook and the meadow, like beautiful artwork. Tyra looked around. There was a double bed with comfortable pillows and a soft, hand-woven quilt, a small kitchen with a flickering stove to warm up the night, and tiny, glowing yellow lights across the ceiling.

Tyra unpacked and then walked to the village through the tranquil, picturesque landscape and well-maintained farmland.

The village was charming. Its petite houses were timeworn but refreshed with a colourful palette and beautifully decorated. There was an old-fashioned bakery and a small, bustling market with handmade crafts and mouth-watering goods. Main Street was filled with the smell of freshly baked bread and blooming flowers. There was even a community center! The entire atmosphere was serene, even idealistic.

It's so odd, she thought. *It feels like I'm not in Azure anymore. It feels like . . . Moss.*

And then it clicked.

Tyra entered the bakery, which looked like Moss in miniature, and stared at her former neighbour in disbelief, the one who had saved them from the beasts' attack. She was a good-looking woman of average height in her early sixties. She was a bit round. Her brown skin glowed like the moonlight with an inner warmth. She had short, curly black hair and a childish smile. Her kind eyes resembled black cherries. No other beauty could ever compete with kindness.

The lady told Tyra that her family and the others who had fled Moss, some of the first, built the community in the middle of nowhere. They found the abandoned village withering away and rebuilt it step by step.

"Seven years and seven months! Can you imagine? The soil here is bountiful! More and more locals from neighbouring villages who are seeking a more fulfilling life come to live with us each year. It feels like a great sublimation for us all. We provide shelters for teens who run away from abusive households as well as women and men, pets, and children. We have formed an interesting, eclectic community. This place feels like home for many abandoned and neglected souls. Like a big family shaped by orphaned adults. You should consider moving here too, dear."

"Maybe I will. It sounds fantastic! I doubt Mama, Grandad, or Olivia will ever want to live in the countryside, even though they despise Moonvine, but I was born for country life."

"And there's a huge shelter we've built outside for dogs and cats who managed to escape. We brought them with us. There are more animals than people. It's paradise. You should definitely stop by. You'll receive as much love and warmth as a person can get in a lifetime."

"Wow, that's amazing! But I can't visit them. I'll end up leaving with a bunch." Tyra chuckled. "Unfortunately, Mama's not ready for another dog. I doubt she ever will be. She misses Moose terribly. And I'm still not ready to leave her. I mean, *I'm* ready; she's not."

"Moose? Oh, dear. I'm so sorry!"

Tyra turned away and wiped her tears. Then she sighed, feeling anxious. She fidgeted, running her fingers through her hair, which was in a perfect upside-down braid. She felt light-headed. "Is . . . Luke here?"

The fear of the negative answer crawled down her chest while the hope of the positive tickled her tummy.

"I'm sorry, Tyra. Haven't seen them or heard about them since we left."

Tyra nodded, the ache in her heart growing stronger. Before that moment she had grown used to that pain, but now it felt unfair and overwhelming. Dashed hopes could do that. Even those that lasted for but a moment.

"What happened to your friend and her family is . . . there are no words for it. Yes, I've heard about it. I'm so deeply sorry for your loss, child. It's unimaginable. Everything that happened still seems surreal, unbelievable. How can people carry within them such unacknowledged malevolence?"

Tyra told her the other news, and they cried together while sitting on a green velvet sofa.

"Thank you, Mrs. Levamiz, for what you've done for our family. I'll never be able to repay you. But can I at least do something?"

"Oh, dear! The only way to repay the debt of life is to live fully, savouring every moment." Mrs. Levamiz squeezed Tyra into a big, hearty, maternal hug. Tyra melted into the woman's soft, wide arms, feeling like a beloved child for a blissful moment.

"Seeing you, Tyra, alive, safe, and sound is . . . I'm so happy, my dear, so happy. Look at you, all grown up and gorgeous! Seeing you still standing and still fighting, after all you've been through, is the dearest gift you could ever give me. I'm so sorry for your losses. I loved Alma, and I liked your dad very much. He was a good lad. Oh, dear! Too many losses. Too many."

Mrs. Levamiz wiped away her tears. "Okay, enough of sadness. Enjoy your vacation, dear. This land can heal. I know that from experience. Stop by to say goodbye when you leave."

Tyra reassured her that she would. She thanked her again and then went out into the fragrant street with a basket full of delicious goods. Mrs. Levamiz insisted she take it for free.

Tyra spent eight nights and eight days in solitude. She read no novels, only poems, and she spent only a minimal amount of time online. She spent most days walking in the beautiful, nurturing nature and sat beside the brook for hours, having breakfast and then lunch, watching the water in constant flux and movement. She shared her food with raccoons and foxes and watched them play in the meadow with their babies, happy and free as if there were no creeping shadows or fall and then winter.

Tyra watched the wavering flames in a bonfire and listened to singing grasshoppers and hooting owls until midnight. At night she cried her eyes out, hugging the biggest pillow, and then fell asleep, drained.

After four days and four nights, the decision was made, although she wasn't aware of it yet. Tyra spent her last days of stillness processing and accepting her choice. Then she put it aside and let it ripen.

On the fifth night, Tyra danced to the sounds of a crackling fire and to the melody of Elton John's *I'm Still Standing*, immersed in intuitive movements, free of burdens.

The shadow made a nest of verdant leaves and jumped up and down with the excitement of a bouncy toddler, making funny moves from side to side like a wiggly crow.

On the eighth day, Tyra called Kai and invited him over for a long weekend. Oh, how she had missed him! And, on the eighth night, he came. No, he rushed over to see her.

They spent a beautiful three days and three nights, as if the last six months had never existed or if they were gleaming with a dim light on the outskirts of fading memories. Peaceful, intimate, and familiar.

Kai and Tyra visited Mrs. Levamiz and were gifted with the warmest hugs and delicious baked goods. They strolled through the village, savouring ice cream and smudging each other's noses. They roasted marshmallows and danced by the bonfire to the sounds of nature and Kai's humming. They cuddled at night and talked until early morning. And he watched her fall asleep, covering her with his arms.

On the last day, Kai and Tyra wallowed in the lush meadow, swimming in the wildflower-scented waters and tickling each other's necks with chamomile petals.

Then Kai sat behind her, touching her loose hair, which rested in a mermaid braid, massaging her neck, and making her laugh. He was wearing yellow sunglasses. Her emerald chiffon dress fluttered in the summer breeze.

"I love you," he said, mesmerized by her as he had been on the day they met.

Her hair swayed in the air, and she truly resembled Diana, the goddess of the wilderness. As Kai stared at her, he couldn't help but notice that she looked like a snowflake melting on a scorching summer day. She was beautiful in her simplicity.

"I love you too," she whispered with a sad smile. "Do you hate me sometimes?"

Kai giggled. "Of course. Love and hate are related. But I love you more."

He tumbled with her onto the grass, his movements slow and tender. They rolled and rolled until they landed on the soft earth, wrapped in a hug for a long time as they sniffed each other's essence, which was already fading away in the whirlwind.

～

The next week on a warm summer afternoon, Kai came over to Tyra's house with a paper grocery bag and declared he was going to make dinner.

"No one's allowed into the kitchen," he said.

"Well, tell it to Tom Sawyer," Tyra replied, giggling.

Kai immersed himself in his work. He baked sourdough buns and grilled salmon to make the best sandwiches in Azure. Distracted for a moment, Kai left the salmon unattended as he responded to Calla, who was seeking attention.

Kai returned to the sandwiches, and there he was, Tom, the loopy furball, his silly face smudged with savoury salmon. The purring troublemaker had crept into Kai's domain of culinary exquisiteness. Kai yelled and swore, then threw the bewildered hooligan on the floor.

"Oh, boy, what are you so upset about?" Olivia asked from the living room.

"Can you ask him nicely?" Tyra suggested.

"I'm not upset; I'm pissed off. Should I teach this beast a lesson, you ask? Should I ask him nicely? Ha! Impossible. Your beastie is incapable of grasping the simplest cause-and-effect dynamics, so he needs a strong, clear signal consisting only of pure loathing. You don't have to thank me, by the way." Kai smirked.

"You know why Vikings, the ancient Terrans, behaved with their wives?" Tyra called from the living room. "Because they knew if they didn't, their women might slaughter them in their sleep."

Olivia giggled. "Poor kitty. It's not his fault. It's his nature. Some patterns are carved too deep to be changed by mere willpower."

Tom understood everything and sat down under the dining table to contemplate with the weight of a thousand naps how he had turned out to be such a scoundrel and how, of all his cozy lives, he'd ended up in that mess.

Kai felt somewhat sorry, not for the cat but for the salmon. He thought of cleaning it under the water, but there had been witnesses to the salmon robbery, not to mention the whole street had heard him yelling. But Tom was still there. Kai cursed the cat as he washed his bowl, giving him the fish to snack on or choke on. Only when the goofy kitty had had his fill and began to lick his mustache, which was greasy with happiness, did Kai realize Tom's cause-and-effect connection might be inferior, but he was the only one who had gotten salmon that day.

"Share it with Calla, you greedy bastard!" Kai said. He petted Tom with affection and gave Calla her cut.

～

Soon after, everything reversed, as if the happy days and nights had never existed. Tyra would listen to the song *Burn* by David Kushner over and over again, singing in unison with obsessive repetition. "You watched me *burn*. You watched me, you watched me *burn.*"

Kai felt as if he were being swept into a hurricane, unable to escape. He wanted to change his patterns, which were ruining his life, but he was trapped in anxiety, struggling to control the defensive walls he had built around his fear of failure and exposure. He wanted to make her happy so badly that it hurt. But the fact that he didn't know how hurt even more.

Tyra became adrift. She felt as if her true identity was buried under restless attempts to avoid heated conflicts, and a new one had been forced upon her, unable to settle down.

Kai found comfort in his kitchen, inventing garment recipes. On a burning hot night, he made a new type of risotto with chestnuts and chives, humming to Tyra's monologues. "She sang as if she knew me in all my dark despair. And then she looked right through me as if I wasn't there. Killing me softly with her song . . ." Kai sang the famous song *Killing Me Softly* by Roberta Flack.

"You've closed your heart so you won't get hurt, but you will," Tyra whispered. "Everyone does. That's the way of life. I love you, Kai, and I always will. But I don't like myself anymore. I hate how I react, how I behave, and how I feel. I can barely write. I miss myself. It's not good for either of us. We're so miserable here, Kai."

He wouldn't respond.

"We suffer, we hurt, we suffer," she said.

"I prefer to be miserable with you," Kai replied.

If only he knew, that not only could one never make another person happy, but they could also never impose their unhappiness on others for eternity. Sooner or later, each person sheds their dead leaves like an ancient, weary tree—either to return in spring, rejuvenated, or to descend into the abyss of unfulfilled dreams, missed opportunities, and untapped regrets.

"I know," Tyra said. "I've felt the same way, but it isn't right."

And then she left.

Kai felt an enormous ache in his chest. It was as if he were drowning in the obscure waters of grief and loss. Kai wanted to stop her, to ask for forgiveness and make things right, but he couldn't move, and he hated himself for that.

Sitting in the darkest corner of his orphaned room, he felt dejected. Crestfallen. Defeated. Kai's heart was broken.

He hit his hands against the wall and covered his face with sore palms and trembling fingers. He squeezed them and roared.

On her nineteenth birthday, Tyra awoke to an empty house. No balloons or a cake or even disappointment. She walked into the kitchen, following the smell of caramel and lavender. Her glance stopped at the turquoise island with the wooden counter. Three glittering gift bags and a bouquet of lavender flowers awaited her, ready to be opened. Their alluring aroma filled the house, making Tyra's nose itch. She sneezed and then smiled. There was also a plate with stuffed eggs, a cheese platter, focaccia bread, fresh purple grapes, and a porcelain bowl of caramelized cookies. Under the bowl, Tyra found two greeting cards, one from her granddad and one from Olivia. Next to them fluttered a sweet note from her mother:

Happy 19th birthday, Tyra!

I kissed you and hugged you in your sleep. I hope I didn't wake you up. The day you were born was the happiest! I love you more than you know and more than I can ever show. Enjoy your solitude; I know you like it. Have fun with the monsters and writing. See you after work, at night. Love, Mama.

Tyra went to her room, turned on some music, and started writing to the voices of the First Aid Kit duo singing *My Silver Lining.* "I don't wanna wait anymore. I'm tired of looking for answers. Take me someplace where there's music, and there's laughter. I don't know if I'm scared of dying, but I'm scared of living too fast, too slow. Just gotta keep on keeping on . . ."

Oh, to open the wonders of life again!

Tyra spent her day as Scarlett predicted until she heard the doorbell ring, which was unexpected.

She opened the door, and there they were, two siblings, smiling and shouting in unison. "Surprise!"

They hugged her, squeezing her in their arms and saying they had ordered a table in the secret jazz club.

Trudy looked guilty. "I'm so deeply sorry, buttercup, I forgot to buy you a present. I feel so ashamed of myself, but there's nothing I can do now to fix it. It's too late."

"Nonsense! I don't believe in missed opportunities. It's okay. Life gets busy, and we all get lost. It's all good, Trudy. Tomorrow, take me to the secret yoga Nidra class with alpacas. I have no idea what yoga Nidra is, but it sounds fun!" Tyra chuckled.

"Oh, great! Thank you, darling! I've heard about it. It's a body-scan technique with a rotation of awareness. My girlfriend said it's super relaxing."

"Sounds fantastic! Kai, are you in?"

"Nah, enjoy your girls' day out." He smiled as he handed her a present—an album filled with candid photographs of her, taken when she least expected it.

"Oh, Kai! Those are your masterpieces! Thank you!"

He shrugged. "It's your creation. I just happened to be there."

Tyra tried to find the right words. The shots were outstanding. "It's you . . . and me. It's us. And you were able to capture the most authentic moments."

He shrugged. "Life is about moments."

She smiled. "I permit you to use them in your exhibitions, whenever that might be."

"Really? Thanks, Diana. I appreciate it."

After a cozy evening with her favourite people, Tyra headed home with ambivalent feelings. It had been a lovely night, but everything was different now.

As Kai walked Tyra home, she told him about the fight over dishes she'd had with her mother the day before her birthday.

"It was so stupid. Just two tired children." Tyra giggled.

"Just like us," he said, sharing a faint smile.

Tyra tried to squeeze out a smile as well. "Yeah, just like us."

Kai gave her a long hug, then he went down the dark street alone.

Tyra wanted to stop him. Her heart urged her to make a move, but she remained still and silent under the wounded wind, which tingled her waterfall braid and played with her mind.

We will recover, she whispered to her heart. *I got you.*

Tyra had chosen herself, but it was painful.

The following day, the girls visited the alpaca farm to practice yoga Nidra. They lay on the grass, surrounded by their fluffy companions and immersed in deep relaxation. The alpacas roamed about with a lazy charm, their damp noses brushing their guests with odd fascination. A recording of the renowned yoga Nidra teacher, Ally Boothroyd, resonated with a melodious purr. "Could you bring your attention to your sensations without judgment? This is like a full-body massage for the entirety of your nervous system.

Warmth, aliveness. Little micro-muscles, radiant with awareness, shimmering with sensations. The whole body, alive, radiant. Should you wish to welcome deep tissues, the innermost core? Bone, bone marrow. Trillions of living cells, tiny beings. Alive, radiant with sensations."

It was a majestic experience. Such relaxation. Tyra had never experienced anything like it before. She felt as if she were floating in an ocean of bliss.

Weeks later, Trudy visited Tyra with a heavy heart. Tyra sensed it and felt cold. Trudy shuffled her feet. "I'm so sorry, Tyra. We're leaving tomorrow, the three of us. Dad needs a change of scenery. We all do. Kai loves you, but he is what he is. We're moving to Terra."

Tyra didn't answer. Tears crawled down her cheeks, unwelcomed. Her face and lips became pale. She felt as if a freezing chill swept through her.

Abandoned again.

"He can't change right now. Maybe when he gets older, he'll heal his wounds and become free of this excruciating pain that's driving him crazy. Free of anxiety, fear of rejection, and anger. For now, he's incapable of loosening his grip on his defensive walls. He'll fall apart. I love you, buttercup, but he's my brother, and I love him too. I need to help him and our family recover. He's in pain and he's entirely lost. But he loves you. That's all you need to know, okay?"

Tyra covered her face with her hands, her tears silent intruders. "I need to help him. I shouldn't have left him."

"You can't help him, girl. You'll drown in the bottomless well of his pain together. You two are too enmeshed. You reflect each other like transparent water in the lake of your tears. You both project, get hurt, fight, and reconcile. You cry, and he hurts you again. You try to communicate. He struggles and gets defensive.

You both fight. You cry. You adapt. You lose yourself. It isn't a healthy relationship, buttercup. It's a vicious, endless cycle."

"I'll go to clinical therapy. I know it's a new concept here in Azure, but they say it's a must in Terra. This type of therapy has helped millions of their people get their lives back on track. I'll heal us."

"It's impossible. You'll destroy yourself in this futile attempt to compensate for his refusal to heal and communicate. You'll scratch and polish yourself for him until you feel open, weeping wounds inside your heart as a result of self-betrayal. Such wounds are so raw and painful, they're unbearable. And for what? I know, for love. But what about self-love? What about your life? You know I know what it feels like. I barely got myself up from the bottom of the bottom. I don't want you to get there and die for love. The only real love that's worth dying for is the love for your wounded, banished fragments, sobbing inside the chasm of your subconscious mind. Your shadow. For then, you will be reborn."

Tyra didn't respond. She couldn't. She felt frozen and voiceless.

"Don't feel guilty, Tyra. It's not about his grief. Separate grief from the person who's grieving. It's just that grief amplifies everything that needs to be healed. And you've done enough. We would've been crushed without your love and support. You've helped us get through the rawest and most acute months. I'm grateful, Tyra. Kai is too."

Tyra sat on the floor and sobbed, her head on her knees and her arms behind her neck in a protective half-triangle. The breakup was agonizing enough. But total separation? No contact and no hope.

It felt like she was falling into an abyss. The pain and the emptiness were so intense, it felt like dying.

The shadow felt acknowledged but also distrusted.

Tyra hugged her friend, clinging to her for a long time, unable to loosen her grip. "I can't let him go. I love him no matter what."

"But you must."

"What will I do without you?"
"Time will heal the wounds, Tyra."
"Nonsense. Time never heals; it only numbs."

"The heart will break but broken—live on."
– Lord Byron

CHAPTER 14
The Invitation

"What deep wounds ever closed without a scar?"
– Lord Byron

Tyra met her father again in her dreams.

"I miss him, and I miss you. Will this hole in my heart ever heal? I don't wanna feel this way anymore."

"In time. But remember, heartaches are too deep and too sharp to be left unattended. Don't turn away from your broken heart, Tyra. There's no use rushing the healing process. I know you're hurting, and I know you wish your life were different, but this isn't the end."

"I feel like an ancient tree that has lived through centuries and has experienced too many losses. I'm so tired, Papa."

"I know, kiddo. But this is your path. And change and clarity are coming your way. The tree's leaves will turn red soon."

Logan looked out the window.

～

Tyra's scarf returned, turning back the clock to serve once again.

In mid-October, when nature had outdone itself and the

186

landscape transformed into blazing reds and golds, Tyra came home late from work. She put her scarf aside and noticed her family gathered in the living room, perplexed and disoriented.

Olivia was sitting in a yoga position on the plush maroon carpet, nibbling her lower lip. Scarlett was fidgeting on the white faux-leather sofa, her gaze wandering across the room. Ethan was standing in the corner, his hands crossed and his eyebrows pressing toward each other in a vain attempt to shrink the distance. Tyra held her breath. The air was dense and stagnant.

Scarlett frowned. "Tyra, you received an invitation. I thought it was a myth."

On the coffee table lay a maple leaf, red and orange with golden stripes. Glowing spritz was scattered across the room, creating powdery letters that formed a message in the air.

Dear Tyra,

You're invited to join us and live in the Land of the Great Lakes! When you're ready, please follow the leaf. It will guide you to the portal. Just go with the flow. You have four weeks to complete the journey. See you soon!

"Tyra, what are you going to do?" Scarlett asked in a dismal tone. She stood up and waltzed around the room, looking anxious.

"I'll accept the invitation. Will you let me go?" Tyra asked with a hint of hope as she wound her ladder braid around her forefinger. "Will you let me go *fully*?"

"I can't."

"I'll leave anyway."

"I know."

Tyra looked at her grandfather and sister, both of them unshakeable.

Scarlett sighed. "Look, Tyra. I know I've failed you, and I'm sorry. But we're your family, and family is everything. There's nothing else outside. Nothing that matters. No one will protect, support, and love you as we do. We're bound by blood forever.

This bond is unbreakable, unlike others. You should stay, Tyra. This is your life. There's no sense running."

"I'm not running. I'm choosing a different path. And family isn't immortal, Mama. I'm languishing in this gloomy realm. I don't belong here. How could I refuse this opportunity?"

Choosing her path over her mother's demand for infinite attachment felt right. The instinct, the urge to extract a blessing at all costs, felt absurd, but Tyra couldn't help it. What force could be stronger than a person's fundamental will to fulfill their needs? Tyra noticed her belly tightening in protest. Guilt reintroduced itself and giggled, celebrating an ultimate victory inside her ribs.

"A mother wound is the deepest and most complex to heal. Remember that, child," the voice whispered. "Please, voice, will you hush up? I'm tired of you. Let me be happy," Tyra muttered, irritated. "Besides, I don't have a mother wound—I have a father wound." She huffed, scowling with her hands on her hips, then clicked her tongue and walked away.

For weeks, Olivia and Ethan treated Tyra as a stranger. They were appalled and insulted by her decision and aimed to make her miserable. They acted like betrayed children, formed their own VIP bubble, and excluded her from their inner circle as a punishment for her choice. Scarlett also became distant and sombre. Little by little, she joined the others, leaving Tyra to bear the burden of being a family breaker. Tyra had never felt so isolated— like an orphan child—powerless, rejected, and lonely.

Under a shrinking moon, almost invisible to the human eye, Tyra entered a lucid dream when she fell asleep at midnight, cuddled with Tom and Calla by her side. Tyra was in Koda's home again. It looked the same as the real one, vibrant with life, but Koda was nowhere to be found. Tyra felt an ache in her chest. Oh, how she missed him. She hadn't realized how much. The mirror was calling her again. Tyra put on an invisibility cap and went through it.

Oy, I forgot to think about the scene I wanted to visit, and now I can't remember, Tyra thought. *I feel so tired, as if I have lived through countless lives.*

Tyra looked around. She was in a gloomy space. There was only dry soil and a vast emptiness. She turned back. The mirror had disappeared. Tyra shivered, turned around, and saw an odd scene. Floating in the air was an oval head with a neck but no body. The head had short, pitch-black hair and greyish skin that was stretched over its nose, mouth, and cheeks. Its eyes were round, black, and huge with no pupils. They looked at Tyra, pleading with her. She shuddered.

Beside it staggered a blackthorn desk in the dim light. The desk was dusty, its colour faded; deep scratches and dark stains were spread across its surface.

On the desk lay another head, but neckless. It was a female head with wavy, shoulder-length, burnt-copper hair. Its eyes were closed, but they fluttered in an unstable rhythm. It had saggy cheekbones and full, bow-shaped, offended lips. It had the tired skin of an aging woman and two lonely wrinkles beside the chin.

Next to the desk on the ground lay an animal. It was curled up in a circle, resembling a middle-sized dog with previously white, shaggy fur that stuck out like pine needles. His face was oblong, his eyes closed and motionless, and his breathing faint, almost invisible.

Neither of them could communicate, but they were suffering. Powerless, boycotted, excluded.

Tyra looked back in search of the mirror. It showed up and then disappeared again. She felt an urge to search for it, to call to it, but she hesitated, pondering.

Tyra looked at the first head. It was communicating through his eyes. The three figures looked so miserable. Tyra took a deep breath as she hugged herself, then approached the desk.

"What are your names? I'm Tyra."

Then she heard a voiceless male sound, or maybe it was just a thought. "Anthony, Miranda, and Demis."

"How can I help you?"

Silence.

"You don't know?" She examined each of them closely. "Well, first, having a nose and lips is essential." She stepped closer and stroked Anthony's face with maternal tenderness. The skin looked strained and wrinkled. "I bet it hurts like hell."

Tyra closed her eyes, attuned to her new acquaintance. Her hands were shaking as she stroked the slick skin, which was unpleasant to touch.

She opened her eyes. "It will hurt way more than now. But it will heal in time. Are you ready?"

Anthony nodded, then pressed his eyes shut.

Tyra closed her eyes again and heard a muted, agonizing scream in her head.

She shivered. "Oh, poor you. It's unbearable. I know. I'm so sorry."

Tyra opened her eyes. Anthony stared at her with a faint smile, his breath deep and his skin red and sore, an expression of boundless relief and gratitude in his eyes. His nose was hawk-shaped, and his lips were narrow. Tyra kissed Anthony's forehead and then turned to Miranda. Miranda was not reactive. She dwelled in oblivion.

"What are your needs?" Tyra scrutinized Miranda as she stroked her dying hair. "Poor girl. You look like . . . like guilt and fear." Tyra removed a curl from Miranda's face and tucked it behind her ear. "Your hair needs a wash and some care, my dear."

Tyra heard a murmur behind her. She turned around and found a basket filled with luxurious hair and skin products and a majestic blend of essential oils: passionflower, jasmine, sweet pea, jojoba, apricot, bluebells, and rosemary. Inside was also a bottle of pure rose oil, a silver comb, a bamboo brush, soft towels, and a silver bucket with an unlimited supply of water. A shimmering golden shampoo ladle lay beside the bucket.

Tyra washed Miranda's hair and brushed the tangled strands with her fingers, massaging and soothing her scalp. The water cascaded to the ground, carrying away guilt, fear, and self-doubt.

Miranda opened her eyes. They were big, deep, and beautiful, the colour of black cherries. She looked at Tyra with a timid sparkle on her face, full of love and appreciation. Tyra wrapped Miranda's hair in a towel and applied skin care products on her salty, trembling cheeks.

"Hello, girl. Let's use the serum now and leave it under this plush towel for a while. Look how pretty you are." Tyra took a small hand mirror from the basket and held it up for her friend. Miranda blushed and twinkled.

"It's going to be okay, girl. I promise. I'll take care of you. And you're not alone. You have Anthony and Demis. You belong, Mimi."

Mimi released a large, diamond-like tear. It flowed down her dry cheek, rejuvenating her tired, pale skin.

"Thank you," she said in a timid, quiet voice. "And I have Koda."

"You know Koda?" Tyra asked, dazed.

"I will," Mimi replied, smiling.

Tyra nodded, her eyes twinkling with joy. "I need to help Demis, but I feel as if it will be much harder."

"Yes, but don't worry. He's got us now. We'll take care of him when you're gone."

"I will never leave you again. Not really."

Tyra cleansed Demis's fur with some brilliant powder she discovered in Mimi's basket and brushed him as if he were a frail fledgling. Her hands moved with attentive delicacy. Demis's coat transformed, becoming like snow, soft and cottony. His tail swayed in gentle liveliness. Demis opened his eyes with apparent effort and looked at Tyra with love. His tears moistened the soil all around.

"That's okay to be sad," she said. "I'm here now."

The four heard the voice humming the song *Broken* by lovelytheband: 'I like that you're broken, broken like me. Maybe that makes me a fool. I like that you're lonely, lonely like me. I could be lonely with you. Every one of us is a little broken.'

Tyra stared at Demis and saw a basket emerging from the darkness behind him. She took a shaggy, feather-soft, cream blanket out of the basket and covered Demis with gentle, considerate movements.

"You can rest as long as you need. No pressure, love. I know it might take time. That's okay. No rush to be happy again."

Tyra lay down beside him in a tender hug. The soil was damp and a bit puffy.

They stayed in that nurturing hug for an hour. *Moonlight Sonata* was playing softly, and the voice was humming in unison. Tyra fell asleep.

When she opened her eyes, she saw Anthony transform into a beautiful raven. His dark blue-purple feathers gleamed in the sunlight. Tyra gasped in wonder. The entire scene had changed. Tyra was in a vast, marvelous field covered with blue and purple irises.

"I love it, love it, love it! Okay, love it!" Anthony sang, swirling and swaying around as he showed off his brand-new wings. He peeked under one wing, then another, and went crazy in ecstatic disbelief of what had just happened.

Tyra laughed and clapped in delight.

"Morning, Tyra," a timid female voice said, and then it hooted.

Tyra looked up and saw a beautiful barn owl with white feathers and vertical light brown bars. The owl had a round face and deep, dark, enigmatic eyes.

"Mimi?" Tyra asked, bewildered.

"Yes, that's me. Come and visit us sometime." Mimi laughed like a gentle bell as she floated above Tyra, landing on her left shoulder.

Tyra petted her, amazed. "Where's Demis?"

Mimi pointed toward a pile of irises. There he was, sleeping on top of fragrant flowers. His whiskers and closed eyes twitched as he whimpered in a deep sleep, his breathing shallow.

Tyra woke up alone in a dark void. "A dream within a dream," she whispered.

Her eyes searched for the mirror, but it was nowhere to be found. Exhausted, she sank to the dry, itchy soil and, finally, began to cry.

Tyra felt so small and fragile, so abandoned and isolated.

Then she heard whispers behind her, but she was too drained to turn around.

Moments later, she sensed gentle, strong hands lifting her up like a child. She opened her eyes. Kent was holding her in his arms, making a protective circle around her petite body as he looked down at her with loving kindness. Kent was in his gigantic form—round, mellow, and grounded. Tyra nestled in and clung to his stalwart, unwavering body. She nuzzled her nose into his soft, soothing tummy as she heard a lulling purring from the mirror. Tyra wanted to stay in that nurturing hug for much longer. So, she waited, melting in her monster's arms.

Tyra! It's time to get back, Cami's melodic, smooth voice said in her head.

Kent stretched his arms and pushed Tyra out through the mirror.

Tyra was in Koda's home again. Koda was sitting in his rocking chair, smiling.

Tyra dashed toward him, wrapping her arms around his shoulders and clinging to him.

"Okay, okay, child. You're gonna smash me!" He laughed as he twisted her loose, wide braid.

"Oh, Koda! I missed you so much!"

"I know! I missed you too!"

"I need to get back. Demis isn't well yet."

"No worries, sugar. I'll keep an eye on them. Demis needs time to recover. Cami and Kent will take care of him too. Grief is the hardest thing to heal, and it comes in many forms. Your grief is almost complete, although it never goes away. It simply doesn't affect us the same way when we complete its circle in allowance."

Tyra shuffled her bare feet. The moss carpet felt like home.

Koda nodded with affection. "I see. You can visit them in your dreams, Tyra, but not only then. They live inside your mind. It's good to see you, sugar."

Tyra woke up again. Tom was lying circled at her feet and Calla at her head. Tyra noticed the first signs of the waxing moon through the window and closed her eyes. "The voice said . . . you said . . . But I don't have a mother wound! I have a father wound."

Then she heard Koda's voice. "Are you sure, sugar?"

"I probably have both," she mumbled as she fell asleep.

The shadow made itself comfortable, snuggled up beside Tyra. It had become a little softer and a little lighter, and it purred and snored like a kitty.

Tyra slept in peace, undisturbed. White and brown feathers floated around her, sneaking under the bed by dawn. Through a dreamless sleep, Tyra heard some lyrics from *The Shadow and I* song by Yehuda Poliker:

"Outside, it's possible to be liberated from all fear only when my shadow and I are together."

Tyra slept through the entire weekend.

Tyra sat at the kitchen with her family, eating dinner in silence—tortellini salad and scrambled eggs with spinach and parmesan cheese.

The silence was strained, and Tyra grew tired of it. "There are only four days left. I understand you're upset. You disapprove. You can't accept it. I get it, and I'm sorry. But can we try to spend our last days in peace?"

"What are you talking about?" Olivia asked in an innocent voice. "You made your decision. It's all good. We're acting completely normal. Let's not make a fuss about it. Obviously, I'm unhappy that you're leaving, but you make your own choices now."

"I do," Tyra mumbled, "but you make it sound as if it's bad or odd."

The atmosphere was stiff. The other three had been making meals, talking, and laughing as if Tyra had already left.

Tom, Calla, and Zeus grieved in advance. They followed Tyra everywhere, offended and apathetic.

"Oh gosh, I can imagine. My beasties, my baby lizard. I'm so sorry to leave you. Separations are like super-bad, feisty guys. I wish I could take you with me, but they need you, my little monsters. Take good care of the trio, will you? We'll have to part ways, my babies, but not just yet. It's too early to turn sour. There are still days pure and untouched by melancholy. It would be better to savour them, right? It's so damn hard. My heart aches for you, guys. And for me. Hugs?"

She covered them with love.

The four weeks had flown by in a flash.

Tyra made a tattoo of an owl with her favourite quote from "Alice in Wonderland": "It's only a dream." She was afraid that her mother would find out, and she felt as if she were forced to hide it. *Forced?* she thought. *Such absurdness.* She frowned. *By whom? All I can see is me.*

When the halo moon cast a soft glow over their townhome, the family gathered for a farewell dinner, sitting on plush cushions around the walnut coffee table. Scarlett made Tyra's favourite dishes—tomato soup, homemade pizza, and blueberry cake for dessert. Delicious.

They ate in silence and unease once again.

Tyra savoured her mama's pizza—paper-thin with homemade dough and delicious sauce—and wondered if she would ever taste it again.

Then her gaze found the twitching maple leaf. It looked so delicate, so brittle. No one dared to touch it.

"Wait! There's a leaf. Let me put it aside first!" Tyra cried while Olivia poured gazpacho soup into a ceramic bowl. *Why are we eating here instead of at the dining table like normal people?* she wondered.

Startled, Olivia covered the leaf in magnificent red liquid, causing it to crumble and turn into a kind of porridge.

"Oh, Tyra! I'm so sorry! Oh, boy, I would never do that on purpose. Never!" Olivia was in shock. She tried to collect the tiny pieces of what remained, but it was too far gone. She sat on a deformed, overstuffed bean-bag cushion. "I never intended to ruin it for you. I was mad, but I would never do that. Oh, boy. I'm so sorry. We have to think. There must be something we can do."

Tyra's vision became blurry, and her head began to spin while her mind refused to accept or try to make sense of things.

How much could happen to one person? Tyra couldn't think, hear, or talk. The hustle and bustle around her echoed in her ears like a distant memory of a grim joke. Ethan was half numb and half restless. In his heart, he wanted her to be happy, one way or another. Olivia covered her face with her red mushy hands, unable to move. Scarlett entered her childlike mode and stared at the messy, overburdened coffee table.

Tyra got up and dashed to her room. She crashed onto her fleecy greyish pillow with fading yellow gorse flowers and fell into a deep sleep. Her shadow squeaked, reshaped, and compressed into a flat, smudgy ball.

"Tyra, time to wake up," she heard Logan say. "Go to the garden and gather the apples. Remember what your cow told you about the apple tree? Use it to find your way out of this mess. Wake up, Tyra! Do something, now!"

Tyra woke up, her brain foggy. Ethan was sitting beside her, stroking her hand with unusual tenderness. Tyra held his warm, sturdy hands and cried until she could cry no more.

"I'm so sorry, Tyra, about everything. Could your tree help

somehow? After all, it possesses unbeknown powers that are hard to deny." Ethan stared at Tyra. "Olivia's devastated."

"I love you too, Grandpa."

Ethan didn't move, but his breathing began to deepen and soften.

"I think it's a good idea. I'll fetch an apple. I'm hungry, anyway."

Tyra left her grandfather lost in thought and went to the garden. She picked an apple and took a bite.

"Olivia, Grandpa, Mama! I'm going to the Land of the Great Lakes!" she shouted.

"The great object of life is sensation—to feel that we exist, even though in pain."
– Lord Byron

CHAPTER 15
The Ash Tree

"Only those who will risk going too far
can possibly find out how far one can go."
– T. S. Eliot

Tyra's room looked blue. The moonlight slipped through an azure window, tinting the fading peach-cloud walls.

Olivia bustled around, hugging her niece here and there. Her curly hair was swaying, her cheeks were red, and her hands were sweaty. "We only have a couple of hours left. The journey's long and stressful! Hurry up, Tyra! Let's get you ready! Find a way to stay connected. Don't wear your scarf too often. Give people another chance, Tyra. I wish we had more time—the days I've wasted." Olivia sighed. "You're strong-spirited, Tyra. I know you're going to be okay. I'm certain. The crisis is over. You've endured so much pain and look how strong life has made you!"

"Oh, lucky me," Tyra grumbled. Then she chuckled. "I already miss you."

"That's not normal. I'm still here. You can miss me when you can't see me."

Olivia scrunched her brows, hid her lips, and puffed her

cheeks. The grimace was half funny and half spooky. The girls burst out laughing.

Olivia clapped herself on the forehead. "Wait, I'll be right back." She ran to her apartment across the street.

Scarlett packed some clothes she had made for her daughter, the unique collection of scarves she'd gathered over the years from authentic boutique shops, a sleek, glossy family album, the teal-blue blanket, Tyra's favorite book, *Dandelion Wine* by Ray Bradbury, which she'd bought for her last birthday, and the apples.

Mother and daughter didn't talk or look at each other; it was too painful. But then Tyra had spotted her mother's emerald earrings, which Scarlett loved the most, inside the bag. "Mama, these are your favourites. I can't take them." Tears tingled her eyes, making them dewy, and her voice became tender.

"They'll go perfectly with the ring your father gave you. It's my choice, *Tara*," Scarlett said with unconcealed affection. It had been years since Scarlett had used her daughter's middle name. She used to, when Tyra was little. It was softer, cuter.

"Mama, I don't wanna leave you, but I must go."

"I wish you'd stay, Tyra. But you've made your decision. It's hard for me to let you go, you know? How will we communicate? Is there a video phone? I don't know. It feels unreal that you're *actually* leaving. We were supposed to spend our lives together, side by side." Scarlett frowned. "I'll walk you to the tree," she announced with a timid, childish smile.

"Oh, Mama, thank you!" Tyra felt a tickling sensation inside her chest. Such a relief! She sighed and smiled.

Tyra held her transformer scarf, staring at it with hesitation. Then she found a small box made of sunstone with a tungsten lock and mulled it over for a moment. The scarf transformed in unison with her thoughts into a tiny piece of silk fabric, even before Tyra could grasp her decision. She sighed with gratitude and placed the scarf inside the box, then locked it and put it into the weightless bag, relieved.

"Voice?"

"Yes?"

"I hope I can find Luke someday. They say other realms have open borders. Did they really move to Terra?"

"Yes, for a while."

"Will we ever meet again?"

"The future is veiled behind the haze, invisible to people. Full of disillusionment and wonders."

"More riddles, thanks."

"I'm not the one to foretell *your* future, child."

Tyra strained her ears and noticed the sound of her grandfather's footsteps in the kitchen. She heard the subtle whisper of the food being cooked. Alma used to say, "The food you cook talks to you."

Tyra paused and listened. Butter was getting caramelized in the skillet, and melting chocolate was fizzling. The water was muttering, the ceramic dishes clashing.

Tyra entered the kitchen and saw her grandfather making her an early breakfast of crepes and poached eggs, her favourite.

"Oh, good. Here, Tyra, look at the counter. I want you to take my father's watch, my diamond pen, and your grandmother's silk gloves. Take good care of yourself, Tyra. Keep in touch." Ethan pointed to the kitchen island, then he flipped an amber crepe in the air.

"Thank you, Grandpa, for everything." Tyra stopped and pondered, feeling anxious. "What if I don't find what I'm looking for? What if I never find *my* people? What if I don't belong there either?"

"We're as good at foretelling the future as that 'oracle' you went to with your mother." Ethan grinned. "We *wish* we could control the flow of life, but often we don't. So, bear the unknown, as hard as it may be. No use overthinking it."

"Thank you, Grandpa."

She hugged him. Ethan's hug was warm and strong and made her feel safe and loved.

Olivia entered the kitchen, out of breath. "Tyra, I wanna give you this silver fork that I adored when I was little as a reminder of me. And a kaleidoscope I never allowed you to hold when you were a kid. I know you want it; you want it so badly, eh?" Olivia giggled. "And my mama's quilt. I insist you take it. No objections."

Tyra felt touched. She took the items with gratitude and put them into her weightless bag, along with a squishy doll, her pinkish suitcase, the monsters' pillows, Alma's spider-like shawl, the alpaca poncho, the teal blanket, six pairs of shoes, the white-gold ring with glowing emerald, Kai's album, and other treasures.

After the royal breakfast, Tyra squeezed her two beasties with love. "I'll miss you so, so much."

Then Zeus left his safe corner and climbed onto Tyra's fore-head, curling up there. Tyra laughed, stroking him. "I'll miss you too, darling. So, so much."

Calla and Tom snuggled on her legs in a black-and-white circle. Tyra moved with great care and cuddled with her loved ones on the mellow maroon carpet. With her four limbs, she made a bigger circle in which her white and black fur babies purred loudly. Zeus moved to her shoulder, and they stayed like that for a while.

Tyra hugged her aunt and grandpa. "I love you," she whispered. Then she took her mother's hand and went out into the foggy, dreamy street lit by dim lanterns.

When they reached the nearest corner, Tyra heard Olivia's voice echoing in the mist. "You can miss me now since you can't see me. I love you. Have fun!"

Tyra smiled, her smile lingering for a while after that.

When they left the city, Tyra tossed an apple onto the ground, and it rolled, leading the way to the forest with the ancient tree. They walked all day, following the apple through numerous villages, resting in local coffee shops, or lying on the grass.

"What do you think, Tyra? I think I'm growing to like the idea of our brief adventure. I get to spend more time with you." Scarlett touched Tyra's shoulder with her fist and giggled.

"Absolutely! I think this is awesome! But the butterflies in my stomach are having a party, that's for sure. I'm leaving this realm! I still can't believe it. I've dreamed about this moment my entire life. I just never noticed. But it's not easy for me to leave you, Mama."

Scarlett sighed and turned away.

When they approached a dense, vast forest, dusk had already settled in, bringing a chill to the air and filling it with moisture. It smelled like butternut cookies. Weird!

"What are we going to do in the dark?" Tyra asked. "We don't know how long until we get to the tree. We have no shelter and no food, and I'm hungry and cold."

"No worries. Check out your bag, Tyra." Scarlett flashed a wily smile.

"Oh my gosh, Mama! You're a genius!" Inside her bag were two sleeping bags, a thermos, a plaid picnic blanket, mosquito repellent, hand warmers, layered clothing, a lantern, a huge umbrella, a fire kit, raincoats, and a woven basket filled with goodies. Her tummy grumbled at the sight.

Scarlett shrugged. "I'm a mum."

The weather was surprisingly warm and dry for November, but the night was dark, the wind rustled in a hushed whisper, and the forest looked spooky. They heard distant howls and growls, bats screeching, and an owl hooting. The twisted branches looked even creepier at night as they creaked, groaned, and swayed. Tyra shivered. Scarlett looked restless and even more scared.

Suddenly, the forest fell silent. The wind died, and their crunching footsteps became louder. The stillness of the night was even more frightening.

Then Tyra heard the voice, humming the shadow song again: "My shadow's inside me, shaking me. Scarier than ever. It asks where are you taking me? I'm replying, where are you escaping?

Why always defensive walls? Why the shadow when the light is within?"

"Great timing, voice," Tyra muttered.

They walked for another hour, using the lantern to light their way.

Finally, they settled beneath a massive oak for a nocturnal picnic. They built a smokeless bonfire, spread the picnic blanket on the ground, and savoured their late and cozy supper: crusty country bread with Camembert cheese, olives and nuts; bell peppers and cherry tomatoes with baked veggie sticks; grapes, macarons, and a blueberry pie for dessert.

They wrapped themselves in the fuzzy blanket, the one with the daisies on it, and ate in silence, looking at the sky, which was sprinkled with luminous stars, their shoulders touching. The only sounds were the sounds of nature.

They woke up early the next morning to the songs of bustling birds and found themselves in a spectacular forest. Radiant, awakening. The morning dew and a hazy, sparkling mist coated the trees and flowers. The air was clean and vibrant. Purple butterflies swirled around Tyra, making her laugh as they tickled her. The smell of moist soil, mixed with ripe berries, flavoured chestnuts, and damp moss, awakened distant memories from Tyra's happy life in her homeland.

Alma's cozy living room in Moss was warm, and it circulated a mixed scent of lavender, lilies of the valley, freshly baked cinnamon buns, and steaming coffee. Olivia, Scarlett, and Tyra sat on comfy, magenta bean-bag chairs beside Tyra's grandparents, who were snuggled on the sofa. Yellow torches illuminated the room with a cordial ambiance. It was a nice evening—one of many. There was chatter, laughter, and warmth. The cinnamon buns were divine.

Life is about moments.

The flashback made Tyra homesick. Whenever she tried to restore the recipe for these buttery, mouthwatering buns, soft and a bit crunchy on the outside, it was futile. It was impossible to recreate memories.

Tyra flinched and returned to reality. She looked around and smiled. That moment with her mother was also special.

"Tyra, look around! It's beautiful," Scarlett said in awe. Withering leaves rustled and whispered under her dark green boots.

Tyra yawned and stretched. It felt so good. "Where do these cherry trees come from? I mean, it's bizarre. We're in November!" she said as she sprawled under the cherry tree.

Oh, how wonderful to feel alive again!

"Well, I don't know. The weather certainly doesn't fit in November's schedule either."

"Mama, look, there's a bluebird I've never seen before. I like your singing, dear."

Scarlett chuckled.

The bird turned and looked at Tyra, then chattered with even more enthusiasm. *Weird,* Tyra thought and then gave it some breadcrumbs.

Tyra made an infinity braid, stretched again, and looked down at the earth, burying her sleepy feet into the squishy terracotta soil. The forest was still wrapped in a hazy veil. She inhaled the scent of wet wood and wildflowers.

"Tyra, look! So funny." Scarlett pointed in the opposite direction.

Tyra turned around and saw the ancient tree half a mile away. It was an enormous, marvelous ash tree, unlike any other. Its grand, sturdy trunk was shaped like an infinity symbol. It ascended high into the sky and split into two loops, one above the other. Its perfectly balanced, symmetrical, intertwined loops were encompassed by four foamy, crystal-clear brooks, each following one of the four cardinal directions—north, south, east, and west. The tree's lavish branches swayed and twinkled in the wind. Now and then the leaves changed shape and colour and made a soft rustling sound. At times they remained unchanged, feather-like and smooth. Purple and a bit waxy. Just regular ash tree leaves.

Scarlett and Tyra stood in stunned silence; their eyes wide. They looked like happy youngsters who had just discovered their own wonderland.

Scarlett frowned with a hint of a smile. "I think there should be some sort of limit for so many intense emotions in a row."

Tyra giggled.

They enjoyed a light breakfast, gathered their belongings, tidied up, turned the leftovers into compost, and spread it around the blackberry bushes.

Tyra fed chipmunks, squirrels, and the peculiar blue birds. Then she closed her eyes and inhaled the aroma of the morning forest. "I wish we could freeze this day and last night, make like an interactive album we could fetch in a minute of nostalgic gloom and reexperience these moments."

Scarlett smiled. "That would be nice. Tyra, who knows when we'll meet again? I feel like it's too much for me."

Tyra noticed an aching sensation of awkwardness and a faint trace of guilt. "I'm sorry for leaving you, Mama, but I have to go. This is *my* way. You're gonna be okay, right?"

Beloved, unloved daughter.

Scarlett looked at Tyra with the grief of an abandoned child and then turned away. Deep down, she knew it was best for Tyra. But an inner controversy created discomfort in her body and disarray in her mind.

Scarlett picked up the bag and headed to the ash tree. Tyra followed her mother with a nagging heart. Still, her belly purred with eager anticipation of the adventure ahead.

Beside the ash tree, they discovered an elegant oak chair with an image of a young stag burned into it. Under the tree, Tyra noticed a tiny dowry chest made of tanzanite, a luminescent, deep-blue, rich-violet gemstone with a touch of burgundy. On top of it was crafted a number—888. Tyra opened the chest and gasped. On the bottom was a silver ring inscribed with a delta symbol. Tyra examined the shimmering symbol and tried to remember where she had seen it before.

"Mama, I think I saw this symbol on my apple tree. How odd, don't you think?"

"It's a symbol of change," Scarlett murmured.

Then Tyra heard cheerful barking, accompanied by melancholy music. The barking sounded like a greeting. She closed the chest. "Did you hear it?"

Scarlett nodded, a bewildered look on her face. "I did."

They walked around the tree and then stopped, confronted by a peculiar scene. A little boy, about eight years old, was sitting there all alone, his back against a vast tree and his legs tucked in. He was playing a light-blue harmonica. His companion, a boxer-mix puppy, rushed to greet them with a crazy mambo-rumba dance. The puppy approached Tyra, his purplish tongue lolling out like a jumbo leaf. He jumped, leaped, and hopped like a bouncy furball. Tyra burst into laughter, then picked him up and surrendered to his endless tongue, which made sure her entire face was groomed and well nourished.

Scarlett came closer and sat next to the boy. "I'm Scarlett," she said, smiling.

The boy gave her a curious look. "I'm Theo."

"How long have you been here all alone?"

"I'm not alone. I'm here with Tai Chi," Theo said, pointing at his ginger energizer. "We just got here this morning."

"Where are your parents, dear?"

"Dead."

"I'm so sorry." Scarlett sighed. "And the others?"

"There's only me and Tai Chi." Theo shrugged as if to reassure her that that was okay. "My mama gave me this compass." He nodded toward a tangled ball of red wool. "She said there's an ancient tree I must find and that I must ask it for protection and shelter. She said the tree can transport me to another world where people treat orphans with kindness."

"A compass?"

"Yes. It'll show you the way, my mama said. You just roll it across the ground and then follow it. She also left me this pendant with a Val Knut symbol on it. Mama said it's a symbol of a mother's love and that it'll always protect me." Theo showed her a square black obsidian on sturdy white lace with three interlocking white triangles carved into the middle of the stone. "My papa gave me this on my last birthday," he added, pointing at his harmonica.

Scarlett spotted a creamy, two-pam-length teddy bear wearing a red shirt and green pants. Theo noticed and petted the bear. "This is Beary. He's my friend."

"I'm glad he found his way to you." Her eyes sparkled as she smiled. The bear was the first stuffed animal she had made for orphans.

Tai Chi ran over, sniffed, and snatched it.

"Tai Chi! No! Give it back!" Theo dashed to retrieve his friend from the dog's slobbery mouth. "You know Beary's off limits! No! Leave it. Now!" Theo took Beary away from Tai Chi and hid him in a secret compartment of his soft brown leather backpack. He tossed Tai Chi his squeaky ball and then searched the ground for some branch.

"You must be freezing," Scarlett said with a mother's concern. She took out the fuzzy blanket with daisies on it and covered the boy as if she were hugging him.

"Not really. It's warm and safe here under the tree. But thank you. The blanket is soft and cozy. I like it." Theo smiled with relief.

Tyra gazed at him with affection and tenderness. His light-brown straw-like hair peeked out of a grey cotton bucket hat, and his amber eyes looked much older than they should have. "It's yours now. I've had it since I was about your age, and it hugged and sheltered me whenever I needed it. Now, it'll be your comforter."

"Won't you miss it? I can't take such a dear present," Theo said with the voice of a young man.

"I want you to have it. I think Tai Chi might like it too."

"He would like it very much, yes. Thank you. What's your name? I need to know the name of the girl who gave me such a gift."

Tyra's mouth twinkled with joy. "I'm Tyra. Tyra Tara. I'm so happy to meet you, Theo."

"Thanks. Me too. If I'm honest, I don't like to get attached nowadays. Goodbyes are painful."

Scarlett shivered. A wave of compassion mixed with sadness filled her chest.

"People disappoint, and people heal," the voice whispered. "They hurt, and they love."

"Different people?" Theo asked.

"Different and the same," the voice replied.

"Odd," Tyra said to the voice.

"My well of astonishment has run dry," Scarlett said. "This forest is talking to us, I guess." She rolled her eyes and shrugged.

Theo chuckled.

"Great, it's not only in my head," Tyra said. "Such a relief. They can hear you now. Yay!"

"I belong to no one and everyone," the voice said.

"Who are you, though?" Tyra asked.

"I'm the Earth Mind, the Well of everything that was, is, and will be. I am everything that has been felt, thought, sensed, heard, written, comprehended, pondered, and mulled. I'm everything that has been created, everything that has been lived through. I'm the Vault, the Chasm of Universal Mind, the Well of Human Wisdom."

"More riddles. Splendid." Tyra shook her head and rolled her eyes.

"Who are you talking to, Tyra?" Scarlett asked.

"No one. Just mumbling to myself."

Tai Chi grew tired of chasing chipmunks and being scolded by a particularly irate squirrel, who threw an array of nuts at his head in a burst of anger. The puppy looked as if he were giggling. Satisfied with the outcome of his well-planned conspiracy, he was ready to calm down. He hopped on his buddy's knees and fell asleep in his arms.

"Are you hungry, dear?" Scarlett asked.

Theo giggled. "Only for sweets."

Scarlett smiled and handed him a piece of blueberry pie and the last macaron.

Tyra chuckled. "I know that feeling, sweet tooth. I used to hunt for chocolate and cookies in our house. Mama would hide them, so I wouldn't eat them all at once. She liked giving me sweets when I was having this crazy urge: 'Oh, give me, give me, give me!' And I'd always find it—always. No matter how complicated her hidden spots became, I'd go straight to this spot if some kind of current led me." Tyra blinked at the blissful memory and laughed.

Scarlett smiled, then her brow furrowed with concern. "Theo, darling, why are you sitting here? We can help you. We have yet to figure out how to get to the other side, but we will. Can I see your leaf? There may be some valuable information. We, well, we lost ours."

"Vitos says little kids, especially orphans, don't need an invitation. He said we're welcome. But I don't particularly like orphanages. Vitus said it's different on the other side, but still. See? I've already been in one. I didn't like it. When I found Tai Chi and brought him in, they refused to accept him, although he's an orphan too. So, I took the ball of wool, and we snuck out before dawn and headed to the forest. I spent six months in the orphanage before I met him. I was scared to run away at first, and then I got even more scared of the journey itself, and I didn't know where it would lead me. I gathered courage only when they didn't take Tai Chi in. It became simple. So, here we are. I'm glad you're here. Perhaps we can cross it together. Vitos says the orphanages there are nothing like those in Azure. I trust him."

"Of course, dear," Scarlett said. *Such an intelligent boy*, she thought. "But, who's Vitos?"

"Greetings, dear Scarlett and Tyra!" a deep voice said. "Welcome, welcome, welcome!" The voice filled the forest with calming softness and a sense that everything was going to be okay. "I'm Vitos, the ancient ash tree. I've been waiting for you last-minute birds."

His mellow laughter stirred a delicate dance of falling leaves. The leaves were in their fancy outfits. Maple, olive, golden wattle, mango, palm, oak, beech, silver birch, elm, willow, cypress, cherry blossom, cedar, fern, pine, and many more. Such a marvelous kaleidoscope of waltzing, masquerading leaves of all shapes and shades.

Theo leaped with delight. He stretched his arms and tried to catch some. Tai Chi went crazy, jumping on crackling piles of colourful treasures. Tyra lay on the ground and made an angel with her limbs, allowing the leaves to cover her as if they were a safe, tingling blanket. Scarlett watched them with careful joy. She couldn't help but close her eyes and smile.

"Will you come to live with me?" Tyra asked.

Theo pondered his answer.

Tyra clicked her tongue. "Hmm . . . see? I've never had any siblings or cousins. I feel like you, me, and Tai Chi belong together."

Theo smiled with a hint of hesitation, then turned to Scarlett. "Aren't you coming too?" He liked her very much.

Scarlett sighed. "No, it's just Tyra. I'm sorry, little pie. I wish I could."

Theo whispered something in Tai Chi's ear, then turned to Tyra. "We accept your invitation, Tyra. It feels right."

Tai Chi tried to dig Tyra out of a gigantic pile of leaves.

Vitus waited, letting the kids have their fun. "Are you ready for the adventure, children? Prepare for everything, expect nothing, and you'll be good."

Tyra stood up, wiping fragments of leaves from her knitted deep-ocean jacket and skinny jeans. "Vitus, could you please tell us about this world?"

"Mm-hmm. You'll have the orientation once you land there.

We're running out of time, kids, but I assure you, you'll both have access to a communication device. By the end of this day, you'll be able to chat and share your stories." Vitus giggled, looking at mother and daughter with kindness.

Scarlett and Tyra exhaled in relief. Theo smiled with pleasure.

Vitus shook his leaves, creating another cascade of circling canopy. "As you know, there are a myriad of realms on Earth. Many coexist in harmony and strive to learn from one another's mistakes. For example, people almost gave up on networks and social media in the Land of the Great Lakes. Well, let's say it's not prevalent. They call it a content diet. But it's easy for those who have access to magic, right?"

"What kind of magic?" Theo asked.

"You'll see. Different lands have different types of magic. At times they overlap, and at other times they intertwine. People like to collect it and use it for their needs. We're all fond of sharing. It's beautiful." Vitus became serious. "It is time, my little friends. Tyra, I invite you to grab the chair and the ring. Theo, my dear, would you put Tai Chi inside your backpack? Put the bag up front and climb on the second loop."

Theo shuffled his feet as he glanced at the ground, palming his weary brownish backpack.

"Oh, Vitus," Scarlett protested, "it's too dangerous for a little boy to climb this high. Isn't there another way? Can't they go together?"

A wave of gratitude washed over Theo's heart. He would never be afraid of heights or climbing. But being alone felt uneasy. After the brief but weighty connection he'd just encountered, it would feel like another disappointment.

Vitus took a deep breath. "No worries, Mama." Its branches leaned down and lifted the boy.

Theo settled atop the first loop and gasped in awe as he clutched his wriggling backpack. Magnificent northern lights lit up the sky, accompanied by soft music.

Meanwhile, Tyra was arguing with the voice. It whispered in a teasing manner so only Tyra could hear it. "Flitting from hell to hell. Oh, human nature, as old as time."

"What? Why are you frightening me?"

The voice giggled. "That's my nature."

"But you've helped me, like a billion times!"

"That's my nature too."

Tyra smiled with affection.

"Now, Tyra," Vitos said, "prepare to use your ring. Place the chair in the middle of the lower loop and take your place on top. We must hurry. The portal's closing soon."

Tyra opened the dower and retrieved a glowing silver ring. She held her mother in a long, tight hug as if she intended to steal a glimpse of her omnipresence. As if she were trying to grasp an imprint of her spirit and keep it forever. Tyra sniffed Scarlet's fluttering turquoise scarf, as soft as silk, to remember the fragrance and keep it in her memory compartments.

When Tyra settled on the giant chair in the middle, Scarlett gripped her daughter's hand and held it for a long, slipping-away moment. Tyra felt a knot crawl from her tightened tummy to her voiceless throat. Her neck became strained, her eyes foggy, and her puffy lips trembled. She rubbed the bridge of her button nose and sniffled.

The shadow made itself comfortable in the vacant left corner.

Tyra blinked as she touched her neck. She shook away the unpleasant sensation and straightened. "Theo, it's going to be okay. I got you."

Theo smiled and nodded. He felt calm and secure, his oldish eyes carefree and boyish.

"Scarlett, I hope you'll let go of overgrown branches. Puck, my pointy-eared friend, will guide you on your way home. I can assure you, when he's on a business trip, his mischievous nature is at rest." Vitos giggled. "Tyra, remember, only when you've surrendered the grip of desire and embraced stillness has your life begun to unfold. Stillness leads to guidance. Theo, my little friend, hold onto your heart as tight as you're holding your wiggling puppy.

Unguarded hearts keep us safe. Farewell, dear friends! See you some other day. Tyra, put the ring on your right finger on the count of four. One, two, three, four."

Click, snap, clap. In a flash, Tyra was in the Land of the Great Lakes.

Scarlett stood in the middle of a noiseless, solemn forest, where only a moment ago, near a marvelous tree, a happy commotion had prevailed—the little boy with his bubbly puppy, the northern lights, picnicking under the night sky, and her daughter.

"There is freedom waiting for you,
on the breezes of the sky.
And you ask. "What if I fall?"
Oh, but my darling, what if you fly?"
– Erin Hanson

TO BE CONTINUED . . .

Acknowledgments

I want to thank my family for supporting me through this fantastic journey and for their insightful input as my dedicated beta readers, especially my daughter, who read and reread this book many times. She grew tired of the myriad revisions, but she continued to help her mama. Thanks to her, Koda was saved from transforming into a groundhog who, frankly (despite his undeniable cuteness), had no chance of replacing Koda's charm and complexity. Jerry is also her co-creation.

I also want to thank my husband and daughter for demanding an extension of Koda's chapters and pointing out the essence of missing settings and limited dialogue in the first drafts.

To my husband for his constant support and encouragement throughout this project and for discovering the perfect illustrator for my book cover and the upcoming illustrations.

Thank you so much to my son for his valuable suggestions and supportive feedback on my writing style, which gave me hope and the determination to continue my work. Thank you to all three of my favourite people for their courage to delve into the depths of my psyche through these pages. I know it wasn't easy since they've seen the hardest parts from the past be reborn and take shape. Thank you for giving me a sense of home.

I am also very grateful to my aunt for motivating me and for inspiring me to believe in myself, both as an author and a person, and for never giving up on me.

A special thank-you to my book cover illustrator, Svetlana Rudikova, for bringing my characters to life and enriching this book with her incredible talent and dedication. Her artistry and unwavering diligence have added both visual and emotional depth to the story, and I feel incredibly fortunate to have worked alongside such a talented and inspiring artist. I'm deeply grateful for the sincere connection we've built along the way, and it feels as if my book mysteriously found its way to the perfect artist for this task. It was as if our paths were destined to cross, coming together to bring this book to life. An additional edition featuring her fantastic illustrations is on the way.

I want to thank my editor, Kevin Miller, whose sharp eyes, patience, and dedication brought clarity and finesse to these pages. I am grateful for his insights, hard work, and thoughtful feedback, and for filling this journey with laughter and making it easy and fun. I know how my struggles with grammar must have challenged and even tried to sabotage his work, especially when I insisted on keeping some ambiguous structures and meanings.

I'm also grateful to FriesenPress for their thoughtfulness and commitment to excellent editing services. The reliability and genuine passion of their team truly stand out, making this collaboration a true pleasure.

Thank you to my friends for being my shelter during difficult times, for supporting my work, giving me hope and direction, and for always making me feel at home.

I want to extend my deepest gratitude to my therapist for her support and compassionate guidance and for walking with me on this journey of healing.

A special thank-you to Goenka, the teacher of Vipassana meditation technique and to the Quebec Vipassana Meditation Centre for an unprecedented opportunity to learn and practice this profound method of self-transformation.

And to my mom, whose early death during the challenging times of the pandemic shattered my world, forced me to face my own shadow, and triggered my awakening.

About the Author

Natalie lives in beautiful Ottawa with her husband, two kids, two cats, and a dog. With a bachelor's degree in behavioural science and a teaching certificate, she has also studied literature and enjoyed writing essays in all her studies.

Natalie has recently discovered mindfulness, which has revived her long-held love for Jungian psychology.

Her pets have been active participants through her joys and struggles, and she often wonders how people can navigate life without a furry companion.

Natalie has been crafting stories in her head throughout her life. Her husband has tried to convince her to put them on paper, which she has finally done after two decades of marriage.

She's a tea person, but she's addicted to coffee. Don't ask; it's complicated.

While she's never been a fan of cakes, Natalie appreciates cookies.

∾

Many events in this book are inspired by her own personal journey, although all the characters, places and incidents are fictional. Natalie had a strong bond with her grandmother, which is reflected in Tyra and Alma's relationship.

She's agnostic but respects any beliefs that don't cause harm.

Her cats, Tom Sawyer and Shira, are prototypes of Tom and Calla, and their whimsical friendship with Jonas, a shaggy, black-

and-white pyredoodle, resembles the one that Calla and Tom formed with Zeus.

Her late dog, Tai-Chi, a boxer mix, will continue to live through this book. His adventures will be told in the second book in *The Land of the Great Lakes* series.

~

Get in touch with the author:

Instagram: n.z_kaminsky_author

Facebook: N. Z. Kaminsky

Manufactured by Amazon.ca
Bolton, ON